I'M GONNA MAKE YOU LOVE ME

GWYNETH BOLTON

Genesis Press, Inc.

Indigo Love Stories

An imprint of Genesis Press, Inc.
Publishing Company

Genesis Press, Inc.
P.O. Box 101
Columbus, MS 39703

ISBN-13: 978-15857-291-5
ISBN-10: 1-15857-291-4
Manufactured in the United States of America

First Edition 2006
Second Edition 2009

Visit us at www.genesis-press.com or call at 1-888-Indigo-1

DEDICATION

To my mother,
Donna Pough
Your devotion and endurance showed me the meaning
of unconditional love. I thank God every day for giving
me a mother like you. Because of you, I know what love
is. I love you.

To my husband,
Cedric Bolton
Your love has made me a better woman, and I look
forward to spending the rest of my life with you. You
make me want to sing along with India Arie because
you certainly are the truth. If I am a reflection of you,
then I must be fly, because your light shines so very
bright. I love you.

ACKNOWLEDGMENTS

First, I want to thank God for granting me a gift and allowing me to share it. I want to thank my mother for encouraging me to read and fostering in me a love of the written word. I'd like to thank my husband for not complaining too much when I had to write. Thanks to all of my family and friends not mentioned by name, but dear to my heart. My thanks go out to my dear sisters: Jennifer, Cassandra, Michelle, and Tashina. And my thanks also go out to my nieces, Ashlee and Zaria. Thank you, Aunt Lois, for always being in my corner. My thanks also goes out to Aunt Helen and Aunt Lynn for encouraging me throughout my life. I want to thank my in-laws, the Boltons and the McClouds. I want to send a special thanks to Lily Payne, LaTisha Nwoye, and Jennifer Thorington-Springer, who each read versions of this novel at various times and encouraged me to get it out there and keep writing. I'd like to thank my Minneapolis critique partners: Allison Carmody, Kristin Cleary, and Jennifer Hubbard. You ladies rock! I'd also like to thank my new Syracuse critique partners Arlene Wu, Suemarie Simpson, and Jennifer Talty, for their moral support and good friendship. I want to thank Helen Crump who read an early draft of the manuscript and provided wonderful feedback and encouragement. My thanks also goes out to Cheryl Johnson and Yolanda Hood for being fellow academic African-American, romance-reading sisters who didn't laugh when I said I'd like to write one. And finally, I'd like to thank the Genesis Press family, especially Angelique Justin and Deatri King-Bey. Thank you, Angelique, for being an Acquisitions Editor with so much flavor and insight that you could see the diamond in the rough and know that the story was special enough to be shared. Thank you, Deatri, for your dynamic editorial skills and the way you helped me to polish this novel so that it shines. It has been wonderful working with you both.

CHAPTER 1

"It's just so archaic—a throwback to the dark ages or at least pre-enlightenment!"

Grimacing as he watched his wife brush her hair, Kyle thought about the best way to respond to her statement and decided humor was the way to go. "Well, I don't know, Karen. Seems like you could bump it up to at least the Victorian era. I don't think people were arranging marriages for their children in the dark ages."

Fixing the bowtie on his tuxedo, he gave her a smile as she stopped brushing her hair to glare at him.

"It's not funny, Kyle. Really, black folk just don't do this kind of thing. We don't pick spouses for our children."

Sighing because he thought they were through with this discussion, he tried to think of yet another way to get his wife to understand what she clearly did not wish to understand. Having long since made the deal with Jonathan Whitman that allowed him to regain control of Taylor Publishing, he was too far in to back out. Whitman made him an offer he couldn't refuse—a chance to save the Taylor legacy, business, and family name.

"You'd be surprised at what black folk do, especially *our kind of people*. It's about control, breeding, and family. I've heard stories about mergers in my family that did not start out based on love as we like to think about it." Untying his failed attempt at a bow, he tried again. "Believe it or not, those mergers were the very mergers that brought the family the most success. *Love* didn't get my parents anywhere."

Were it not for his father's gambling and bad habits, Kyle wouldn't have even considered the offer. In many ways, they were lucky the Taylor name still meant something. A scandal like the one his father had left would have annihilated a lesser family.

The overly indulgent lifestyle his own father had led almost ruined the family name and made Taylor Publishing vulnerable to a hostile takeover by Whitman Enterprises. Whitman offered a chance to earn it back, albeit at a high cost.

"Well, my father is a Kansas City barbecue king, and although I grew up well-off and attended all the *right* schools, I was not among that elite group of *your kind of people*. So, forgive me if I don't understand this!" Karen put the brush down, crossed her arms over her chest, and narrowed her eyes on him. "Those two kids who you and Whitman hope will one day marry *cannot* even stand each other. They argue every time they are near one another!"

Kyle sighed. He knew the children didn't get along and hoped the childhood rivalry between his daughter and Whitman's son would eventually go away.

"You know," Karen's voice calmed to a whisper, "if your family arranged a marriage for you, or if you didn't have the guts to date and fall in love outside of your tight-knit group of black elites, you and I would not be together now."

"Probably not. If my life had followed the path I started out on, if my father were half the man he should have been…" Stuttering slightly, he closed his eyes in search of the words that would make her understand.

"I have a chance to rebuild my family's legacy. To do all the things my father wouldn't or couldn't do."

"And it will only cost your daughter's future. Her right to choose who she wants to fall in love with? Don't you see it's crazy? And did I mention, Alicia *can't stand* Darren Whitman? The two of them are like oil and water!"

"What I see is that if I don't try this, my child won't have the lifestyle she deserves. I can't abide with that, Karen. I won't! She will have the world and will grow up in a world where the Taylor name still means something." Reaching out and touching her shoulder, he continued, "They are kids now. Most boys and

girls don't like each other when they are young. She
might grow to like him, even love him one day."

Karen lowered her gaze. By the way she clenched
her teeth, he could tell she was simmering. "I don't
like it, Kyle."

"It will work…It has to work. When you think
about it, what more could two parents wish for? Our
daughter will marry one of the richest men in the
world. Could it be so bad for our little girl to grow up
and become Mrs. Darren Whitman?" Hearing his
own voice, he realized that in addition to trying to
convince his wife, he was trying to convince himself.
Things had to work out.

Letting out a ragged breath, he continued,
"Jonathan Whitman is letting me run my family's
company. I'm making a lot more now than what I
made when I was trying to work my way up the
corporate ladder. Taylor Publishing is my legacy. The
dinner party that we are hosting this evening is just
the start of the big things to come. Think of the
important people who will be here. I'll have a chance
to build the company back to its original luster. I
know I can do it. It's my birthright.

"I'll get to run it for now, and once they are
married, part of the company will revert back to the
Taylor family. Once there is an heir, another part of
the company will revert to the Taylor family. Doing

this will give Alicia and her future children the family's legacy."

Straightening his slouched shoulders, he shrugged and sighed. Things were truly out of his hands. "If Alicia grows up and decides she just cannot marry the young, rich man her daddy picked out for her, then we'll lose everything. Don't you see I had to try? I *have* to try."

When his wife finally turned her gaze back to him, he used his own expression to plead with her to understand. He hoped one last time that she did and that they would not have to rehash this discussion.

Alicia giggled as she eavesdropped on her cousin Kendrick and his friends, Darren and Troy. The three boys irritated her to no end, and she awoke each morning thinking of ways to ruin any idea of fun they might think up. The thing an eight-year-old girl with braces and pigtails hated most were twelve-year-old boys who teased her and pushed her around at whim.

Each of the older boys annoyed her, and Alicia could not decide which boy annoyed her most. Her cousin came to visit every summer because her father said Uncle Kelvin was a loser like the grandfather who died before she was born. Darren Whitman and Troy Singleton were just boys who came around whenever Kendrick was in town. Troy lived right across the street in a big red brick house, and Darren lived in a huge mansion in Bloomfield Hills.

The rich boy, Darren, was the one she decided she hated most of all. Not only was he rich and a pain, he was also the meanest. He tugged her pigtails anytime she got within arm's reach and called her names like metal-mouth, brat, and antenna head. The nerve of him calling anyone names when he was so bony and his voice went all low and then high, sounding like tires screeching all the time.

The boys were planning to come inside out of the heat and watch a stupid karate movie on the VCR. Racing into the family room of their six-bedroom classic Tudor home in Palmer Woods, Alicia turned on the TV.

"Get out, metal-mouth; we want to watch a movie on the big screen!" Darren barged into the room followed by Kendrick and Troy.

"I'm watching it, so you can't." Gripping the remote control in her small hands, she gave the boys her best attempt at a threatening glare.

"Come on, Licia, you have a TV in your room. Let us watch our movie in here." Kendrick's request was just a little nicer than Darren's.

Letting out the kind of exasperated sigh she saw glamorous women give in the movies whenever someone was getting on their nerves, she replied,

"What part off 'no' don't you understand? You have a TV in your room. I was here first. Get lost."

"I'm tired of this! Give me the remote and get out of here, brat!" Snatching the remote, Darren yanked her left pigtail extra hard before walking away.

She let out a loud, piercing scream, and her mother, Karen Taylor, came running from upstairs where she was supervising the help and getting ready for a big dinner party.

"What is it now? You children know I am busy getting things ready for Kyle's dinner party. I really don't have time for this." Karen placed her hands on her hips and gave each child a pointed stare.

No visible tears accompanied Alicia's sobbing. "I was here first watching something, and they came in bothering me. I was here first, and Darren hit me. He's mean and horrible! Mommy, they know the rules. But they don't care." Burying her face in her dainty hands, Alicia dramatically fell on to the sofa.

"Boys, was she here first?" Karen said in her no-nonsense tone.

Almost tempted to peek up from her production to watch, Alicia didn't want to risk having her mother's tone turned on her.

"Yes," the boys murmured in unison.

"Well, you know the rules. Go and watch TV in Kendrick's room until Alicia is finished."

The boys followed her mother out of the family room with Darren bringing up the rear. Lifting her head just in time to stick out her tongue at Darren, she relished the view of his face twisting up in anger.

The show that was playing, like every other show, was a re-run and didn't interest her. Her best friend Sonya was away at Jack and Jill camp for *two weeks*, and Alicia had no one to play with or talk to. Although Alicia was also a member of Jack and Jill, her father felt she was too young to go away for two weeks. So she amused herself day after day.

Deciding to go and spy on the boys again, she got there just in time to follow them out to a huge cluster of oak trees that extended just a few yards from the backyard of their home. The backyard was huge, and just behind it was what the kids felt was a mini-forest. It didn't have nearly as many trees as a forest, but for kids living in the city, it was just as good. Forbidden to go back there alone, Alicia reasoned she wouldn't *really* be alone. She would be with the boys, only they wouldn't know it.

Darren kicked the rocks with all the force his twelve-year-old feet could muster. Unaccustomed to not getting his way, he focused his anger on that metal-mouthed brat Alicia. He was almost tempted to call his driver and go home, but there was nothing to do there and no one else to play with.

He really loved spending time with Kendrick and Troy. They were like brothers. In fact, they'd made a blood brothers' pact in their secret spot earlier that summer. They were now headed to their secret spot to come up with ways to make sure the brat didn't ruin the rest of the summer. They stopped under the dark shade where oaks met so closely they almost made a circle.

"Well, she did it again. She messed up a perfect afternoon." Vocalizing what they all thought, Troy was the first to speak.

"Well, we could spend the rest of the summer at one of your houses." Bowing his head, Kendrick kicked a rock.

Irritated, Darren pointed out, "If we do that, she wins. No way is that little brat going to win. It's us against her! We can't let that metal-mouth win."

"It's like she always knows what we're going to do next, and she beats us to it," Troy complained.

A slight noise in the bushes drew Darren's attention. Motioning for the boys to be silent, he caught a glimpse of the yellow ribbon at the end of Alicia's long, curly pigtail as she darted behind a tree.

"That's it, brat! When we catch you, you're toast!" he yelled.

Alicia let out a high-pitched scream and took off running. The boys followed, but she was fast. They each took different directions, hoping to corner her. Gaining ground, Darren had her right in his sight. Glancing back at him, Alicia did not see the big rock in her path.

He watched as her foot hit the big rock, and she tumbled to the ground. He stopped in front of her and saw that she was holding her leg, and crying. It wasn't the loud fake sobs that she had let out earlier, just streams of tears down her cheek. He sat down beside her and put his arm around her.

"It's going to be okay, Licia. Can you move your leg? Can you walk?" He had heard people on TV ask people who were hurt if they could move the injured body part.

Alicia moved her leg and continued to cry. The others came running up from different directions.

Throwing up his hands, Kendrick groaned. "Oh, man, this is guaranteed punishment for at least a week."

"She's hurt her leg. You two go get your aunt and uncle, and I'll stay here with her." Guilt-ridden, Darren wanted to make sure that Alicia was okay.

The other two boys ran back to the house, and he talked to Alicia while waiting. He could have sworn that he even made her smile—either that or she was grimacing from the pain.

Relief washed over him when he saw Mr. and Mrs. Taylor come running through the woods followed by Dr. Samuels. They were all dressed in fancy clothes, and he knew that he and the boys were going to be in big trouble for interrupting the dinner party.

He smiled down at Alicia. "See, I told you everything would be okay. Here's your mom and dad." He waited until the adults got there before removing his arm from her shoulder.

While examining her, Dr. Samuels asked if she could move her leg and Darren smiled.

Mr. Taylor picked Alicia up to carry her back to the house. The doctor had said she had a bad sprain, and she wouldn't be running around for a while. When Darren was on the verge of feeling sorry for her, Alicia lifted her head from Mr. Taylor's shoulder and stuck her tongue out at Darren. Furious that he had wasted his time being nice to the little metal-mouth brat, he kicked a rock.

CHAPTER 2

Six Years Later, Andover, Massachusetts

Preening in the bathroom mirror of her hotel room and running her tongue across the smooth surface of her teeth, Alicia relished in the fact that she was finally free of the retainers that had made her preteen years a drag. Smiling what her father called his Bentley smile because he claimed he would have been driving one a long time ago if she'd had been blessed with her mother's smile instead of his, she practiced tilting her head and batting her eyes.

The years of torture—from braces to retainers and all the metal-mouth jokes in between—had been worth it. She was on her seventh or eighth pose when Sonya came bursting into to bathroom.

"Alicia, what is taking you so long? Oh my goodness, look at you preening and posing in the mirror like you're some kind of fashion model. Would you hurry up so that I can get ready for the graduation?" Sonya folded her arms across her chest and leaned against the doorframe.

"Well I have to get ready, too. I don't know why you're in such a rush to see those stupid boys graduate.

So what! They managed to graduate from boarding school. Big deal!" Alicia turned to face the mirror again.

Everyone is sooo excited about this graduation! In Alicia's opinion, her father paid too much attention to her cousin Kendrick already, always talking about how Kendrick was the future of the family—the future of Taylor Publishing.

She thought back to when she was younger, and she had asked her father what she was going to do in the future to help the family. The weird expression that darted across his face had worried her. Then he picked her up, tickled her, and told her that little girls didn't have to worry about things like that. Even though she had laughed uncontrollably as she always did when her daddy tickled her, she hadn't felt very happy.

"Listen, darling, it takes time to be beautiful." Alicia flung her long, curly, black hair and batted her eyes.

Sonya gagged and faked vomiting. "Listen, girl, our parents let us stay in a hotel room by ourselves because they thought we were adult enough to get dressed and be on time. Now I know that you're just barely fourteen and not a mature high school student like myself, but I do hope that you will hurry up so that we are not forced to sleep in our parents' suites."

Sonya's tone was pseudo-condescending, and she even pointed her finger as she spoke.

Then, tossing her own long, chemically straightened, light-brown tresses and putting her hands on her hips, Sonya walked over to the mirror and studied her own fair-skinned complexion, which sported a range of copper hues because she, unlike Alicia, was allowed to wear makeup.

Alicia smirked. "Ha, ha, ha. Just give me three minutes. I'm almost done."

By the time they finished calling all the names of the 240 graduates and the fifth speaker finished speaking, Alicia thought she might leap from the balcony to end her misery. When the graduates finally made the procession out of the auditorium, she got glares from everyone around her because she thanked God a little louder than she meant to.

She tried to walk ahead of her family in hopes of losing them. However, her father was determined to keep her in his sight the whole night. She was just as determined to get away from him as soon as she could.

"Oh, I have to go to the restroom. I'll catch up to you guys as soon as I'm done." Pulling away from her parents, she motioned for Sonya to join her in the restroom.

"Girl, I'm going to find my brother. I can't wait to congratulate him. I'm so proud of him!" Sonya ran off with Mr. and Mrs. Singleton to search for Troy.

Traitor.

"Alicia, we're going up the hall to find Kendrick." Barely sparing her a glance as he spoke, Kyle's eyes roamed the crowded hall for Kendrick. "His mom couldn't make it, and my sorry brother didn't even try to make it. I'm sure he's wondering where his family is."

He turned his attention to her. "You better find us as soon as you get done in there. If I have to come back for you, you will be sorry." The tone of his voice showed that he had had enough of her antics for one night.

Karen touched Alicia's cheek and pulled Kyle away. "Hurry up, Alicia honey, as soon as we find Kendrick we're taking him out to dinner. Your daddy's just a little hungry. That's why he's so cranky. Come on, Kyle, let's find Kendrick."

As she entered the ladies' room, Alicia huffed because she couldn't believe Sonya went after Troy instead of helping her make her getaway; it was always better for the two of them to get in trouble together. Troy wasn't even worth all the hoopla.

She peered in the mirror and pulled out her lip gloss, which was the extent of her make-up. She managed to talk her mom into letting her wear lip gloss with a tiny tinge of color. She was wearing her favorite—blush red.

Straightening her red mini-dress and opening the bathroom door, she examined her matching red pumps for tissue. Too many people were caught thinking they looked good all the while wearing tissue on their shoes. She was so busy checking her feet that she didn't see the guy coming out of the men's room next door, and she walked right into him. Strong arms held her.

"Whoa, pretty girl, you might hurt someone."

She glanced up into the most beautiful, dark eyes she had ever seen. He resembled her favorite soap actor Hans Moore. His face was clean-shaven, and his skin looked like golden honey. He was wearing dress slacks, shirt, tie, and carrying his graduation gown over his left arm. Something about him seemed familiar. He was so tall and cute that she found herself staring.

Oh no. I'm staring like a geek.

"Excuse me. I'm sorry. I wasn't watching where I was going." She smiled, trying to remember one of the sexy smiles she'd practiced only a couple of hours earlier, but she couldn't think of one.

Glancing down at her feet in order to break the gaze of his deep, dark brown eyes, she tried to calm herself.

"It's okay. I take all the blame. Listen, I have to run and meet my folks, but please tell me I'll see you later at the big party tonight at Club Retro?"

When she got up the nerve to look at him again, he smiled, practically throwing Alicia off balance. She had never seen a smile so perfect. His smile went all the way up to his eyes, and she swore she could see sparkles in them—almost like the fake stars in the eyes of cartoon characters.

"I didn't know about the party, but now that I do I'll be there." She managed to bat her eyes and flash a smile as she turned around.

Trying to walk away smoothly to find her folks, she didn't dare look back because if she turned around and saw him watching her, she was sure she would trip or fall and embarrass herself.

The sexy young woman in the red dress mesmerized Darren. When she looked up at him with those stunning hazel eyes, he almost couldn't think of a word to say. He kicked himself because he didn't think to get her name or even tell her his name, or that it was his party.

He had seen many striking women, but this one had it all and then some. He felt drawn to her. There was *definitely* something about her. Her complexion was a soft shade of milk chocolate, and her hair was jet-black, long and curly. When she smiled, her whole face lit up. Her legs went on for days. The little red dress left just enough to the imagination, the way it hugged her curves and closed in around her narrow waist.

Somewhat disappointed that she hadn't turn around as she walked away, he knew that he would have loved to see that dazzling smile again, and he had to see her again. Not that he believed in love at first sight or anything like that. Although, he had a gut feeling that she was just the girl to make a believer out of him. He gave one last glance at her perfectly round retreating behind, turned and walked right into his father.

"It's about time I found you. You know we have reservations, and we have quite a bit to talk about tonight before your little party. Your mother and I will be leaving tonight. I have a very important meeting in the morning that I cannot miss." Jonathan Whitman awkwardly patted Darren's shoulder. "We are very proud of you, Son."

"Thanks, Dad. Where's Mom?" He searched the crowded hallway for his mother.

Jonathan hesitated for a moment. "She wasn't feeling well, so she went back to the suite. I figured you and I could have dinner and talk about some things alone."

"Oh. Okay. We don't have to go out if you don't want to. I know you're busy, and if you would like to get back to Mom, it's cool. I could try and catch up with the Taylors or the Singletons. I'm sure they wouldn't mind if I tagged along." He tried to hide his disappointment at the fact that his mother wouldn't be joining them.

He knew that his parents probably had had an argument and that his mother was off somewhere upset. He didn't know why they stayed together, and he certainly didn't see how they'd ended up together. If their marriage was any indication of what married life was like, he would *never* get married.

"Nonsense, Son! I will take you to dinner. This is a major milestone in your life. You are becoming a man." Jonathan gave Darren's back one last hesitant pat and led him out of the auditorium to the limousine waiting out front.

There wasn't any conversation, just brief awkward glances during the ride to the restaurant. The two were so unfamiliar with each other that the dinner, while not as silent as the limo ride, dragged on in strained, stilted conversation.

Jonathan kept questioning Darren about his mood. And, rather than say that he was a little nervous about spending the summer working at Whitman Enterprises, Darren decided to mention the beautiful young woman he just saw.

Darren had never seen his father so frustrated. He figured that mentioning the girl would make his father stop asking his probing questions.

"Son, you know our family history? You know that I am one of the richest men in America? We come from a long line of strong, hard-working black people." As he sipped his water, Jonathan observed Darren with an expression that was new to Darren.

"Yeah, Dad," he answered. Half listening because he had heard the speech many times before, he couldn't believe his father was going to start that again.

"You also know that when there is this much power and wealth in a family, something must be done to maintain control of that power. Each person is expected to make certain sacrifices—to fulfill certain obligations." Jonathan's eyes never left Darren's face.

Darren simply stared. *This* was a part of the speech he had not heard before.

"My grandfather started a tradition of choosing the mates for his children—mates who would add to the growing stature of our family. As you know, your mother's family is a very prestigious family with a rich history and legacy. My father arranged my marriage to your mother when I was a young man. And a young lady has been chosen for you. This young woman is beautiful, smart, and she comes from a prominent black family."

Darren felt himself run through a series of emotions from perplexed to shocked to angry in a matter of seconds.

"Are you saying that I am supposed to marry some woman I don't even know? That's crazy. No way. This is America. It can't be done. I won't do it!" Talking so fast he could barely catch his breath, Darren slammed his hand on the table.

Surveying the restaurant and monitoring those around him, Jonathan tapped his own fingers on the table, and his gaze narrowed in on Darren.

"Anything can be done if you have enough money, Son. And as for your bride-to-be, you do know her. You grew up playing at her house in the summer."

"Who?" After thinking for a minute, Sonya came to mind. Troy's sister Sonya was about a year or so younger than him, and he'd played at the Singleton's home often as a kid. "Not Sonya, not Troy's sister?"

"No, Darren. The girl who I have chosen for you is Alicia Taylor." A triumphant smile sprung from Jonathan.

Pigtails and braces materialized in Darren's mind's eye. A grim expression came across his face. "Not that bratty little girl! God, Dad, she must be about twelve years old. Christ, that's robbing the cradle."

"She is fourteen, and turning into a beautiful young woman, I might add. You won't be robbing the cradle. The wedding is to take place well after she turns twenty-one."

"Dad, this isn't fair. I don't like her, and I'm not going to marry her. She's probably still an annoying, spoiled little brat. No, I'm not doing it!" His mind went to the beautiful girl in red who he'd bumped into earlier. "Suppose I meet someone in college who I really care about and want to marry?"

"That is precisely why I am telling you of your obligations now. So that you can be careful and not make any mistakes!" Jonathan Whitman's voice was forceful. Observing his son thoughtfully, his face and tone softened. "Life is seldom fair. Cheer up. Enjoy your single years! You have lots of time to enjoy yourself. I'm not saying that you can't come to care for some other young woman. I am simply telling you that you *will* marry Alicia Taylor."

Darren's throat went dry. He took a big gulp of his water and glared at his father.

"By the way, the Taylor girl does not know about the marriage yet. I assume her father will be telling her in the coming years. So, if you see her, don't tell her. Her parents should be the ones to talk with her initially, just as I have talked to you."

Eyes narrowed to slits, Darren finished his water. His lips curled into a snarl as he thought that the last thing his father had to worry about was his talking to that little pest Alicia Taylor.

Alicia's eyes roamed Club Retro in awe because she had never been inside a real club before, complete with strobe lights and a hot DJ. The party her mystery guy mentioned was Darren Whitman's. His rich daddy had actually rented out the entire club for him and all his boarding school buddies to celebrate.

She was shocked when her dad—after a couple of glasses of champagne toasting his golden boy Kendrick—actually agreed to let her attend the party with Kendrick, Troy, and Sonya. Those silly boys were good for something, she reasoned, especially if it meant she would get a chance to see that sweet-smiled cutie again.

As soon as she walked out of the restroom, she saw *him* walking into the club. They caught each other's eye at the same time, and she could have sworn she felt her heart skip a beat when he smiled at her.

He walked over to her and smiled as his hand lightly brushed her cheek. "Well, it must be my destiny to meet you, pretty girl." He smiled, but she noticed that his eyes didn't light up the way they had earlier.

"Well, I guess if you believe in destiny, we must be destined to meet. This is a huge club, and I doubt that

I would have found you. It's pretty packed in here."
Hearing her feeble attempt at conversation, Alicia
figured she would have to work on her conversational
skills if she were going to be able to date all the young
men she planned to date—*once she was officially
allowed to date*.

They made it appear so easy in the movies;
however, she couldn't think of one witty or clever
thing to say. "So—" she started.

"So, how about you and I go find someplace quiet
to talk? I'm supposed to be meeting some friends here.
But I'm sure when I tell them that I met the girl of my
dreams, they'll understand." He smiled, and she
noticed a dimple in his left cheek.

Following him to a vacant part of the club, it
briefly crossed her mind that she should be afraid
because she didn't know him. *Although there is something about him that makes me feel like I've known him
forever…*

Confident and self-assured was the aura he gave
off in those black slacks and cream shirt. He must
have removed the tie he had on at the graduation. The
top two buttons of his shirt were open, and he was
sporting a more casual look.

She would follow him just about anywhere. When
she noticed that he was watching her intently, she
turned away shyly. The way his eyes slowly traveled
her body sent a shiver down her spine.

Could you actually shiver just by having someone look at you? With those eyes, she supposed so.

He pointed to a table off in a corner in the empty section of the club and asked her if she wanted to sit. She quickly realized that she had better sit before she lost it and her knees gave out just from his looking at her.

He pulled the chair out for her, and she eased into it. When he took the seat next to her, she turned to face him.

"So, I take it you graduated today?" Steadying her voice enough to form a question, she mentally kicked herself because he'd been carrying his gown when she saw him earlier in front of the restrooms.

"Yes, I did. I have a summer of freedom, and then it's off to college. I take it you were here to see someone graduate?"

I could always lie about why I was at the graduation. If he knows Kendrick, it would only be a matter of time before he found out how old I am. Cursing her age, she smiled at the fine dark-eyed angel who seemed captivated by everything about her.

"Well, I was attending the graduation of my wack cousin. I'm sure you know him and his even wacker friends. There probably aren't a lot of black people attending your school."

His face lit up, and this time the smile reached his eyes. "No, sweetheart. There aren't a whole lot of black people at Andover. In fact, there were only about twenty in my graduating class. So, I definitely know your cousin. Who is he?"

Biting her lip, she tried to suppress the soft sigh of defeat that nonetheless escaped her lips. The gig was up. "Umm, Kendrick Taylor. My cousin's Kendrick Taylor from Michigan." When she was brave enough to raise her eyes again, she noticed him staring at her with even more intensity.

She knew for sure that it couldn't be because her cousin had spoken about her. This was her first time visiting the school. If her cousin had a friend that gorgeous *ever,* she would have *definitely* remembered him.

Darren couldn't believe the words that had just come out of the beautiful young woman's mouth. Having been a close friend of Kendrick Taylor's for most of their lives, he knew that Kendrick only had one cousin. Staring at her, he tried to find some semblance of the bratty little girl with pigtails.

After gazing into her eyes, he knew he had seen that stunning shade of hazel before in the young Alicia, Mr. Taylor, even Kendrick. And those curly jet-black locks that were once tied up in pigtails were a link between Alicia and Mrs. Taylor.

Stunned, Darren felt that if he tried to speak he would stutter and make a fool of himself. He leaned forward, lightly brushed the lips that had him mesmerized the entire night, and touched top of her head gently.

Based on the smile that curved her lips, Darren could tell that she enjoyed the brief meeting of their lips. It was clear she hadn't had a whole lot of experience kissing by the slight tremble in her lips. He watched her reactions, and he could see her getting a little nervous under his gaze.

"Are you crazy?" she finally sputtered.

Darren leaned back in his chair. Distance was the best thing because he didn't trust himself not to kiss her again, and he knew that if he did it would be more than a slight brush of the lips.

Her wack cousin and his even wacker friends, huh?

"I see you still have that smart mouth, little Licia. What happened to your braces?"

Darren watched her face as she tried to process what he had just said. It was funny to watch her try and piece together how he could possibly know that she used to wear braces. Frowning, she studied him, and her mouth dropped. She closed it and opened it again. She squinted her eyes, and then they grew wide. After the facial theatrics, she smirked and brushed her hand across her lips in mock disgust.

"Well, Darren Whitman, I think we had better join the party. My cousin, Troy, and Sonya have been searching for you all night."

CHAPTER 3

Six Years Later, Detroit, Michigan

Alicia rushed down highway 75 in the airport rental SUV, not wanting to be late to the wedding rehearsal. After taking the hardest test of her college career, she'd had to drive all the way from South Hadley to Boston in order to take the flight she booked last minute, which thank God had been delayed.

Knowing that her father would have a fit because she was late for her own cousin's wedding rehearsal, and her best friend would have a fit because she couldn't manage to make it on time, Alicia drove a little faster than the sixty-five miles per hour speed limit.

The fact that she was attending Mount Holyoke College and could not plan all the activities that the maid of honor was supposed to take care of, made her just a bridesmaid. She felt slighted by Sonya's decision to let one of her chapter sorors be the maid of honor. Showing up late to the rehearsal, Alicia reasoned, would only make Sonya believe that she had made the right choice.

Her father wanted her to reschedule her test or arrange to take it earlier, but she insisted that she could take the test and still be on time for the rehearsal. Readying herself for the "I told you so" speech, she maneuvered the rental SUV in the tight space between another SUV and a luxury sedan.

She hopped out of the truck and grabbed the red leather jacket that was no more a match for Detroit in February than it was for South Hadley. Not exactly winter fare, it looked good, especially when she wore the low-ride, boot-cut jeans she was wearing and the matching red leather boots.

She laughed to herself, unable to believe that Sonya had actually pulled it off and gotten Kendrick to propose, let alone make it down the aisle. In Alicia's opinion, Kendrick—like the rest of his no-good friends—would fight marriage until his dying breath. It amazed her that Sonya could be so patient, but she got her man.

The rehearsal had already started when she burst into the sanctuary of St. Luke's Episcopal. Taking a seat in the back so as not to disrupt things, her actions were to no avail. Everyone turned around to see who had entered, and she was the center of attention.

Alicia smiled weakly and waved. Everyone turned back around and continued with the rehearsal, but her father made a point of narrowing his eyes and glaring at her before he turned. She knew right away how the conversation at the rehearsal dinner would start.

Thinking of the rehearsal dinner reminded her that she hadn't eaten a thing since the bagel she'd had for breakfast before she rushed to class. At that moment, her stomach growled. Sifting through her purse, she searched for the pack of peppermint candies she knew she had and couldn't find them. She became so absorbed with finding the mints that she didn't notice she had become the center of attention yet again.

"Alicia!" Kyle Taylor snapped.

Raising her head to find all eyes on her, she responded meekly, "Yes?"

Kyle narrowed his gaze on her again and spoke sharply. "The reverend is talking to you."

"I'm sorry I wasn't paying attention, Dad. Excuse me, Reverend?"

Reverend Richardson shook his head, frowned, and appeared even more irritated than Kyle. "I said that you can join us, and we'll run through the rehearsal one more time for your benefit."

Closing her purse, Alicia slid out of the pew and walked up to the front of the church.

"Nice of you to join us, Alicia," Reverend Richardson's tone was half-joking and half-serious. "It's good to have you back home."

Alicia smiled at the reverend. "It's nice to be home. Thank you, Reverend. Sorry I'm late. My flight was delayed."

"Well let's get started, shall we?" snapped a tall woman with a short-cropped blonde Afro and incredibly striking features. "We don't have all evening. We can catch up with trivial information at the dinner. If we keep talking about this now, we'll all be late for the dinner reservations."

Alicia recognized the woman from conversations with Sonya. She was Deanna, the wedding coordinator. *Wedding Coordinator from hell would be a more apt description*, Alicia thought. But it wasn't her wedding, so who was she to judge?

"Now, the bridesmaids and groomsmen will enter in pairs. Right foot, step! Left foot, step! Slowly! Walk in time with the melody. You should be arm-in-arm, and try to look natural! Happy! This is a joyous occasion!" Deanna barked.

Alicia thought it was a contradiction to walk slowly, arm-in-arm, to the beat of the music, smile, all the while concentrating on right and left feet and still be natural, but she wasn't about to say that.

Surveying the sanctuary as all the other bridesmaids and groomsmen lined up with their partners, she assumed that the guy left standing alone would be her partner. Her eyes fell on Darren standing off to the side, leaning on the front pew and staring at her.

Shoot. Her mouth went dry, and she swore her heart skipped a beat.

She examined Darren as nonchalantly as she could and couldn't contain her gulp.

Is it possible that he could get better looking?

He'd grown a couple of inches taller, and his body had filled out in all the right places. Eyeing his broad shoulders in the brown suit jacket and his chest, she thought, *Pecs, pecs, and more pecs.*

He wasn't overly muscular, but Alicia could tell he was no stranger to the gym. Walking over to him, she held out her arm. When he took it, they walked toward the back of the church.

As soon as Darren's arm touched hers, she felt tiny bolts of electricity travel from her arm to her toes. Determined not to talk to him, she knew she was being petty and should just get over her childhood issues, be a bigger person and all that stuff. The fact that she was paired with him was going to make her life difficult, especially since she couldn't seem to control being so very aware of his presence.

She hadn't seen him much over the years. She had actually tried to avoid seeing him whenever she could. The only reason she was at the wedding was because Sonya was her best friend and she wouldn't miss her best friend marrying the man of her dreams for anything in the world, especially when that man was her favorite cousin. Otherwise, she would have dodged him the way she had successfully dodged him from the summer she was fourteen and heard him say words that broke her young and impressionable heart.

Whenever she heard bits and pieces about him from Kendrick or Sonya, she always pretended as if she couldn't care less. She knew that he'd stayed in DC to get his MBA from Georgetown, and he was now working as second-in-command at Whitman Enterprises.

Must be nice to have a plush-cushy job just handed down to you. Even as she thought those words, she knew that Darren Whitman would have been a success even if he weren't to the manor born. As much as she tried not to be impressed with the man he had become, she couldn't help herself. *He's just an impressive guy. One I need to stay far, far away from for my own good.*

When she was sixteen, her father arranged for a *special* college-aged young man to escort her to her debutante ball. When she'd found out that the young man was Darren Whitman, she refused to go.

Neither she nor her father budged. Kyle Taylor still complained about it every now and then. Alicia, on the other hand, took pride in her position as the first Taylor woman in over one hundred years not to have been formally introduced to society.

Her plans to stay away from Darren Whitman couldn't last forever. Sure, she could have been a brat and refused to be paired with him for the wedding. Instead, she opted to try and ignore him. It was harder than she thought would be.

She was glad that he didn't try to make small talk. It was all she could do to walk—no step—down the aisle with her arm locked in his. His arm was so hard she could swear she felt his muscles flexing through his shirt and suit jacket.

She made a mental note to tell Sonya and Kendrick off for pairing her with Darren.

Sonya knew how Alicia felt about Darren Whitman. And it was Kendrick who held her while she sobbed her eyes out that summer when she was fourteen. She clearly remembered how her heart broke when she heard Darren say that he wouldn't be interested in her if she were the last woman on earth. Sure, she was only fourteen, and he was about to go to Howard University for college. But she really liked him, and she thought that maybe he liked her, too. She had run from her favorite eavesdropping place in tears, and her cousin Kendrick came to her rescue.

Kendrick let her cry on his shoulder, told her she was smart and pretty and would have all sorts of boys her own age knocking down the door when she was old enough to date. Most importantly, he told her that no boy was worth her crying over. That night, she decided her cousin wasn't so bad after all. They had gotten along ever since.

But now—now that he and his bride-to-be have betrayed me—well…

Alicia caught the demon wedding planner frowning at her. She forced a smile and kept her eyes in front of her.

What kind of cologne is he wearing? He smells so…so…manly.

If only she could stop inhaling. His smell was intoxicating.

She and Darren were the second pair to head down the aisle. There were exactly ten bridesmaids, the same for the groomsmen. The number seemed huge to her. She doubted that Kendrick and Sonya were even close friends with all those people. She didn't recognize the majority of them.

When she got married, she would not have one of those big society weddings. Instead, she wanted to have a small, intimate ceremony in a little white chapel filled with candles. She had planned the wedding when she was fourteen and in love with Darren. Sometimes she still had dreams about her own wedding day, from the exact dress she'd wear down to the groom. It irked her that she was currently walking down the aisle with the man from her dreams. She desperately tried not to think about her reoccurring fantasy wedding and groom.

She knew that she would have to fight her father to have a small wedding—*if* she ever found a guy to replace the one she had imagined marrying when she'd initially planned the wedding. *The guy I have to ignore and stay far away from*, she reminded herself.

Letting go of Darren's arm when they got to the front of the church, she felt the same warm and tingly feeling she felt when they first latched arms. She stood on the bride's side, and he stood on the groom's side. While she tried her best not to pay him any mind, every now and then, she would slip and glance at him, only to find him watching her.

Annoyed by his open staring, she couldn't wait to go to the bathroom and check herself. *Is my hair sticking up? Is my lipstick smudged? What is he looking at?* The thought that he could be staring because he liked what he saw crossed her mind briefly, but she dismissed it quickly. *Nope, I'm not the last woman on earth*.

She shifted and slanted her eyes in a way that read "stop staring." He didn't stop and she frowned. The wedding planner tilted her head, and Alicia gritted her teeth in a tight-plastered smile.

The way his eyes moved over her body would have left her insulted if it were anyone else. Since it was Darren, she found herself confused.

Flustered, she moved her hand across her head in an attempt to smooth her hair. A wide grin came across his face, and he appeared to be seconds away from bursting into laughter. Her frustration was clearly some form of amusement for Darren.

The rehearsal dinner was worse than Alicia had thought it would be. Her father would not let up. He was on her case about everything.

"So tell me, Alicia, what were you doing with him? What possessed you to go out in public with that hip-hopper? I'm paying good money to send you to Mount Holyoke, and you are out globetrotting with that Flex Diddy Towns." Kyle Taylor had her cornered at the end of the table. His hazel eyes were flashing, and his fair complexion reddened in anger.

Alicia thought she saw veins popping up along the receding hairline of his sandy-brown wavy hair.

Everyone else enjoyed dinner and polite conversation while Kyle read her the riot act. Sighing, she tried to figure out a response that would have a calming affect. So far, she hadn't had any luck. "It's Flex Towns, Dad. Just Flex. You must be getting him confused with P-Diddy. You're mixing up your rap record label moguls and super producers." She offered a weak smile.

"I don't give a damn what his name is, Alicia! What are you doing attending rap awards shows? Is this what going to that Mount Holyoke is teaching you?"

She had never seen her father so disturbed. If he didn't calm down, he could have a stroke or something. He looked fit, healthy, and very young for his age. Even the picture of health that he was, he could stand to calm down a little.

Wondering what he would do when Flex showed up at the wedding as her date, she almost regretted inviting Flex. She didn't want her dad to have a stroke or anything. When she invited Flex, she reasoned there was no way she wanted to show up at the wedding without a date. Having a date was crucial; however, her dad's reaction had her second-guessing.

She was almost tempted to call Flex and tell him that he didn't have to come. He was flying in to repay her for attending a couple of events with him.

She'd met Flex when she was interning at *Source Magazine*. She'd had tickets for one of his release parties, and he wasn't really enjoying his own event. When she'd made a comment about it, in the smart-aleck way that she was prone to, he thought she was interesting because she was one of the only women there not throwing herself at him. They went out a couple of times and shared quite a few kisses; however, there were no sparks, no passion. Against her will, Darren and the tingles she felt when he touched her arm came to mind. *Perish the thought*!

Flex was an excellent kisser, and Alicia was sure that he was willing to forgo the passion and take her to bed. In her heart, she knew she would wait for the whole package. When she decided to become intimate with a man, she wanted all of the passion.

She and Flex decided that they made better friends anyway, and she did him the favor of attending a few events with him when he was in-between what he called his "model-chicks." That worked out fine for Alicia.

"Dad, we're just friends. He asked me to go to the *XXL* awards show with him, and I had a break in my class schedule. It's not like I skipped class like you wanted me to do, so that I could make the rehearsal dinner." She spoke in a whisper. Kyle was making her the center of attention; and despite how she came off to others, she really *did not* like being the center of attention.

Sighing, she continued, "Good grief, you act like I'm failing all my classes or something. I'm on the Dean's List every semester. I'm graduating a year early. What more can I do? Can't I pick my own friends? I'm twenty years old!"

He glared at her and said between clinched teeth, "I forbid you to see him again, Alicia! He is not the kind of guy you should be dating. If you had gone to Howard or even Spelman instead of Mount Holyoke, we probably wouldn't be having this problem."

Unable to believe her father was still being so unreasonable, Alicia gritted her teeth. To hear him tell it, there would be world peace, an end to world hunger and angels would get their wings in heaven, if only she had attended Howard like the rest of her family.

"Kyle," Karen Taylor snapped. "We can talk about this when we get home. This is not the time." Karen's deep-dark chocolate complexion didn't turn red like Kyle's, but the way her eyes flashed and her words ended with sharp enunciated clips, it didn't take a genius to see her anger.

Deciding that a little distance might not be a bad idea, Alicia got up from the table and went to the coat check. She was leaving the rehearsal dinner before either she or her father said something that they would regret.

As she waited for her jacket, she turned and saw Darren coming toward her.

The evening couldn't get worse, could it?

"So, Licia, I see you've still got it."

His cocky demeanor was as irritating as it was attractive. It was going to be a long weekend.

She gave him a thorough once over as well. *Dang, he's fine!*

He'd grown a mustache, and his eyes still held that beautiful sparkle when he smiled. He still had skin like rich golden honey, and his head held thick black waves. The deep brown suit he wore appeared to be made just for him. *As rich as he is, the suit probably is made just for him.*

"What do you mean by that, Darren? And what are you doing following me?"

"Still full of yourself. What makes you think I'm following you? Maybe, I was headed out to the restroom and decided to stop and speak to you since you have been trying your best to ignore me all day." He studied his nails for a moment and glanced back at her with a wry expression.

"I haven't been around you all day, Darren. And to ignore you, I would have to be aware that you exist." She tried to keep her voice in a calm matter-of-fact tone, but between the spat with her father and Darren's smart-aleck comments, she was about to snap.

His eyes lingered over her before he finally shrugged. "I'm just trying to make conversation. But if you can't move beyond the past then…" Displaying a wicked and dangerous smile, he held out his hand. "Let's call a truce, shall we?"

Staring at the hand as if it would explode any minute, she thought, *what's his deal?*

No way would she shake his hand. "Hmm… I don't think so, Darren. I like things fine the way they are." She grabbed her coat, put five dollars on the counter, and walked off.

"Licia," Darren called after her.

Alicia turned around and tilted her head.

"So what's really going on with you and Flex Towns?" Even though his posture suggested that he couldn't care less, when she looked in his challenging eyes, she felt as if they were urging her to respond.

The look in his eyes sent sensual shivers down her body, and *that* scared her. Giving him her sassiest smile that she hoped read "Wouldn't you like to know," she burst through the door and into the crisp Detroit night.

CHAPTER 4

It wasn't as if Darren disliked weddings, he just felt weird walking down the aisle with Alicia. She was beautiful in the red, low-cut, off the shoulder bridesmaid gown. The red and white rhinestones at the center of her cleavage pulled his eyes to her very full bosom. The curve of her breasts peaking out of the top of the dress made his imagination go off in places that he was sure were not proper in a church.

Her normally curly hair was straightened and pulled up in one of those elaborate hairdos. He couldn't keep his eyes off her. Thinking back to the night of his high school graduation when he thought he was meeting her for the first time, Darren remembered that she'd been wearing a red dress then. The color red combined with her milk chocolate skin did something to him.

Darren knew he was staring at her, and he could tell that it unnerved her. Ever since she blew into the church late yesterday wearing those jeans and that tight little sweater, he couldn't help staring. All grown up—in all the right places—she was taller, and her legs still went on for days. Those jeans had hugged her hips perfectly.

Darren didn't think that he could have a more intense reaction to her than he had when she was fourteen. He was tempted to get to know her better—the grown-up her. It was about more than how breathtaking she appeared. Based on everything he'd heard about her from Kendrick and Sonya, Alicia Taylor was a woman well-worth knowing. She was still smart, brave, and just willful enough to make things interesting. Based on their history, however, it wouldn't be easy pursuing her.

Then there was the issue of Flex Towns. When he heard about Alicia being seen out on the town with the rap producer, he didn't know what to think of it. At first, he thought it was a good thing. If she was involved with this Towns character and she was serious about him, Darren didn't have to worry about the stupid arranged marriage. Then he *saw* her again.

Now he wasn't so sure how he felt about Alicia and Flex. The only thing he knew for sure was that he didn't want to be forced into marrying her. *That* he would fight.

As he watched her standing there holding those carnations and smiling at Kendrick and Sonya, he figured that he owed it to himself to find out what it was about her that got to him. It could be quite the experience getting to know her better, if she allowed

him to get anywhere close. It had been a long time
since the laughs and long talks they shared the
summer she was fourteen. Knowing that she was
catching feelings didn't stop him from hanging out
with her when he could get away from Kendrick and
Troy. He liked talking with her. Even then, she was
way smarter than most girls his age. When Kendrick
finally questioned him about the attention he was
paying Alicia, Darren chose cool points over truth. He
hadn't counted on Alicia overhearing them.

Alicia caught him staring at her and glared at him.
Trying to focus on the ceremony, which was almost
over, he couldn't believe that Kendrick was actually
doing it, breaking up the crew. Kendrick was
marrying Sonya, and Troy was *letting* him. Amazed,
he shook his head.

When Sonya and Kendrick began their on-again-
off-again romance in college, Darren was sure that it
would *not* end up in marriage. Kendrick was more of
a player than all of them. After Sonya called it quits
during her senior year while Kendrick was in graduate
school, Darren just knew that was it. He guessed
Kendrick couldn't stand seeing Sonya with other guys.

Darren's eyes shifted to Alicia, and he noticed her
gaze out at the wedding guests and smile. His eyes
followed hers, and he did a double-take. She was
smiling at Flex Towns.

What the hell is he doing here?

From what Darren could see, Flex had a couple of bodyguards with him. One was sitting behind him, and the other was sitting in front of him.

He is going to need those bodyguards if Kyle Taylor gets as heated as he was last night.

Darren wondered what Alicia could possibly see in Towns. He wasn't one to check out guys, but Flex Towns wasn't exactly a super stud. He was fine if you liked the dark-skin-baby-dreadlock-type. The brother was talented; he made good music. He just didn't seem all that special to Darren.

Darren shook his head and turned his gaze from Flex to Alicia, only to find her frowning at him. He narrowed his gaze and she rolled her eyes. He mused that one day her eyes would get stuck like that and it would serve her right.

The reception was a blast, a perfect combination of high-society and good ole black folk fun. The DJ played a mix of music, and everyone had a good time. They did every line dance from the electric slide to the cha-cha slide to the booty call. The only thing Darren didn't enjoy was watching Alicia dance with Flex Towns most of the night.

She was magnificent on the dance floor, the way she moved her body to the music had more than a few men eyeing her. It irritated Darren that Flex Towns was enjoying her so much.

Glancing across the ballroom, he noticed that he wasn't the only one obsessed with Alicia and Flex. Darren's father and Alicia's father were having a heated conversation, all the while staring at the dancing duo. Taking a stroll across the ballroom to see what the two men were discussing, he had a feeling he could guess what they were talking about, and he was right.

"Kyle, you need to tell your daughter about her obligations now! How long has she been seeing that hip-hopper?" Jonathan Whitman's tone held its usual condescension.

"She says she's only gone out a couple of times with him and that they are only friends. I'll tell her when the time is right." Kyle Taylor watched his daughter nervously.

"Just when will that be? She'll be twenty-one next year. What are you waiting for?" Jonathan's tone turned menacing. "You know, you've done a wonderful job building up your family's company. Letting you run it was a smart investment for me. The community needs an outlet like *Black Life Today*. It would be a shame to lose it. It would also be a shame to see you lose it all like your father did. Especially when it's right in your hands!"

"You don't have to make threats! I know what I'm doing. I know my daughter. And I don't think she is anywhere near serious about that Flex character." Mr.

Taylor moved his arms back and forth vigorously as he spoke.

Darren couldn't believe his ears. The two fathers were standing there discussing their children's futures as if they didn't have a say. His mouth snapped shut once it occurred to him that he was standing there listening with it wide open.

"And just what the hell does that have to do with anything, Kyle? We had a deal. You need to go over there and tell your daughter what is expected of her."

"No!" Darren didn't realize that he had spoken aloud until the word came out.

Both men turned and stared at him.

"Son, this doesn't concern you. You should go and enjoy the wedding." Jonathan sliced his hand through the air in manner of finality.

"The hell it doesn't! It more than concerns me. And I will say this, if you tell Alicia about this ridiculous scheme you two have to make us marry each other, Alicia won't be only the problem. I won't go through with it." He bit out the words and folded his arms across his chest. He knew for sure that he didn't want to marry someone he didn't love and who didn't love him.

"I won't have Alicia think that she has to marry me or risk her family losing everything. And I *won't* have a loveless marriage." Darren cringed at the thought of ending up like his parents. "If Alicia and I decide to get married, it will be our choice, and it will be because she has decided that she loves me and we can't live without each other." As he spoke the words, he knew he would *only* marry Alicia for love, *never* for money.

Jonathan started laughing. "What the hell does love have to do with it? Listen, Son, this really doesn't concern you. This is a business discussion between myself and Mr. Taylor."

"Jonathan, I think we should hear the young man out. He seems to have a point." Mr. Taylor eyed him with wonder.

"You would think that because you're too scared to tell your child that she has an obligation." Jonathan ran his hand across the salt-and-pepper waves on his head and gave Mr. Taylor a pointed stare.

"It's not that. I just don't think that this is the right time. She'll be graduating in May, and then she's going into a Master's program. I'll tell her at her graduation."

"What is she getting a Master's for? She doesn't need an MA to be Mrs. Darren Whitman!" Skin flushed in anger, Jonathan shook his head in disgust.

"She won't be Mrs. Darren Whitman if I decide not to go through with it. And I promise you this, if you tell her about this crazy mess that you two have created, I will *not* marry her." He spoke as firmly as he could. He didn't know why, but he needed his father to understand him more than he ever had before. He had feelings for Alicia, feelings that he now wanted to examine. Everything he'd heard about her during the past six years made her intriguing, made him want to find out more about her. He didn't want whatever chance he had with her tainted by his father's plans.

"If you decide not to fulfill your obligation, Son, as much as it would pain me, you will be disinherited." Jonathan stared Darren in the eye.

Darren couldn't believe what his father had just said. Paralyzed in shock for just a moment, he recovered quickly. He hadn't considered the possibility of his father disinheriting him. The thought of losing everything made him suddenly weary, but he refused to back down. Unwavering, he kept his gaze locked with his father's.

"If that's what you have to do, fine. You raised me to be a man, and I would have to take responsibility for my actions. I'm simply offering a way for us all to get what we want."

Do I want Alicia?

The question echoed in his head, but he wasn't ready to face it yet. Often, he thought about when he graduated from high school and was home for the summer. He'd had so much fun talking with her before she'd overheard what he'd said to Kendrick and Troy about not liking her. She had stopped talking to him and cut him off completely. He found himself thinking about her often when he was in college, wondering if she was still spunky and full of sass, wondering what it would take to tame her wild personality. Just thinking about his memories let him know that he was more than a little interested in getting to know the grown-up Alicia, her feelings, thoughts, and dreams.

"If you all give me some time to make Alicia see that we are meant to be together, then I get a wife who loves me, the Taylors get Taylor Publishing, and you get to continue to improve the family pedigree." *That ought to hold them off until I can figure things out.* The threat of losing his inheritance was a variable he hadn't considered. All he wanted was a chance to get to know a young woman he found himself attracted to without her feeling as if she were under some obligation to be with him. He never thought his father would disinherit him, and he wasn't sure how he felt about that.

Jonathan studied him briefly before turning to Mr. Taylor. "Well, Kyle, does Darren's plan work for you?"

Mr. Taylor had an expression on his face that was in between fear and relief. "If Darren can make this work out where they fall in love, then I say go for it."

"All right, Son. We'll try it your way. Just remember if you fail, Alicia *will* be told, and you will either marry her or you will no longer be the sole heir to Whitman Enterprises."

The only thing that concerned him was ending up in a loveless marriage. His growing attraction to Alicia prompted him to take his father's challenge. If there were a chance that everyone could get what they wanted, he had to take it.

"Deal." He turned and walked directly onto the dance floor, keeping the dancing temptress firmly in sight.

How hard can it possibly be to make little Licia fall in love with me?

Alicia had to admit she was having a wonderful time at the wedding reception. The music was jamming, and her father hadn't cornered her once to talk about Flex and why she had invited him to the wedding. Then again, with all the wedding pictures, her bridesmaid duties, and the fact that she and Flex hadn't left the dance floor in a while, she hadn't had a free moment for her father to get on her case.

That was fine with her. If she could make it through the rest of the weekend and safely escape to South Hadley without incurring her father's wrath, then she would be all right.

She'd noticed Darren staring at her a couple of times and wasn't sure how she felt about that.

She knew that Flex was probably tired of dancing, and he was being a good sport. He was one of those reformed rough-neck types who didn't do a whole lot of public dancing. After hanging out with him, she concluded that he didn't surround himself with many people, and his work ethic didn't leave him a lot of time to date. He didn't even seem interested in it really. Sure, he bedded and wooed his fair share of beautiful models, but it seemed as if his heart was elsewhere. However, he did have an image to uphold, and, unfortunately, that meant having a pretty girl on his arm at certain events.

Alicia's minor in Women's Studies and her feminist—albeit third-wave feminist—leanings made her cringe at the thought of being someone's arm candy. It was different with Flex because he was such a cool guy, and she thought of him as a dear friend. The fact that she needed a date to Sonya's wedding also played a small part in her agreeing to go to so many events with Flex. Although she told herself that it had nothing to do with the fact that she knew Darren would be there, deep inside she knew better.

And who better than a handsome, famous producer and record-label owner to have for my date?

Her schedule at Mount Holyoke didn't leave her much time for dating. And the fact that it was an all-girls' school didn't leave many options.

"So, are you having a good time at this little old wedding in the Midwest?" Alicia asked. The DJ was playing a smooth R&B tune, and she did a little half glide as she spoke.

Having teased her countless times about being from Middle America, Flex laughed. "It's cool. Detroit isn't bad. I'll be back out this way in April for some promotional stuff for the label."

"Really, when in April?"

"I'll have to check. I think around Easter weekend."

"Easter weekend? Won't you be spending that with your family?"

Flex shrugged and kept time with the beat. "Nah, it's just me and my pops really. And we don't get along that well. We don't do the Easter thing."

Alicia frowned. As much as she complained about her own family smothering her, she didn't know what she would do if she couldn't be with them on the holidays, or if they didn't get along. Her heart went out to Flex.

"Well, if you need a home-cooked meal while you're in the area, you can swing by the Taylors. My mother makes the best ham and potato salad you ever tasted. Don't get me started on the greens and candied yams."

"Well, that sounds like it would be too good to miss. I might just have to take you up on that, Shorty." Flex spun her around.

Besides the fact that Flex was a good friend, she secretly had to admit she also liked having the press wonder about their relationship and having such a handsome and famous guy want to hang out with her. It was an incredible ego boost. Unfortunately, it was not *very* feminist. *Sooo un-feminist*! Even by her third-wave, hip-hop feminist standards, she was at risk of having her feminist card revoked.

Although they would probably only ever be good friends, she thought it might be a good idea for him to meet her folks. If they could see how cool Flex was, maybe her dad wouldn't be so upset the next time he heard about her hanging out with Flex.

She almost didn't want the evening to end. Needing to let loose and dance, she only wished that she had on a more comfortable outfit. The bridesmaid gown was beautiful, but the way she felt like dancing, jeans and tennis shoes would have been more appropriate.

As the song ended, so did her good time. Darren Whitman approached them on the dance floor and asked Flex if he could cut in.

How antiquated and sexist is that?

Instead of making a scene, she took the high road by simply smiling and taking Darren's hand. She felt a sharp tingle shoot up her arm as soon as she touched him. Flex looked like he was tired of dancing anyway.

"I'm gonna go and make some phone calls. I'll catch up with you in a few, Shorty." Flex's lips brushed hers and she smiled.

Turning to Darren, she responded, "Fine, I won't be long."

Darren had a frown on his face, and his eyebrow was slightly arched.

Figures the DJ would pick this moment to start the slow jams!

She decided to be cordial. Once this song was over, she would politely bid Darren Whitman farewell. It was easier to ignore him when she wasn't dancing in his arms; however, she was a trooper, and she was determined to do just that. She was all about self-preservation and if she came off as rude, she didn't intend to. There was really no way around it if she was going to be able to protect herself. Darren Whitman would not be able to break her heart again. Having heard what a player he was, she had to steel herself and not allow those old teenage feelings to resurface. Smarter, wiser, and having dealt with a couple of players since she was fourteen, she was not going to let Darren Whitman of all people make her another conquest. Once the dance was over, she would get as far away from him as her legs could carry her.

She had to admit that she liked Alicia Key's song "You Don't Know My Name." It had a nice soulful feel to it.

Enjoying the music as she had all night, she couldn't help but notice how good Darren looked in the winter white tuxedo with the red tie and cumberbund. Closing her eyes, she quickly opened them again.

There was something about dancing so close to Darren, with his strong arms holding her around the waist and her eyes closed that felt a little *too right* for her comfort. His chest was so firm and hard against hers. He was holding her so tight, she felt like she could count every ripple in his body—and he had lots of ripples. Worse than the ripples and the tingles they gave her was the lump in her chest, the one that yearned for things she knew she could never have with him.

She frowned.

"So, Licia, how have you been?" Darren's voice, the one that used to screech when he was twelve, was now deep, smooth and right in her ear.

Alicia restrained the urge to shiver. "Fine."

"That's nice. I never thought that Kendrick would be the first one to get married, but he was. The wedding was nice. It could have been cheesy. You know, with them getting married on Valentine's Day and all."

Listening to his small talk was difficult because it made her think of the summer he broke her heart. They used to talk and hang out, and she'd hoped that they would have eventually been a couple, even dreamed of marrying him and had her dream dress picked out. All of that was before she overheard him tell his friends that he wouldn't be interested in her if she were the last woman on earth. She inhaled and quickly regretted it, knowing she would never be able to get that cologne out of her memory.

Is it possible that manliness has a smell? Can't he just shut up and get this stupid dance over with?

"Yeah." She didn't trust herself to give more than one-word answers.

"And when Kendrick told me that the colors were going to be red and winter white, I thought for sure that they were taking it *too far*." Darren started laughing.

He had a nice laugh—a sexy laugh.

She fought the urge to swoon. "Yeah, well, red and white are Delta colors." Her voice sounded squeaky in her ears.

"And Kappa colors," Darren said matter-of-factly. "I guess that's to be expected when you have a Delta and a Kappa getting hitched."

Then, as if they both realized that he was also a Kappa and she was a Delta, they each let out nervous laughter.

"Anyway, it was nice to see everyone again. I hadn't seen some of the groomsmen since our party days at Howard."

"Well, I didn't know any of the other bridesmaids. Most of them were on line with her when she pledged at Howard, right?" Since he was being so pleasant, she lowered her guard slightly and gave into the small talk.

"I think so. I can't believe you got out of going to Howard." Darren pulled her closer and his arm slid a little further down her back. Taking a deep breath, this time she did shiver.

"I was kind of looking forward to checking for you in your freshman year. How did you get your father to let you go to Mount Holyoke?" Darren used that deep sexy voice in her ear again.

She smiled. "I only applied to Mount Holyoke. Then when he used family connections to get me into Howard at the last minute, I refused to go. He was pissed because every generation of the Taylor family has attended Howard since 1905, blah, blah, blah. But I wanted to go to Mount Holyoke." *No need to mention the fact that there was no way I was going to be on the same college campus with you.* "He said if I wanted to go to an all girls' school, I should have picked Spelman."

"Well, do you like it at Mount Holyoke? Where in Massachusetts is that anyway?"

"South Hadley." Alicia noticed that the Alicia Keys song had stopped playing, and they were now dancing to some old-school Luther.

It feels so nice in his arms, but this is the last dance.

"What do you do in South Hadley? If it's anything like Andover was, it must be boring."

"Well, I mostly study and go to class. I did manage to pledge Delta last year. But it was rough. I had to drive all the way to U-Mass Amherst and pledge the citywide chapter. I only did it because I knew my mom wanted me to pledge her sorority."

"Oh, so you don't balk at all traditions? Just the ones that your father insists on?"

Judging by the way his gaze narrowed and his voice clinched, Alicia could tell he was remembering that she refused to attend her debutante ball because her father picked him as her escort. He had come all the way from DC to escort her, and she had refused to go.

"It's not like that. I just…" *Why am I explaining myself to him? Who is he to pass judgment on me anyway?* "It's really not any of your business." She started to pull away, but Darren held her tighter.

"Don't leave in a huff."

Feeling the heat rise from her neck to her cheeks, she *hoped* it was because she was pissed.

"We can change the subject."

"Good." She returned to one-word responses.

"So, you never answered my question last night. What's up with you and Flex Towns?"

Alicia sighed and started to pull away. The DJ had started playing another song anyway, and Darren's company lost its luster.

"Okay, you don't want to talk about that either. That's cool. But, I don't think he's the right guy for you."

Alicia squinted her eyes and pursed her lips in a manner meant to warn Darren off the subject. While it was interesting that he was so concerned, she was not going to have *him* telling her who she could and could not be friends with.

Darren babbled on, bent on continuing to voice his opinion as if he had been asked. "First of all, he's too old for you. What is he thirty-four, thirty-five?"

"Thirty-three."

"Second of all, he runs with a rough crowd. I heard his record label was started with drug money. Didn't he belong to a gang?"

Fed-up, Alicia pulled away successfully this time. "Oh, cut it out! I could believe this coming from my father, but you?"

"Listen, I don't want you to get mad. I'm just concerned." He chuckled and ran his hand across his chin. "I just wanted to see how serious you were about the guy because I would like for us to get to know each other better. Are you cool with that?" His eyes narrowed as if in challenge.

"I know everything I need to know about you, Darren Whitman. Since I'm not the last woman on earth, I'm sure you are not interested in seeing me on any level."

He smirked and opened his mouth to say something that she was sure would push her way past pissed when one of the sorority sisters grabbed the microphone and started singing, "Calling all sorors to the floor, ohh Delta. We got one here, but we need some more, ohh Delta."

Welcoming the save, Alicia thanked God for the sorority's tradition of singing the "Delta Sweetheart Song" to the bride. "Well, I have to go and serenade the bride. It was nice dancing with you. Oh, and by the way, I am not interested in seeing you again."

Tempted to add *ever*, she knew it would be a lie. It was unsettling just how much she wanted to see him again. She walked away, clapping her hands and singing along with the other sorors that had already started forming a circle around Sonya.

Nonchalant and cool, she tried not to look at Darren. Then she couldn't help it. She glanced back, and he was watching her.

CHAPTER 5

Alicia could barely stay awake in church the next morning. The reception lasted well into the night and long after Kendrick and Sonya left for their honeymoon. After successfully dodging her father and avoiding another encounter with Darren, she went out to a new club downtown with Flex and didn't creep into her parents' home until well after four a.m.

When her father woke her up to go to church as if she were still a little kid, she couldn't believe it. Perky and chipper, he spouted some nonsense about if she was able to party all Saturday night, she could get up and praise God on Sunday morning.

Her mother—usually the sane one—totally agreed with him. They wouldn't even stop to let her get a caramel latte.

The sermon went well past twelve-thirty p.m., and Alicia caught herself dozing off several times. Clearly enjoying her tired state, Kyle didn't even give her his usual irritated stare. Church was her punishment for staying out all night with Flex.

When the reverend finally ended his sermon with the benediction, she was the first person out of the pew. Kyle quickly grabbed her shoulder and guided her toward the long line of parishioners waiting to greet the reverend. All she wanted to do was take a nap in the backseat of the family's luxury sedan.

Just as they were inches away from the door, Kyle noticed the Whitmans.

"Jonathan, good to see you."

She frowned. They'd just seen them all day yesterday at the wedding and reception. She could have gone a while longer without seeing Darren again, especially since he appeared all rested and full of energy when she felt like crap.

"Well hello, Kyle, Karen, Alicia. How are you all doing this morning?" Patricia Whitman's voice always sounded false to Alicia, as if she were trying to make everyone think that she was happy. The tall, light-complexioned woman flashed a strained smile.

"Kyle." Jonathan Whitman nodded his head. Stern, he rarely ever smiled. He and Darren resembled one another, but the father's features were harsher. He had the same build as Darren, but everything about the older man seemed hard-edged and severe.

"Well, look at you, Alicia. Aren't you lovely? " Mrs. Whitman had her signature plastic smile on. "You have grown up beautifully. You really have. You're just a little woman now, aren't you? Oh, Karen, you must be so proud to have such a beautiful daughter."

"Yes, I'm very proud of Alicia," Karen said. "She's on the Dean's List every semester at school. She's graduating a year early. And she's already been accepted into several graduate programs. She makes me more than proud." Karen smiled graciously, but it was clear to Alicia that she didn't want to talk to Mrs. Whitman anymore than Mrs. Whitman wanted to talk to her.

Alicia recognized Karen's fake voice. She knew Karen wouldn't participate in any of the women's groups and clubs that women like Mrs. Whitman frequented if it wasn't for Kyle.

"Yes, that's lovely, really." Mrs. Whitman's eyes glazed over, and she turned to her husband.

"So, Alicia, when are you heading back to Massachusetts?" Darren's gaze was so intense it almost made Alicia forget she was in the church.

"I'm flying out this evening at seven." She tried to be pleasant and civil even though her attraction to him unnerved her.

"I was hoping to spend some time with you before you left. Can I take you out for brunch or lunch today?" he said with cocky assuredness.

What is the point of getting up early and trying to get some religion when the devil is so busy working through the likes of Darren Whitman?

"I think that's a wonderful idea," Kyle chimed in. "You guys can go and have brunch right now. You really don't get a chance to hang out with your friends when you come home. I think it's really nice that you are going to get a chance to catch up with Darren."

Somehow, her father had turned into a walking beer advertisement. She halfway expected to hear *"here's to good friends…"*

And who said that Darren Whitman is my friend?

"Thanks for the offer, Darren, but I'm really tired, and I was planning to go and take a nice nap before heading out to the airport. Maybe next time?" Putting on her best polite smile, she turned to walk away.

"You can nap on the plane, Princess. Plus, your mom and I were planning to take a nice romantic Sunday drive. You go out with Darren, and he can take you home afterwards. Is that okay with you, Darren?" Kyle was already leading Karen away as he spoke.

"That works for me." Darren's tone was nonchalant, and he eyed her as if he was daring her to make a scene by protesting.

Her eyes narrowed and she forced a smile. "Well, far be it from me to turn down a free meal. You are treating, aren't you, Darren?"

"Of course, Licia. I wouldn't have it any other way." He put out his elbow and waited for her to link arms with him.

"Okay, Mom and Dad, I'll see you later. It was good seeing you both again, Mr. and Mrs. Whitman."

Cutting her eyes in Darren's direction, she walked past his extended elbow and out the door.

Darren pressed the automatic opener to his burgundy Italian sports car. When he opened the passenger side, Alicia climbed in, and he couldn't help but notice her long, shapely legs as he closed the car door. Her sheer navy blue stockings resembled poured-on silk. He would have paid money to be that simple navy blue wrap-around dress she was wearing.

He'd noticed her the moment she and her parents had walked into the church and knew that he had to figure out a way to spend some time with her. He wanted to get to know her better, get to know the spitfire that bucked family tradition and went to the school she wanted to attend, the debutante abstainer who dared to go against her father's wishes. Seeing her again and talking with her made him want to talk with her more. He thanked God that they were in church and Mr. Taylor was helping him out. If they were outside of the holy walls, she would have had no problem telling him what he could do with his brunch.

He got in the sports car, cranked it up, started driving and tried to think of something to say. She wasn't saying anything, and he took that to mean that she was too pissed to talk. He understood her being upset. The way things went down in the church, she had more than a right to be upset. Under ordinary circumstances, he would have had no part in such a scam of a setup. It was the second time in a matter of days that he was doing something totally out of character to appease their fathers. Disgusted, he made a mental note not to make it a habit. Planning to make it up to her later, he just hoped that she would let him.

One thing he knew about her was that she couldn't stand being told what to do. In fact, as far as he could tell, the quickest way to get her to do something was to tell her not to do it. Stubborn and hard-headed as a kid, she was just as willful and determined as an adult—and he found himself intrigued by that.

He'd made a huge mistake at the reception telling her that he didn't think Flex was right for her. She liked to make up her own mind, and he had to see if he could repair the damage that he and her father did by warning her away from Flex Towns. Just thinking about Flex kissing her lips last night irritated him.

Turning to sneak a peak at her as he reached a stoplight, he almost laughed aloud. No wonder she was so quiet; she was sleeping, peaceful and calm. He turned, noticed that the light had changed, and kept driving.

Using the quiet time to strategize, he drove past the Rhythm Kitchen Café in Greektown—where he intended to take Alicia for brunch—and headed toward 375 instead. He bypassed the rest of downtown in order to get to his loft on Kirby Street quicker. She slept the entire way, and he hoped she wouldn't pitch a fit when she realized he had taken her to his place instead of a restaurant.

After he pulled into the underground parking garage of his building, parked, and turned off the ignition, Alicia opened her eyes and sat up like a baby that wakes up as soon as the car stops moving.

Rubbing her eyes, she surveyed the area. "Where are we?" She stifled a yawn.

"I decided that I'd cook you something to eat. That way you can nap while I make it." *What woman can resist a man who cooks for her?* He'd have her eating out of his hands in no time.

"Oh, so you just decided to take me to your place without asking me if I wanted to go? I agreed to eat with you in a public place, Darren Whitman, not your little private pimp shack." Alicia made no effort to remove her seat belt or any attempt to follow him as he opened his door.

"Oh come on, Licia, you're obviously tired. I'm trying to be nice. I figured you can take a little nap, and I can cook you a nice meal. We can talk and catch up once you've rested, then I'll take you home." Wondering if she gave Flex this hard a time, he tried to keep a positive demeanor.

Taking a deep breath, he said, "I don't have a secret agenda. I'm just trying to be nice. I know you didn't want to go out, and your dad and I sort of backed you into a corner. So, I'm trying to make it a little more relaxed."

Her eyes trained in on him, and her lips twisted to the side. Smiling his best Boy Scout smile, he could almost see the wheels in her mind working overtime before she tried to stifle another yawn.

"Well, I guess you're not a serial killer or anything, and my parents do know that I'm with you. Okay. I am tired, and it is your fault that I'm not in my bed sleeping now. Can you cook? I'm not trying to get food poisoning." She eyed him suspiciously, but her tiredness won out.

He laughed. "Come on, girl. Let's go upstairs. You'll see how I burn."

Alicia took off her seatbelt and opened her door. "Yeah speaking of burn, just don't burn the place up. I don't want to die from smoke inhalation while I nap." She got out of the sports car.

"I expect a full apology when you taste my delicious meal." He decided that he would warm up one of the entrees that Dorothy, his housekeeper and cook, had prepared and frozen for him to have on hand whenever he had unplanned guests.

Judging by Alicia's comments, she wouldn't be impressed with the scrambled eggs, microwave bacon, and sausage he'd intended to wow her with.

They took the elevator to his loft, which was on the top floor of a recently renovated factory building. His was one of four lofts in the building and was on the top two floors.

Darren showed Alicia upstairs to the bedroom area that sat on a suspended platform above the rest of the loft. He liked the layout of the loft because the spacing allowed him to have an open area in the rest of his home and still have his sleeping quarters remain private. Alicia glanced at his king-sized bed.

Taking off her coat and those sexy navy pumps, she eyed his bed. "Do you have an extra blanket? I'd hate to mess up your bed."

"You can get under the covers, Alicia. I don't mind." He couldn't take his eyes off her legs.

Again, she stared at the bed, and then looked at him. "Umm, no offense but, I don't know what's been going on in those sheets." She shrugged. "I'll just use my coat."

Is she being rude because she's sleepy, or is she trying to push me away? I know when a woman is attracted to me, and she is definitely attracted. Is she trying to resist her attraction?

"Licia, my sheets are changed daily. Dorothy is very good about maintaining that. Do you really think I would ask you to sleep on a dirty bed?"

"Oops, my mistake. Must be nice to have good help." Snickering, she pulled back the blanket and sheet. "Ooo, Downy fresh and Snuggles soft." She got into the bed.

She fluffed the pillow under her head. "Hmm, nice high thread count, impressive." After one good yawn, she was out almost as soon as her head hit the pillow.

Darren shook his head and went down the spiral staircase that led back to the first floor of his loft. He decided to catch a little of the Pistons game before he heated up one of Dorothy's specialties. The arroz con pollo with a little baby spinach salad on the side would work fine. All he'd have to do was put the dish in the microwave, open the bag of salad, pour on some balsamic vinegar dressing from the bottle, toss, and presto—instant impressed woman.

The Pistons were playing the Lakers, and the game was close—twenty to fifteen, Pistons. He had been a fan of the home team since the days of Isaiah "Zeke" Thomas. They were having a good year, and he hoped this would be the year they brought the championship back to Detroit again.

The city could use another championship. So many things were happening. The city was becoming vibrant again, and it was ripe for change. There were so many facets to it that people from elsewhere didn't think of.

When most people thought of Detroit, they thought of the riots and urban devastation. They thought of Motown, black music, singing, and dancing. They thought of rags to riches, white hip-hop stars. They thought of the automotive industry and deindustrialization.

They never thought of rich, black executives like his father. They didn't think of young black mayors making moves to insure urban renewal helped the city and its inhabitants. They probably never thought of historic districts like the Palmer Woods neighborhood where the Singletons and the Taylors lived. Detroit was a city full of things that Darren bet many people hardly thought of.

They definitely never thought of elite black blue bloods like the Taylors, steeped with so much family history and pedigree that even rich and successful men like his father wanted a piece of their own to claim.

Deep in thought, he almost forgot about warming up the food. The game was almost at the end of the second quarter. Satisfied that the Pistons were still winning, he turned the television off and went into the kitchen to work his magic.

Everything smelled wonderful when he finally headed upstairs to wake Alicia. She was still sleeping. Balled up like a little kitten, she made the cutest little murmuring sounds. He sat on the bed beside her and touched her arm. She turned over and literally leaped into his arms.

Alicia was having the most delightful dream about Darren. They were back at Club Retro, and instead of brushing her lips and patting her on the head like he did when he found out who she was, he proclaimed his undying love and kissed her passionately. For some reason, instead of the fourteen- and eighteen-year-olds they really were when it originally happened, they were their current ages. He was wearing the tuxedo that he wore in the wedding, and she was wearing her brides-maid gown.

The kiss felt like magic. He started slowly by lightly brushing her lips with his. The light brush deepened when he softly nibbled her top lip, and her bottom lip. He stared at her in a way that made her insides turn to mush. The intensity of his gaze and the kiss were almost too much for her. Alicia found herself trying to express what she felt in words, but the only things that came out were murmurs and moans. She felt the tingles again—all over. She was finally able to at least say his name, and she

*found herself breathless as his mouth claimed hers again
and his tongue wrestled with hers for control of the kiss.*

"The food is getting cold," dream Darren said.

*"What are you talking about? You know the club
doesn't serve food."*

*"Come on, Licia, baby, wake up, you're letting the
wonderful meal I prepared for you get cold. The food is
getting cold. Wake up, sweetheart."*

*Alicia tried to process why dream Darren had stopped
kissing her to talk about food. Then delicious smells
wafted past her nose along with a whiff of Darren's
cologne.*

*Umm, dream Darren smells just like the real Darren,
good.*

She frowned. *This sure is a vivid dream. Hey!*

Alicia opened her eyes and found that she was in
the real Darren's arms, and her lips felt like they had
been thoroughly kissed. She narrowed her gaze on
him. "What do you think you're doing?"

"I came in to wake you up for lunch, and you
opened your eyes and literally jumped into my arms.
We kissed until I realized that you weren't totally
awake. Sorry about that."

Trying to get her bearings was beyond difficult.
"You know, I did not come to your house to be
molested." She pulled away from Darren and tried to
sit up in the bed.

The space was too limited to successfully maneuver because he was still very close. "Can you get off me, please?"

Darren sat up and ran his hand across his chin. Eyeing her appreciatively, he murmured, "That must have been some dream you were having."

Shoot! "I don't know what you're talking about, Darren Whitman. All I know is that I was sleeping peacefully until you came and attacked me with your lips." Alicia eyed the lips in question, and her mind went back to his kisses. She suppressed the urge to kiss him again by getting out of the bed and straightening her dress.

She stepped into her pumps, walked over to the mirror, and straightened her hair before turning to face Darren again. "So, you said that you were going to feed me. Let's see if you can really cook." It was best to change the subject and move away from the kiss topic.

Eyes narrowed, Darren shook his head. "So, you're not going to tell me what you were dreaming about. I mean, judging by the fact that I heard you say my name, I think I can safely say *who* you were dreaming about. I sure would like to know *what* you were dreaming about."

He got up from the bed. "I understand if you want to keep it a secret for now. I just wanted you to know that if you share your dreams, I just might be able to help make them come true."

Cocky and arrogant, too, she thought. She thanked God she didn't have a lighter complexion, because she knew that if she did, she would have turned ten different shades of red. The heat traveled from her neck to her hairline as it was.

Deciding to play it cool, she walked from the mirror to the bed where Darren was standing. She tilted her head. "So, you want to make my dreams come true?" Her voice was almost a whisper.

"Yes. If you're willing to share them." Darren brushed her face with his fingertips.

Alicia smiled. "So, you'll make my dreams come true only if I tell you what they are?"

"I want to be sure to give you what you want."

"Umm, that sounds nice. I might be able to work with that."

"Really?"

"Yes, really. I'll remember that in case I ever feel the urge to share all my dreams with you."

"Really." Darren placed his arms around her waist.

"Yes, I'd love to start with the dream I was just having, but I don't think you really want to hear about that. Do you?" She licked her lips, wrapped her arms around Darren's neck and gazed up at him adoringly.

"Oh yeah, sweetheart, I'm all ears."

"Well, I wasn't dreaming about you really. You were in there. But I was dreaming about Denzel. Denzel and I were kissing when you showed up. That might be why you heard me say your name. In my dream, I said your name and told you to get lost because you were interrupting my flow with Denzel. So, do you think you can make that dream come true—minus the part where you walk in? Can you hook a sista up with Denzel?"

Trying to keep a straight face, she almost lost it at the sight of the perplexed expression that crossed Darren's face.

Darren's lips curled into what passed for a smile. He used the hold he had on her waist to turn her around, led her toward the stairs, and whispered in her ear, "Just remember, whenever you're *really* ready tell me your dreams, I'm here waiting to make them come true."

The sound of his sexy whisper almost made Alicia lose her footing. It was a good thing Darren still had a firm hold of her waist.

CHAPTER 6

Darren watched Alicia closely as she ate the arroz con pollo and spinach salad. Judging by the way she half-closed her eyes and smiled after each bite, she enjoyed the meal. She didn't seem to suspect that he hadn't prepared it. Letting his mind wander back to the kiss they shared, he wondered if she was as moved by it as he was. He had no idea she was sleeping or he would never have kissed her. When she reached for him and touched her lips to his, he was a goner until he realized she had no idea what she was doing. That didn't sit well with him at all because he wanted her fully awake when he kissed her.

Alicia took a sip of her iced tea and smiled. "No way in hell did you cook this, Darren."

Her words ripped him out of his musings. He gave her his best "I'm innocent" face. "Licia, you insult me. Do you really think I would lie about preparing a meal for you?" Watching the way her eyes worked him, he almost laughed at her mock seriousness.

"I think you would lie about just about anything and everything. I especially think you lied about preparing this meal, which by the way was delicious. You must give Dorothy my thanks."

"Okay, now I think I really am insulted. I try to create a nice vibe here with a lovely meal and salad." He reached back and grabbed the remote control off the rich mahogany wood console and pressed play. Soon Musiq Soulchild's "Love" played in the background. "Nice relaxing music. Hell, I even let you nap in my bed while I slaved in the hot kitchen. And the best you can do is call me a liar? I don't know, Licia. For a deb, you are sure lacking in the manners department. Didn't your charm classes give you etiquette lessons on how to behave when you're a guest in someone's home and they have treated you as superbly as I have?" Trying to keep an indignant tone, he barely kept a straight face.

Alicia started clapping and laughed. Her laugh sounded like music to Darren. It started in her throat, and by the time it came out of her mouth, it took on a bell-like quality. Her face was radiant with laughter, and he was so enthralled that he didn't mind that she was laughing at his expense.

"That was marvelous. Bravo, Darren, bravo! That was almost Oscar-worthy. I don't know which performance to give the nod to, you as a cook or you as an insulted host. Oh hell, I'll just give you a double nomination. Both performances were superb." Alicia's throaty laugh tapered off, and she took another sip of her iced tea.

After she stopped laughing, she sighed. "And we both know that I was never officially a debutante."

Darren remembered the year his father told him that he had to escort Alicia Taylor to her debutante ball. Darren had feigned resistance, but secretly looked forward to spending the night dancing with her.

Most debs had college-aged escorts, so he would have enjoyed the evening with her with no ribbing or jokes from his friends. He even planned to plant some seeds and put things in motion so that when she arrived at Howard as a freshman, he would be able to get to know her better.

She refused her debut, and she didn't attend Howard. If he didn't know better, and didn't know that she was just being her independent and willful self by choosing her own path and not allowing her father to choose a path for her, he would have thought that she was deliberately avoiding him.

"Would it have been that bad to attend the ball with me?" Wanting to keep the mood light, he was also dying to know why she basically stood him up back then.

"At the time, yes, it would have been." Unblinking, her voice was matter-of-fact.

"What about now?" He saw her startled expression.

Like a professional actress, she suppressed it so quickly that if he were not so in-tune with her he would have missed it.

Interesting.

Smiling, she swiftly changed the subject. "Now, we find out why you lied and tried to take credit away from dear, wonderful Dorothy."

Okay. Fine. I can roll with this...for now.

"Okay, what gave it away?"

"Well, first of all, I find it hard to believe that a man who doesn't do his own laundry or make up his own bed prepares his own meals. But I do realize that there are some rich guys who can do all of that and can out cook even the best chef, so I'm not stereotyping you."

She grinned. "But come on, Darren, you can't really expect me to believe that you can cook. Whenever would you find the time between all the work you do at Whitman Enterprises and all the women you are seen out and about with? You probably don't have a minute to sleep, let alone cook."

Got you!

"So, you have been reading about me and following my career, huh? I knew it. You want me, don't you?"

Frowning, she narrowed her gaze.

He could tell that she wouldn't admit her interest in him. He could wait her out though. By the time he was done with her, she wouldn't be able to deny her feelings for him.

"You are probably the most arrogant jerk in the world, Darren Whitman. I would have to be blind not to know what is happening in your life. You are only in just about every issue of *Black Enterprise* and all the society pages. What functions *don't* you attend?"

Darren inhaled deeply and tried to cut the edge he felt creeping into his voice. "Well, I can say for sure that you won't catch me at some hip-hop awards show or CD release party for the newest gangster rapper."

"Oh that's rich, so very rich. I take that back. You are *definitely* the most arrogant jerk in the world." She folded her arms across her chest.

"Again with the insults, huh? Fine, I'll take that as a compliment coming from a stuck-up, conniving, little daddy's girl who is clearly trying to get attention by dating a thug." He folded his arms across his chest.

Her eyes become so narrow they almost closed. Her lips turned up in what resembled a snarl. Then, as if nothing had happened, her face went blank, and she stood up.

"I'd like to go home now, if you don't mind, Darren. I have to pack, and I'd like to spend some time with my folks before I head back to school. Thanks for the lunch. As I said, it was superb."

Darren couldn't take his eyes off her. When she stood up, he couldn't help but notice how the navy blue dress hugged every curve on her body. He was tempted to walk over and untie the straps on the side of her dress that held the dress on just to see the dress let go of her curves. His mouth felt dry. Things were going fine until he teased her about having feelings for him. Yes, she was definitely resisting her attraction. He tried to think of the words that would salvage the afternoon.

"You can't leave mad, Licia."

The glance she shot him read, "You want to bet?"

"Listen, obviously we've got some weird energy thing between us that needs to be investigated. I'm brave enough to explore it. Are you?"

She just stared at him.

He got up from his chair and walked over to her. He noticed her stiffen when he got close enough to whisper in her ear. "You have been driving me crazy ever since I was twelve, and I think it's about time we put all that energy between us to good use. Are you game?"

Alicia turned around and gazed deeply into his eyes. He did everything he could not to pull her into his arms and finish the kiss they started upstairs.

"For the record, Darren, the only energy we have between us is an intense dislike. I think that if we were to explore it, one of us would definitely get hurt, and it wouldn't be me." Her eyes were sharp and piercing, as if she used them to make both a threat and a warning.

Interesting.

"Your proposition, while amusing, has to be declined." She stepped away. "Now, if you will please either take me home or call me a cab. I really have to go."

Walking past him, she grabbed her coat and strutted over to the door. Grabbing his keys and jacket, he joined her. He opened the door and Alicia walked out without giving him a second glance.

Difficult!

Silence was the best strategy to ensure a safe ride home, Alicia decided. If Darren made one more smart comment or wisecrack about her, she would pop him upside his head, which could cause him to lose control of the car. So she bit her tongue even though she wanted to tell him off.

Who does he think he is anyway? He doesn't know the first thing about me! Daddy's girl? Seeking attention?

Struggling to think of what she ever saw in him when she was a teenager, she figured that the hormonal changes that she was going through at that time must have had an impact on her brain. She had a better read of him when she was eight and hated his guts. She found it mildly amusing that he was claiming to have an interest in her now.

She glanced at him. His square jaw line was set and determined. His Adam's apple seemed to be pulsating. He stared straight ahead and held the wheel with his right hand while the other tapped his knee.

Somebody's a little upset. Good. How dare he cop an attitude when he should be apologizing?

She sighed.

Darren sneered at her and pulled off the highway onto the shoulder.

"What are you doing?" She folded her arms across her chest.

"We need to talk."

"We are *so* finished talking, Darren. Take me home, or I will get out and walk."

The expression on Darren's face said, *Go ahead. I dare you.*

She decided that she would rather walk than spend another minute with him. When she reached to open her door, Darren grabbed her arm. "Let go of me, Darren."

"You're not walking, Licia. Stop acting like a brat and listen for a change."

"If I'm such a brat, Darren, why are you even bothering to…to… just exactly what is it you're trying to do? Why this sudden interest in me? Have you run out of conquests? Do you need a new challenge?"

She watched him as he watched the cars whiz by. He didn't seem to be trying to think of anything to say; rather, he appeared to be trying to calm down.

She knew that she would be able to tell if he lied. He might be a bonafide player, but she was nobody's fool. The two relatively short relationships that she'd had in the past, one in high school and one in college, had taught her how to read the signs. The chinks in her heart were almost worth the knowledge she gained. She would not be played again, and her heart couldn't take it if Darren were the one to play her.

"Can we just call a truce and agree to get to know each other?" He tapped the wheel again.

"Right now, I think you're sexy as hell, and you know just how to work my last nerve. So why don't we just stop fighting it? Maybe I can come visit you in Massachusetts when I'm in Boston on business. Right now, I just want to get to know you a little."

Resigned, she shook her head. "You know what, Darren, you must have forgotten that I used to eavesdrop on you, Kendrick, and Troy all the time. I even used to listen in on Kendrick's phone calls when I was bored. I know a player move when I see it, and those lines, while classic, are hardly working." The yearning lump in her chest started to throb, but she bit out a laugh in spite of the ache. "Take me home before I miss my flight."

"What do I have to do to get you to see that I'm serious?"

"Do *you* even believe that you're serious, Darren? Come on." Laughing again, she mimicked, "'I think you're sexy as hell.' Give me a break. I think I heard Troy whispering those same wack lines in some poor girl's ear when he came home for break one Christmas."

She watched him carefully as she laughed and hoped that he would just drop the conversation and drive. She wasn't ready for this. She remembered that summer when she was fourteen and pining for him like a longing lover in a Christina Rossetti poem. Even though it was silly, she was afraid of being hurt by him again. Any other player she could handle and maybe even give as good and she got. Not Darren. Somehow her instincts told her that he could very well break her heart in a way that would never mend.

"So, I'm just going to have to prove it to you." Darren started up the car and stared at her in a way that made her feel like he could see all of her inner organs, even her soul.

"Yes, Darren. You are going to have to prove it to me, and trust me, you'll be bored before you get a good start." The tingling sensation returned just from his gaze, and she fought the urge to fan off the heat building from her neck to her face.

Darren shook his head and pulled back on the highway. Alicia simply stared out the window, just a little unsettled.

CHAPTER 7

Darren sat in the living area of his loft, staring at his telephone as if it would suddenly start talking to him. For a moment, he thought it actually had spoken to him. It was his own subconscious telling him to go ahead and call Alicia.

It had been almost two weeks since he'd gotten Alicia's phone number in Massachusetts from Mr. Taylor, and he had yet to use it. He told himself that he wasn't calling her because he wasn't interested in her. She had too much attitude. She was just too much work—too much stress and drama. The truth was he liked her little attitude, most of the time, just not directed at him. The other truth was he loved her spunk and wanted to talk with her to see if she was still as witty and insightful as she used to be.

He thought of all the beautiful women he had dated over the years, and if he was honest with himself, none of them compared to Alicia. He never found himself wondering what they would say about this subject or that. He wasn't intrigued by their different opinions or political views, mostly because they never shared, just told him what they thought he wanted to hear. *I'll never have to worry about Alicia just telling me what I want to hear. That's for sure.*

He wondered how everything became so twisted. When he impulsively made the bargain with his father and Kyle Taylor, he figured it would buy him some time. He refused to be forced into a loveless marriage. He'd just wanted a chance to get to know her and possibly woo her without the arranged marriage hanging over their heads. Losing his inheritance wasn't even an option he'd considered until his father's threat. He had no idea what kind of life he would have if he weren't the heir to Whitman Enterprises. Being the heir had always represented security to him. Faced with the very real possibility of disinheritance had him wondering if being the heir wasn't really more of a crutch.

Then there was the attraction he felt for Alicia. There was a glimmer, a hint of something that he wanted to find out more about. Certain that she felt something for him too, so far he had no problem getting some kind of reaction out of her. The problem was that most of the time it was a negative reaction. Wooing her had its drawbacks because the more he tried to get her to open up to him, the more he opened himself up to her.

He figured that he would call her and she would get all indignant and ask him how he got her phone number and why he was harassing her, blah, blah,

blah. She might talk to him for a few minutes, but it would be far from a nice, civil conversation.

No, it's not worth it to call her.

Darren rose from his black leather sofa, walked toward the kitchen area, and made a smoked turkey sandwich on wheat with lots of dijon mustard, tomatoes, and lettuce. Biting into the sandwich, he changed his mind. He wasn't hungry, so he left it on the counter, went back into the living room, turned the TV on, and flipped through the channels.

Over four hundred channels and I can't find anything on the tube to take my mind off her.

He turned off the TV. It wasn't as if he was afraid of Alicia. Hell, he wasn't even afraid of rejection. Women had turn him down before—not many, but a couple. It was never a big deal. There were plenty of women in the world.

So what is the big deal? I like a good challenge, don't I?

Alicia was proving to be just that. If he did decide that he really liked her and couldn't live without her, there was that arranged marriage thing. No, he couldn't imagine making her be with him. He didn't know what he would do if it came to that. Although there was something almost comforting about knowing, even if he would never play that card, in some small way, Alicia was already his.

Thinking it, however, did not make him feel good. In fact, it made him feel like the arrogant jerk that she'd accused him of being. That scared him the most of all.

Am I my father's son? Will my life end up like his? All the money and power I can dream and a beautiful wife who hates my guts? No way. I couldn't bear that.

Then again, he was a Whitman, and they didn't give up without a fight.

We always play to win.

Darren picked up the phone.

Let the games begin.

Alicia was sitting at her computer working on the capstone paper for her minor in Women's Studies. She was writing an essay on black masculinity and using Kevin Powell, Mark Anthony Neal, and bell hooks to form her critique.

When she first started the minor in Women's Studies, she did it as a form of rebellion. Her father worried that she was going to become one of those bra-burning, man-haters, and she figured the minor would give her just enough knowledge to show him how problematic his views on women's rights were.

Her minor ended up being more interesting than her major; however, the BA in English and the MA she planned to get were going to bring her one step closer to her ultimate goal—running Taylor Publishing.

Kyle Taylor probably thought that she didn't have any interest in the family business since she interned at just about every magazine and publishing house but Taylor Publishing. Alicia, however, was building her resume so that when the time came, Kyle would have no choice but to give her a seat at the table.

Although she had long since given up her grudge against her cousin Kendrick, she still felt like she needed Kyle to accept her as a vital contender to one day head the company. After the internships she had with magazines like *Source Magazine* and *Bitch Magazine*, the family's *Black Life Today* seemed a little stiff. Determined, she felt that she could add a fresh perspective on black culture and that she might be able to create a newer, cutting-edge magazine aimed at her generation, that is, if Kyle gave her a chance.

That goal had pretty much driven her throughout her undergraduate studies, and it still pushed her. Being so driven made it hard to develop relationships, and she was fine with that until she saw Darren again. As much as she hated to admit it, he was right. There was something between them, some kind of energy that she found hard to ignore. Oh, how she wished she could ignore it! Out of her league, she knew she wasn't ready to deal with Darren the way she needed to in order to keep her heart safe. All her endurance disappeared when she heard his sweet, deep voice or gazed into his dark eyes.

That's why she liked her friendship with Flex. Even though he was fine with a capital F and could give her the world if she asked for it, she had no desire to ask him for anything. She didn't *need* anything from him. He was the perfect man for a woman on a mission, and he didn't send her heart racing the way Darren did.

If she let herself, she would need Darren with enough intensity to throw her whole program off track. The spark that was thankfully missing with Flex was very strong with Darren. More than the attraction, however, there was that achy little lump in her chest that swelled with need whenever she saw him. The ice around her chest, that being played by two other foolish guys left her with, melted when she was around Darren. Her fear of a total meltdown was the only thing that kept her on her toes.

His decision to pursue her was causing chaos in her life already. The fifteen minutes she had spent thinking about Darren had already distracted her from finishing her paper. She was trying to focus on the computer again when the phone rang.

"Jazz, get that. You know it's for you," Alicia called out to her roommate who was in the other bedroom listening to her reggae and calypso and no doubt practicing her dance moves in front of a full-length mirror.

She'd met Jasmine Stewart during their freshman year, and they'd been friends ever since. Jazz was more inclined to enjoy life; therefore, she wasn't graduating early like Alicia. A serial dater, whenever the phone rang in the two-bedroom attic apartment they shared in a beautiful white Colonial off-campus, it was *always* for Jazz.

Jazz walked into Alicia's room, handed her the cordless phone and plopped on her too-high, over-pillowed, white sleigh bed. "It's not for me this time; it's some guy for you."

Perplexed, she took the phone. "Hello."

"Hello, Licia. How are you?" the deep masculine voice on the other end asked.

Darren.

"Who is this?" Alicia feigned cluelessness.

There was an audible sigh. "It's Darren."

"Darren who?"

She heard teeth suck and another exasperated sigh. "Darren Whitman."

"Oh, Darren Whitman, right. Who gave you my number, and why are you calling me?" Alicia tried to keep her tone matter-of-fact and nonplussed, but she was being flippant and joking with him to subdue the thrill that pulsed through her at the sound of his voice.

"I got your number from your father." His voice sounded a little clipped.

"Oh." For once, Alicia couldn't think of a snappy reply, which was more reason for her to stay away from Darren Whitman. He was beginning to wear down all her resolve after a few dances and a shared meal. *What would happen if I really let him get close?*

"So anyway, I was thinking that since I'll be in Boston later this week, I would love to meet up with you, maybe this weekend, have dinner, catch a show, do some dancing, whatever." He paused. "I could get you a room at the hotel, and you could come down when your classes are done and spend the weekend in Boston. What do you say?"

Again, she didn't know what to say. *You need to say no*, she thought. *I want to say yes.* It was the mind and body split thing on full blast. She almost said "Amen" aloud when the call waiting clicked in.

Saved by the bell. "Hold on a second, Darren, I have a call on the other end."

Clicking over, she half-hoped it would be for Jazz so that she could pull the old, "Sorry, this is an important call for my roommate; I'll call you back" routine. In fact, she fully intended to do that anyway, even if it was a telemarketing person on the other end.

"Hello," she greeted her savior.

"What's up, Shorty? This is Flex. Did I catch you at a bad time?" Flex had a smooth voice that dripped with flavor.

"No, not a bad time at all. What's up?"

"I wanted to know if you wanted to go to the *Source* Awards with me next weekend? I know it's short notice, but I had a schedule conflict that just got resolved, and now I can go. You down to roll with me?"

It was a busy time of the semester, but Flex was a cool person. Determined to find a way to help him out, she also figured it would also give her a chance to do something besides think about Darren. "Let me check my schedule. Hold on." She put the phone down and studied her PDA.

Luckily, midterms were over. Figuring she could make it if she got a lot of work done between now and then, she picked up the phone a little too quickly and pressed some dials as she did.

"Sorry about dialing in your ear, Flex. I've examined my schedule, and I can do you that favor and attend the *Source* Awards with you next weekend. Keep in mind, you'll owe me." Silence was the response to her best saucy voice.

"Flex? Hello," she purred.

Just because there wasn't any chemistry between them didn't mean she couldn't flirt with him. He was fine after all.

There was another too-long pause. "This is Darren."

Shooooot! I must have hit the flash button by mistake.

"Oops, how did that happen? Hold on, umm, let me call you back…" Flustered, she stumbled over her words.

"I'll hold. Handle your negotiations with Towns." His voice had an edge to it that she didn't want to put a finger on.

"Oh, okay, hold on." Alicia clicked over.

"So, Flex, I'll be able to go with you to the *Source* Awards."

"Okay, Shorty, I'll have a driver pick you up and take you to the airport on that Thursday evening, and you can meet me at my beach house. Catch you next week."

"Okay, see you then." Taking a deep breath, she clicked back over. "Sorry about that."

"No problem." He paused. "So you're going to the *Source* Awards?"

"Yes, I am. Would you like a souvenir?"

More silence. "No, I wouldn't. I would like to see you this weekend if possible?"

"Well, since I'm going to the *Source* Awards next weekend, I really have to cram a lot of work and studying in this weekend." Happy to have a legitimate excuse to decline Darren's very appealing offer, the words rushed out of her mouth.

"How about this, you bring all your books with you, and I promise you will have plenty of time to study? We'll just do things that you would have to do anyway, like eat. I'll even send a car for you, so that you can read on the way to Boston and not have to drive."

Could she spend a whole weekend with him and continue to resist him?

What to do? What to do?

She hadn't planned for this. After hearing him say that he would never be interested in her, she figured that he never would be interested in her. Now he seemed to be hell-bent on wooing her. He almost seemed to be daring her to take up his challenge. Never one to back away from a challenge…

"I don't know, Darren. I think we should—"

"Come on, Licia. What's the big deal? If I didn't know you better, I would think you were scared. I know that the Alicia I remember has more guts than to be scared of a few meals and conversations." Something in his voice told her to run at the same time that it lured her closer.

"I promise to be on my best behavior. I won't behave like an arrogant jerk the entire weekend. I won't even try to talk you out of going to the *Source* Awards. Do we have a deal?"

"Fine. Okay. I'll come to Boston and hang out with you this weekend. This is strictly platonic. None of that 'I think you're sexy' talk or 'I want to get to know you' crap. We already know each other, Darren, and I am fine with things the way they are." *Liar*, she chided herself.

"Cool. I'll see you later this week."

"Don't you need my address so that you can send the car? I do hate driving in Boston."

"I already got it from your dad. See you later." Darren hung up.

She hung up. *What in the world happened to my determined resolve?*

"Are you gonna keep staring at the phone like it's some kind of monster, or are you gonna spill it? Who was that deep-voiced brother on the phone? What's up with the *Source* Awards? And since when did you go from having your head in the books to having two weekend trips in a row? If I didn't know you better, I would say that you were trying to take over my mack momma position."

Jazz was lounging on the bed with her face in her hands watching Alicia with what seemed to be a newfound respect. The twists in her natural hair were a deep shade of cinnamon that week, and it brought out the red undertones in her light brown complexion.

She'd forgotten that Jazz was still in the room. Grabbing a tissue to clean her computer screen, she huffed. "You are all in my business."

"That's cause you finally *have* some business worth being in. Spill it. Who was that guy Darren, and what made you agree to go to Boston with him? Is he fine? And what was up with you messing up the call waiting? You definitely need some help with your player skills cause now he knows about Flex. Not that you're serious about Flex anyway." Jazz paused and caught her breath.

"And I'm not even gonna get into that because I know lots of women who would love to be in your place, and you are wasting the opportunity of a lifetime with all this 'friends and no expectations' bull. But I digress, do fill me in." Jazz's speech was rapid and given with that attitude that black women perform best.

"My goodness, you would think you know it all already, Miss Know-It-All. Okay, Darren is just this rich, arrogant jerk who happens to be incredibly fine and for some reason he has developed an interest in me. I've known him since I was a child. I had a brief misguided crush on him when I was fourteen, but wised up and decided he wasn't worth it." She paused and thought of Jazz's questions—questions she didn't know the answer to.

"I'm going to Boston because I am determined to prove that his interests in me are just as fake as he is. Did I mention the brother is *fine*? As far as the *Source* Awards, it's the *Source* Awards! That is more than worth spending the weekend in Miami. Flex is not interested in me in that way."

She had given some thought as to why Flex wasn't interested in her as a serious contender for his heart.

"He is clearly still in love with Sweet Dee. You remember her from back in the day? She was the *baddest* female rapper out. I wonder what happened to her? Anyway, I don't think Flex even realizes that he's still in love with his ex. I like him as a friend and only as a friend."

"So you're still in love with this Darren Whitman guy? How come you never mentioned him to me? I've known you how long? We've been cool for how long? And I don't know about the one guy who can clearly turn your world upside-down." Pretending to ponder the situation, Jazz's mouth broke into a devilish grin.

"Hmm. Come to think of it, even though I didn't know him, I should have known that there was a *him*. I mean it explains why you have been freezing out all other interested guys. What did he do to you?"

"You are just too-too nosy. Who said he did anything to me? And I am not in love with him! Look, I'm tired of this conversation, and I have a lot of work to do if I'm going to make time for this social life you seem so intent on me having." She turned to face her computer screen.

Jazz got up from the bed and took the cordless phone from Alicia's desk. "Well, since you won't talk, I guess I'll call some of our sorors to tell them about these recent developments. Maybe together we can decide why you are suddenly turning into the social butterfly and figure out the extent of this Darren's role in these new developments."

Picking up an ink pen that was sitting on the table, Alicia threw it, hitting Jazz on her denim-covered ample behind. "Don't spread all of my business."

Jazz's bright red finger-nailed hand rubbed her backside. "Ouch! Girl, please, now that you finally have some business to tell, I will definitely be telling it. Happy studies!"

As she stared at the computer screen, she tried to figure out how she went so quickly from plans and order to chaos.

Darren leaned back on his sofa and stared at the blank television screen. The conversation with Alicia didn't go as badly as he thought it would, but it didn't go as well as he had hoped. She would meet him in Boston, but she would also see Flex the following weekend. He wondered just how much of a problem Towns would be.

CHAPTER 8

"I can't believe I let you talk me into coming with you to Boston." Jazz spoke in an overly dramatic drawl as she lounged in the limo and sipped a bottle of overpriced sparkling water.

"Yeah, like I had to pull your arm. Once you heard that we would be staying in a hotel at Copley Place with direct access to non-stop shopping, you jumped at the chance." Thankful that her roommate had a penchant for window shopping and dreaming about the lifestyle she wanted to become accustomed to, Alicia let out a sigh. Jazz's shopping jones and the fact that she was actually from Roxbury and couldn't pass up a trip home made Jazz the perfect shield.

Somewhere between saying yes to Darren and packing her suitcase to spend the weekend in Boston, she got cold feet. Though she still told herself that she wanted to prove Darren was not seriously interested in her, something in the pit of her stomach wanted Darren's interests to be genuine. That scared her. After what he did when she was fourteen, it should have been easier for her to just blow him off. Even if he was seriously interested in her, it shouldn't matter. When she was in high school, Terrence was interested in her, yet cheated with Sue the cheerleader when he realized Alicia wasn't putting out. In college, Paul was so interested in her he failed to mention his wife and kids until the woman showed up at restaurant where they were having dinner. Now Darren. She'd learned from her previous mistakes and would be wiser than to catch feelings for a known and proven player. No, she'd focus on protecting herself and not how fine and sexy he was.

Jazz agreed to come and check Darren out after being bribed with the promise of one item of her desire and a promise that they actually have some fun while in Boston.

She reluctantly agreed to Jazz's terms, even though she knew that Jazz's idea of fun usually involved either partying or shopping. Alicia liked to party and shop as much, if not more, than the average person, but Jazz easily bypassed her in both categories.

With Jazz along, studying would have to take the back burner. At least she would get Jazz's opinion of Darren, and that was worth it to her. All she needed was one person whom she trusted to agree with her that Darren was a fake and a fraud, and she could happily go about the rest of her life.

Jazz took another sip from her bottled water, kicked off her shoes and laid back. "You know, usually, I don't believe in or condone cock-blocking, but since you're being kind enough to buy me a Coach wallet this weekend, I guess I don't mind so much this time." Pretending to think, Jazz placed a finger on her chin.

"You should know, however, that I can't spend the entire weekend babysitting you and your guy. I couldn't go to Boston without visiting my peeps in Roxbury. Mama would have a fit."

"Oh, I love your mama. Girl, you know I couldn't come to town without seeing her. I'll just go with you." Alicia put down the Persuasive Writing text-book she wasn't really reading.

"Oh no you don't! Trust me, when I tell Mama that you're in town with a man, she will understand if you don't see her this time."

Alicia sucked her teeth. "And who said I was buying you a Coach wallet? You better think about a Coach keychain. I'm not buying you a wallet if you're going to take time off."

"I could spend the entire weekend at Mama's. Then, you wouldn't have to buy me anything." Polishing off her sparkling water, Jazz grinned.

"Fine, a wallet it is. You make me sick."

"I love you, too."

The suite in The Westin was posh, to say the least. The bedrooms were filled with rich, dark brown woods and nickel accents. The beds were flanked with luxurious and startlingly white down comforters. The sitting area was decorated in a variety of neutral tones with burnt orange accents for splashes of color.

Sniffing the bouquet of pink and red roses sitting on the counter, Alicia smiled in spite of herself. The card had a handwritten note from Darren telling her that he would stop by her room after his business meeting to see what she wanted to do for dinner. His suite was right across the hall.

"Hmm, nice roses and a card...I'd say your guy is really trying to woo you. Look at this suite. All this and he thought it was just you? Good thing I'm here to help you make use of all this luxury. It would be a shame to let it go to waste." Jazz snatched the card out of Alicia's hand and read it.

"My, my, my, rich and thoughtful, too. I don't know, Alicia. I'm having a hard time seeing the jerk you've made him out to be. Good thing I'm here to check it out. You could be throwing a good one away." Waving the card from side to side, Jazz did a little dance as she spoke.

Alicia snatched the card from Jazz. "Whatever. Listen, you just try to be objective. Don't let these little flowers, the room, and the limo cloud your judgment. I need you to be on point because I feel like I'm losing my objectivity."

"Like you were ever objective where he's concerned? Based on everything you've told me, you are biased against him. You seem pretty determined not to like him no matter what he does." Jazz took a whiff of the roses and put her hand on her hip.

"Are you going to do what I want you to do or not?"

"I'll do exactly what you need me to do," Jazz said with a grin.

Frowning, Alicia was about to tell Jazz that there was a difference between doing what she wanted her to do and doing what she needed her to do when the phone rang.

"Oh, I wonder who that is? Could it be our Prince Charming? Let's see." Jazz rushed over to the phone and answered it.

"Oh, you have the correct room. Alicia's right here." Still grinning, Jazz handed the phone over. "I don't think he's too happy that you brought your roommate on his romantic weekend." Jazz's face showed mock concern.

"Shut up." She snatched the phone. "Hello."

"Hi, Alicia. I'm calling to let you know that I'll be done in about an hour and to see what you had a taste for so that I could make reservations." He didn't sound upset to Alicia, and that bothered her in a way that she didn't expect.

She'd invited Jazz to be an objective observer; however, she realized that if he really wanted a romantic weekend to woo her, he should be upset, and he didn't seem to be.

"Oh, I don't know. Why don't you surprise me? Be sure to make the reservations for three. My roommate Jazz decided to come with me."

"Fine." She thought she heard a hint of disappointment in his voice, but she couldn't be sure. "So, I'll pick someplace nice. When I'm done with my meetings, I'll stop by my room, freshen up a bit, and then come for you and Jazz."

"Cool. I'll see you a little later." After hanging up the phone, she flopped onto the cushy cream sofa where Jazz had landed just seconds earlier.

"What are you grinning at?" Alicia snapped.

"You really like this guy. I can tell. You don't get anywhere near this flustered about Flex. And I haven't seen you give anyone else the time of day."

"That's why I need you. Darren Whitman is not worth all the time and energy that I've been giving him. I told you what happened when I was fourteen." She picked up one of the brown throw pillows and fiddled with its tassels.

"Child, please. You were fourteen. He was eighteen. What did you want him to do, date you? Come on, even if he did like you, he couldn't act on it. They have laws against that sort of thing." Jazz made a dismissive gesture with her hands and sighed in feigned exasperation.

"You didn't hear him." Poised to plead her case, Alicia tossed the pillow aside.

"Please, what did you expect? He was an eighteen year old drinking with his boys, one of which was your cousin, I might add. What was he supposed to say? *Yeah, man, I think your fourteen-year-old cousin is hot. I want to rock her world.*" Her imitation of an eighteen-year-old boy was followed with a Beavis and Butthead laugh.

Alicia picked up the throw pillow and hit Jazz upside the head. Then, she offered reluctantly, "Okay, maybe I can let that go—eventually, one day, maybe. I still don't trust Darren. He, Troy, and my cousin were a bunch of players in college. Sonya gave me the scoop. Plus I've spent all this time trying to stay away from him. Maybe the broken heart I thought I had at fourteen wasn't that big a deal. If I got involved with him now and he broke my heart, I don't think—"

"I know, Alicia, that's why I came. I've dated enough players in my day, and I can tell them apart. I can also tell when a player is ready to stop playing and get serious. I'll be objective." Jazz put her arm around Alicia and rubbed her back. "Now let's get dressed for this fancy dinner that your guy has planned, so that I can earn my Coach bag."

"Coach bag!"

"You get what you pay for." Jumping up from the sofa, Jazz grabbed her duffle bag from where it rested on the extra thick toffee carpet and headed for the bathroom.

Darren couldn't believe he was spending his weekend with Alicia shopping. After hitting all the stores in Copley Place from Neiman Marcus to Tiffany & Co, and almost all of downtown, Alicia and her friend Jazz ended up on the bottom level of Filene's searching for bargain Coach bags: *because true divas never pay full price when they can help it.*

He leaned against a wall and watched as they dug through a basket full of designer handbags looking for a bargain, and was tempted to take them both back to the Coach store and buy every bag in the place if it would have meant they could finally stop shopping.

It was Saturday, and they had been shopping since nine that morning. They were like hunters on the prowl.

Alicia and her friend were leaving on Sunday. Jazz had been with them the entire time, and she was really talkative—talkative and nosy as hell. She asked question after question after question. He decided that she definitely had a future as a talk show host and could give Oprah a run for her money.

In the limo ride to Bob the Chef's Jazz Café for dinner on Friday night, Jazz wanted to know everything from what he majored in while in college to the length of his last long-term relationship. She was so good she even found a way to ask, and got him to answer, how many women he'd actually been serious about in the past.

Alicia seemed to be watching his reactions and paying close attention to his responses to all of Jazz's questions. He deduced he was going through some kind of test, and Jazz was really grilling him for Alicia.

At first, he was annoyed Alicia didn't come by herself; however, being around Alicia and Jazz was showing him another side of Alicia. The two women were close. They played off one another, and the more they talked, the more he learned about Alicia, who became more relaxed and not on guard. He liked seeing the fun and playful side of her.

During dinner on Friday, Jazz spent the entire evening interrogating him about his job, his plans for the future, what traits he found desirable in a woman, if he was dating anyone right now, and if he believed in commitment.

He couldn't even get insulted or irritated by her barrage of questions because she had such a smooth way of doing it. By the time he realized what was going on, she had everything but his Social Security number.

Darren was just about to go and find a chair to sit in when Jazz apparently found the Coach bag of her dreams.

"This is it! This is the one. I knew if we searched hard enough we would find it at a bargain." Holding up a gray leather bag, Jazz danced around in a circle. "This will look *sharp* with that gray pantsuit I just got."

"That's nice. I like that. I wonder if they have it in brown. I could use a nice brown leather handbag to go with those boots I just bought." A woman on a mission, Alicia started rummaging through the stack of handbags.

"I'm sure we can find one in brown here somewhere." Determined and in full pursuit, Jazz took another dive into the bargain basket.

Darren cleared his throat, and both women glanced over at him as if they had forgotten he was even there.

The first to acknowledge his presence, Jazz's tone was apologetic. "Oh, we are being so rude. You must be so bored by now. Are we working your nerves? Should we hurry up? I guess you don't have much patience for shopping, do you?"

There she goes again with the carefully orchestrated questions.

There was such a concern in her voice that Darren almost believed that Jazz was genuinely interested in how he felt.

She is damn good. He could see how she and Alicia became such good friends.

Smoothly, he offered, "No, you ladies take your time. But it's well past lunchtime, and I think you would get more quality shopping done with more energy. Why don't we get some lunch, and come back for more *power shopping*?" He gave her his most charming smile.

"Oh, isn't that nice, Alicia? He wants to make sure we get the most of our shopping experience. That is so nice of him that I think I'll give him a treat." Jazz turned to Alicia and gave her the gray handbag.

"Alicia you go ahead and pay for this, and I'm going to take the T and go visit my mom. I'll probably spend the night with her, so you guys don't bother waiting around for me. You two can go have lunch and spend the rest of the day together without little old me getting in the way."

Darren watched as Alicia's face went from shock to anger to nervous and finally nonchalant in a matter of seconds.

"But, Jazz, why would you want to take the T when we could easily take you after we all have lunch?" Alicia shot him a nervous glance and smiled tentatively. "That wouldn't be a problem would it, Darren?"

About to say that it wouldn't be a problem, Jazz jumped in before he could open his mouth. "Girl, please, Darren wants to spend some time with you. You guys do your thing, and I'll go do mine. We'll have lots to talk about on the ride back to South Hadley. Just make sure you have my purse." Leaving him and Alicia in awkward silence, she trotted off and got on the escalator.

Darren studied Alicia carefully. She shifted from one foot to the other and chewed on her bottom lip. All the while, her eyes stayed on Jazz going up the escalator. If spending time with him was going to make her that uncomfortable, he would just forget about his desires to explore the possibilities of a relationship between them. The last thing he needed was another miserable woman in his life. His mother pretty much had that area covered.

Obviously, Alicia wasn't interested in him, or else she wouldn't have brought Jazz with her. He wondered why she didn't just say no to the weekend or cancel at the last minute like he'd been expecting her to do anyway.

Perplexed and a little annoyed, he finally spoke. "So listen, Licia, if you don't want to spend the day with me, I understand. Maybe this wasn't such a good idea."

It was Alicia's turn to study him. He watched as she scrutinized him with piercing eyes. He thought he saw frustration and a little disappointment before she shrugged her shoulders. Then she got that irritating smart-aleck grin on her face that she always got before she was about to make some equally irritating comment.

"Well, that was easier than I thought it was going to be." Her tone was almost relieved. "You see, Darren, I knew you weren't really interested in me. You gave up your pursuit so easily. All I had to do was make it a little harder for you than you're used to, and you totally caved. I love it! I brought the notorious Darren Whitman down! I'm the woman. That's right." Moving her head from side to side and doing some silly little dance, her voice was almost sing-song.

"You mean this was all a joke to you? Some little game to see if I would stop trying to pursue you because you made it difficult?" Not sure whether to be appalled or delighted, he simply let the new knowledge stew.

Alicia kept doing her little dance and added arm movements to the choreography. "That's right. I won. You caved. I was right. You're a player. You like it easy or you quit. Ha, ha." She continued to chant her little song.

Here he was genuinely trying to take her feelings into consideration, and she was actively playing him just so she could prove that she was right about him.

Two could definitely play that game. She was not the only one who had theories about how someone really felt, certainly not the only one with something to prove. He had a theory about how she felt about him that he wanted to test, and he had just been inspired to up the ante.

Alicia was sort of relieved that Darren was giving up on her. She didn't know if she could take anymore of his suave mack daddy act. He was smooth; she had to give it to him. He had a way of gazing at her that made her think that she was the only woman on earth. Sure that if she had to spend another moment with him in pursuit she would throw all her caution out the window, she almost breathed a sigh of relief when he conceded. He was starting to become a little irresistible.

There should definitely be a law against a voice that made women long for the bedroom. It was so deep and so sweet. The voice made her think of and long to kiss his lips.

Jazz managed to make her realize that she was being a little petty holding him responsible for something that happened when she was fourteen. That didn't make her any less wary of him.

She had never cried as hard as she cried the night she overheard him saying he would never be with her, not when she heard about Terrence and the cheerleader, or when she took the cab home after Paul's wife bum-rushed their date. That night, she vowed that she would never let anyone get close enough to make her cry like that again. A little battle shy, she had spent a lot of time and energy avoiding Darren Whitman, and she wasn't about to let him catch her now. Having a focus and a plan helped out, but having Darren in hot pursuit was pushing all of that to the sidelines.

Even though she was somewhat happy Darren was giving up, the throbbing ache in her chest let her know she'd really wanted to believe that he wanted to get to know her, that he really wanted to be with her, and that he would keep trying until she finally said yes.

This part of her was the same part of her that watched romantic comedies back-to-back on rainy days because she still secretly believed in fairy tales, the part of her that read romance novels because she craved happy endings and hoped that one day her prince would come.

My life is not a fairy tale. If I really think that Darren Whitman is my prince, I need to get my head examined.

Deciding that she might be going overboard with the song-and-dance routine, she stopped and smiled. He had that smirk on his face, and an intense narrow gaze that signaled he was on the verge of severe irritation.

Then, just like that, his smirk turned to a smile. "So, you caught me. I guess my skills are wasted on a woman as smart as you. You win."

"I win?"

"Yes, you win. Obviously, you don't believe that I have purely the best intentions where we are concerned. I admit I was pouring it on a little thick, but you have to admit you were a bit *abrasive*." He paused and twisted his face when he said the word abrasive as if it left a bad taste in his mouth.

"I figured if I poured on the charm you would come around. What woman wouldn't?" He spun around as if to highlight what a good catch he was.

"I guess you're the one woman who doesn't want to be with me. That's cool. I'm done pouring on the charm."

"Thank God! Because your idea of charming is my idea of a fake, phony, wanna-be-mack, played-out-player. Oh, and for the record, I am *not* abrasive. I am usually a very pleasant person."

Darren made a noise that sounded a lot like a laugh, a fake laugh for sure. "I would use a lot of words to describe you, Licia, but pleasant is not one of them."

Indignant, she snapped, "You don't know me well enough to make that call, Darren."

"Oh, I know you well enough." Rubbing his hand across his chin, he gave her a once over. "Not as well as I'd like to for sure, but well enough."

"You know me just about as well as you're ever going to get to know me. I'm ready to go back to the hotel. I'm tired of this."

"Well, unless you're going to hop your ass on the T or flag down a cab, you aren't going back to the hotel right now. I have spent the entire morning and the better part of this afternoon shopping with you and your little girlfriend, and I am having lunch. So, if you want to ride back to the hotel with me, then you will be stopping to have a pleasant lunch first."

Her jaw dropped, then she quickly shut her mouth. Not wanting to spend another minute with Darren, she was almost tempted to take the T or a cab. She took Jazz's Coach bag to the register to pay for it.

Darren followed her to the register. "So what's it going to be, Licia?"

"Get out of my face, Darren." Not bothering to spare him a glance, she searched through her wallet for her credit card.

"Fine. See you around." Darren dropped her bags at her feet, walked away, got on the escalator and left.

By the time she finished paying for the purse, she could barely focus on anything but getting back to the hotel, packing her things and leaving. *How dare he leave me!* Mentally, she called Darren everything but a child of God. She even found herself verbalizing some of the thoughts as she walked out of the store through the revolving door.

A little old lady walking in as she walked out gave her a startled look because she heard her less than flattering reference to Darren, his mother, and sex acts.

She almost went back in the store to tell the woman that she wasn't talking about her, but she stopped when she saw Darren's limo parked in front of the store. Bill, the driver, was already out and holding the door open for her.

"Ms. Taylor." The tall burly driver with red-hair, green eyes, and hands like Paul Bunyan's waited for her to get in.

Smiling as pleasantly as she could, she responded, "That's okay, Bill. I'll take a cab."

Darren got out of the limo. "Get in the car, Licia."

"I'd rather walk." Starting down the street, she only got a few steps.

Darren motioned for Bill to take her bags, and before she knew it, Bill was storing her bags in the trunk while Darren commandeered her into the car.

"Stop manhandling me! I said I'd rather take a cab."

"Maybe you need a man to handle you." Darren used the hand that he wasn't using to grip her arm and push her forward to hold her head down as he pushed her into the limo before sliding in next to her and closing the door.

"So you move from charming right to caveman? Well, I can tell you this; if your charming lacked appeal, then you should certainly realize the rough-neck approach won't work either."

Nonchalant, Darren shrugged before turning away from her. "Who said I'm working at anything?"

"Then why didn't you just let me take a cab? I'm tired of you already."

"Oh, I am beyond tired of you." He cut her a dismissive glance.

"Fine, let me out and you won't have to see me for the rest of the weekend—make that the rest of your life."

"Just shut up, Alicia. We are going to lunch, and then we are going back to the hotel." The finality of his tone made her want to grab him by the shoulders and shake him.

"I don't want lunch."

"Well, I do."

"Well, I don't!"

Darren glared at her and pressed the button to let down the partition separating them from the driver. "Bill, take us back to the hotel, please. Thank you." Making business calls on his cell phone, he didn't bother to spare her another moment of attention.

She opened her mouth to tell him that he was a jerk, but he shot her a glare so harsh she thought better of it. Pretending to gaze out the window, she twisted around in her seat and finally got comfortable as far away from him as she could.

The buildings passed by, and she really couldn't distinguish one from the other. The lump in her chest had a dull, steady ache after the scene in the department store, and she was trying to figure out how she went from being happy that she had finally busted Darren to being pissed off and bullied into a limo. Having lost control, she wondered if she ever really had it.

She glanced at Darren. He continued to talk on his cell, ignoring her. Telling herself that it was fine that Darren was tired of pursuing her because it was getting old anyway wasn't doing a thing to soothe the ache in her chest. He'd called her spoiled, but he was the one who turned into a jerk when he couldn't get his way.

When they pulled up in front of the hotel, she didn't even wait for Bill to get out and open her door.

Snatching the door open, she leaped from the car and brushed past the doorman.

She was in her hotel room packing her things and contemplating calling Jazz to tell her the weekend was over when she heard a knock on the door.

Through the peephole, she saw Darren standing there.

"What do you want?"

"I want to give you your bags. Open the door." The aggravation that laced his voice was palpable.

She opened the door a crack. Darren pushed it all the way open and stormed in.

She balked, "Excuse you. I did not invite you into my room. Just drop the bags and leave, please." Standing by the door, she held it open for Darren to leave.

"Well, since I'm paying for this room, let's just say I'm inviting myself in."

"I can pay you for this room, Darren. In fact, I will write you a check right now. You and your attitude need to leave." She closed the door and tried to squeeze past Darren who was still standing in the entryway.

Sighing, Darren mumbled, "I'm so tired—"

Alicia cut him off before he could finish. "Yeah, yeah, I know, you are *so tired* of me. That line is getting old. If you're so tired of me, get out of my room and leave me alone."

She used her shoulder to move Darren out of her way so that she could get away from him.

Darren grabbed her arm and, before she knew it, she was pinned against the wall, and Darren was way too close for comfort. "What I was going to say before you so rudely interrupted me is that I am so tired of playing games with you, Alicia." His voice lowered. It was a mixture between dangerous and sexy.

Darren took his free hand and cupped her chin. Tracing her lips with his thumb, he covered her mouth with his. His tongue was relentless, and she soon felt as if she had no choice but to let him in. Closing her eyes, she kissed him back with everything in her.

His mouth was searing. Each time it made contact with hers, she felt a jolt of electricity and her insides felt toasted.

She placed her arm around his neck and pulled him closer to her. Darren let go of her arm and used his hand to explore her breasts. He put his arm under her sweater and unsnapped her bra with more speed than she could ever snap one on.

Opening her eyes, she was about to protest; but she felt his thumb ever so slightly circling her nipple. His other hand pulled her closer to him, and she could feel just how much he wanted her. Part of her brain wondered why her instincts were not telling her to stop kissing Darren.

Her nipples tightened, and an ache started in the pit of her stomach and traveled down her thighs. She leaned her head back and closed her eyes; she didn't trust herself to look at him. Lifting her hands above her head, he removed her sweater. Goosebumps popped up on her arms as the sweater and his hand trailed her skin.

She ran her hand over the top of his head while his mouth worked each of her nipples, first one then the other. The ache slowly ebbed, and she felt a release unlike anything she had ever experienced. Her entire body shook, and she had to close her eyes just to get her bearings.

Her legs went limp, and she gripped his shoulders. Things were going fast. She felt like she should either stop him or tell him that she'd never done anything like this before.

Holding her up, he pulled her closer to him as his mouth moved from her breasts to her neck.

He nibbled on her neck until a soft gasp escaped her lips, and lifted her up and carried her to the nearest bedroom. Again, Alicia thought that she should tell him. Then she thought that if she told him he would stop, and she didn't want him to stop. She buried her head in his chest and inhaled; the musky-masculine scent of his cologne made her moan. She planted soft kisses on his face and ran her fingernails gently down the back of his neck. His breath caught, and he placed her on the bed.

Wanting to feel him, she pulled his shirt from its neat position tucked in his pants and slowly examined each of the ripples beneath. She so enjoyed the feeling of his muscles that she couldn't contain the gasp that escaped her lips. This was not supposed to be happening. But she couldn't have stopped it even if she wanted to.

I am in trouble.

He wasted no time taking off her black mini skirt and black tights. He didn't stop until she was completely nude, and then he just gazed at her. Holding his stare for as long as she could, she finally had to turn away. The intensity was overwhelming, and soon her heart joined the other aching parts of her body that longed for Darren.

Saying nothing, he knelt in front of the bed and pulled her hips toward him. Then, he kissed her where no man had ever touched her, and she sighed. His tongue and his lips circled her with such fervor that she could barely control her legs.

Her thighs shook, and his strong hands held on to them with tenderness as the rest of her body began to shake as well. A niggling tingle rose in her, and she exploded. Determined to try and tell Darren that she was so new at this, she closed her eyes, realizing that she had to recover her voice first.

When she opened her eyes, he was gazing at her and taking off his clothes. Fully erect, the sheer size of him gave her pause.

I really need to say something.

He walked over to the bed and positioned himself between her legs. He kissed her hungrily before he entered her. Her body resisted him, and she tried to relax herself so that she wouldn't give her secret away. She didn't want him to stop. Once he penetrated, she took a sharp intake of air.

"Oh shoot," she mumbled. Not meaning to say anything, she'd wanted to play it cool.

Struggling to get used to him inside of her, she opened her eyes.

Horror filled his eyes. Lowering his head, he whispered in a voice that sounded strained, "Licia, baby, is this your first time? Why didn't you tell me?"

She mustered as much brazenness as she could, considering he was so large inside of her and she felt stretched to the limit. "You didn't ask."

Turning her head so that their lips met, she kissed him. "Please, don't stop." She slipped her arms around his neck and arched her back as much as she could.

He moved his hips slowly at first, and she followed his pace. Instinctively, she wrapped her legs around his waist and pulled him deeper inside of her. Control lost, his thrusts came faster and deeper. She bit her lower lip and took all that he gave.

She couldn't believe she was actually having sex, let alone having sex with Darren. She was even more shocked that even though she thought about stopping, she didn't want to. She definitely couldn't tell him to stop when he made her body experience things with an intensity that she had never before felt.

Now that he was inside her, it felt so right that she couldn't think of one reason why they shouldn't be doing what they were doing. Better yet, she couldn't think at all. All she could do was match his thrusts with her own and try not to scream too loudly as the tension that was edging from her inner thighs to the tip of her toes finally released.

She dug her nails into Darren's back as her head moved from side to side. She was trying hard not to scream, and just when she couldn't take it anymore, Darren's mouth covered hers, and she let out a deeply satisfied "aaahhh."

Once she finished her climax, he started to move again.

"Alicia sweetheart, you don't know how long I've waited for this moment." His voice was husky and at least a full octave deeper than normal. The sound of it made her knees weak.

He moved from slow to fast more swiftly than he had before. Soon, she was gripping the sides of the comforter and saying words she didn't even understand. She did manage to hear what sounded like

Darren's voice whisper, "Now baby." Just before she felt a warm release match her own.

At that moment, everything felt so right. Her whole body tingled, throbbed, and went peacefully, blissfully still.

Darren rolled over and took her with him. She rested on top of him as he softly caressed her back. Grudgingly, she admitted to herself that Darren Whitman was always supposed to be her first. As he ran his fingertips across the small of her back, she couldn't help but sigh. She could still feel him inside of her, and that's when she realized that not only had she had sex with Darren, but she had foolishly had unprotected sex.

She tried to pull away from Darren, but he pulled her closer. "Where do you think you're going?"

Rolling off Darren and on to the bed beside him, she whispered, "We didn't use any protection."

Darren let out a guilt-ridden sigh. "I know. I didn't have any, and we were in the heat of the moment. Honestly, I couldn't have stopped if I wanted to."

"What kind of playboy doesn't have a spare condom in his pocket?" She knew that she was lashing out and sapping every bit of the after glow, but she couldn't help it. She didn't want to feel anything except contempt for Darren. The feelings she felt for him were definitely not contempt, and they were extremely scary.

"I wasn't expecting to have sex this weekend, Alicia. I just thought we'd get to know each other and hang out. I didn't plan for this to happen. Now that it has, I think we need to talk about where we'll go from here." Rolling over, he faced her.

"What do you mean 'where we'll go from here?'"

"Well, I'd like to think that maybe it means something that you decided that your first time would be with me. That means a lot to me." His fingers trailed through her hair.

"I wouldn't put a lot of stock in it, Darren. Clearly, I wasn't thinking. Did it look like I was in deep thought to you?"

"Well, I think we need to stop fighting and playing games and really examine what's happening between us, Licia."

"And what would that entail exactly?"

"Well, for one thing, you could call Flex Towns and let him know that you won't be attending the *Source* Awards with him next weekend." Darren's tone was final, and again it disturbed her.

She sat straight up in the bed and glared at Darren. "Why would I do that?"

He sat up, and his voice dripped with irritation. "Do you mean that after what we just shared, you have to ask that question?"

"Clearly, I do. Because you seem to think that you have morphed into Kyle Taylor. The last time I checked, my daddy was in Michigan, and even he knows that when push comes to shove, he cannot tell me who I can be friends with and where I can go with them."

"Oh come on, Alicia. This is not about whom you can and can't be friends with. This is about the fact that Towns obviously wants to be more than friends with you, or else he wouldn't be parading you all over the place." Indignant, his gaze narrowed in on her, and his chest heaved just a little.

"So what if he does want to be more than friends? What if he's planning to take me to bed next weekend? So what? Either we will have sex or we won't. Either way, it's my decision, and I get to make that call, not you. Just because you had sex with me doesn't mean that you have branded me and I belong to you. I *still* get to say what I will and won't do, Darren."

"What the hell do you mean either you'll have sex or you won't? Do you mean to tell me that you would have sex with me one weekend and him the next?"

She got up from the bed a little too quickly. Still sore, she stopped and turned. "This conversation is over."

"Don't go to Florida, Licia."

"I think you should leave now, Darren."

Darren got up and walked over to her. Wrapping his arms around her waist, he turned her to face him.

"I don't want you to go to Florida, and I definitely don't want us to part angry with one another." His lips covered hers, and she almost forgot how irritated she was with him.

Stopping the kiss, she whispered, "Darren, I can't do this."

She stared past him to the bed. Small red blotches now flecked the white comforter. The reality of what just happened between them hit her with force.

Darren turned and examined the comforter. He took a deep breath. "How do you feel?"

"I feel sore, and I don't feel like arguing about Flex or my choice of friends."

"That's fine." Darren ran his hand through the waves in his hair. "We don't have to talk about it now."

"I don't want to talk about it at all, Darren. We're not going to agree."

His eyes narrowed, and he let out a deep breath. "Fine."

CHAPTER 9

Trying to make her flight, Alicia quickly packed for her trip to Miami, dashing around the room and throwing things in her bags.

"So, you're still going to Miami?" Lounging on the bed, Jazz watched Alicia pack.

"Yes, I am." Alicia attempted to get over what happened in Boston. She told herself that it was only because she had to study and focus on her classes so that she could finish her college career in the stellar fashion she started it that she pushed the possible implications from her actions to the back of her mind. Yet somewhere inside, she knew what happened between her and Darren was so far removed from what she thought was her life that she didn't want to deal with it.

For a person who planned everything and was so careful not to get involved with anything that would deviate from her plans, falling into bed with Darren and not taking the proper precautions was ridiculous. It was as if everything that she worried about where Darren was concerned, all her fears about not being in control, were coming to fruition.

"Do you think that's cool? I mean it's clear that you really like Darren. You're not the type to play the field."

When did Jazz turn into an advocate for dating only one guy at a time?

"Flex is my friend, Jazz. There's nothing going on between us. Darren doesn't get to dictate who I can hang out with. It's the principle of the thing." Alicia grabbed a slinky dress she'd just purchased and threw it in the bag.

Underneath all the charm Darren was putting on, she knew that the twelve-year-old bully who used to pull her pigtails was still lurking. Something wasn't quite right. Even though she told herself it was because of his playboy ways that she was keeping him at bay, it was really because she knew that he was just as determined as she was to be in control. That was not going to happen.

So she had to go to Miami with Flex and attend the *Source* Awards. She was not about to let Darren tell her who she could hang out with. It would have been easy to give in and cancel on Flex. But if she had, what would Darren ask her to give up or do next?

Her greatest fears were coming true, and instead of a twelve-year-old torturer who called her names, she was dealing with a twenty-four-year-old, drop-dead gorgeous bully with kisses and caresses in his arsenal.

"Girl, he's been calling you every day. You guys talk all the time. He really seems so into you. I know Flex is *not* into you like that." Jazz sat up, and her voice got serious.

"Flex is my friend. I know he's *not* into me. What's your point?" Alicia tried to keep the irritation out of her voice because she knew that Jazz was just trying to be helpful.

"My point is that Darren *is* into you. I could tell when we were hanging with him in Boston. Why else would he have put up with your annoying friend and all her crazy questions? I know you well enough to know you're in way deep with him."

Resigned that she knew what was best for herself, Alicia kept packing. "All the more reason to go to Miami, Jazz. I need to maintain my autonomy. I am getting in deep, and I need to make sure he doesn't take away all my control."

Nothing irritated her more than the thought of not being in control of her own actions. The fact that she actually considered canceling on Flex and going home to Detroit for the weekend instead so that she could spend time with Darren made her pack more vigorously. Jazz just didn't understand.

Darren sat on the Whitman jet staring at the tickets. He didn't know how his people did it, but they managed to obtain two tickets right next to Flex Towns for the *Source* Awards. Although he had no real desire to attend the awards show, he knew that Alicia had every intention of going just because he asked her not to go. The girl was hardheaded and stubborn.

The Whitman jet was stocked to the hilt with just about every amenity one could imagine, and Darren watched as Troy took advantage of every single one of them. While enjoying champagne and caviar, Troy groaned and complained about how he had to cancel his plans to come with Darren to Miami.

Taking a sip of his champagne, Troy let out a sigh. "You know, I cancelled two very hot prospects in order to come with you to Miami, man. I mean *hot*."

"Right," Darren said wryly.

Tempted to bring one of the sexy models he'd dated in the past to the awards show, to give Alicia a taste of her own medicine, he opted to take Troy instead. Strategy was key with Alicia. Him showing up with a date could backfire big time. Him showing up at all had the potential for the ultimate fallout; however, it was a chance that he was willing to take.

If he could get Alicia to stop fighting him, he could make her see that they had the potential to have something good between them. He had never been so taken away with any woman before that he hadn't even thought about precautions.

Once he'd tasted her, once he was inside of her, there was no way that he could stop. The past few days, they had spoken on the phone and actually enjoyed each other. He definitely wanted to explore the options between him and Alicia further. If they actually ended up falling in love and getting married, that wouldn't be such a bad thing.

Maybe our dads know what they are doing after all.

"Damn right. I'm doing you a huge favor. You owe me big time for this." Troy moved on to the smoked salmon and capers.

"Oh yeah, and a free trip away from Detroit in mid-March to beautiful Miami and a chance to see all of those rap stars you like, not to mention watch some of them perform is not enough to make us even?" Darren asked sarcastically.

Troy smiled. "Not even close. Because I know this isn't about the two of us hanging in Miami and picking up hotties. No, this is about Licia. This is about the fact that she is going to the *Source* Awards with Flex Towns, and you've had the hots for her ever since we started college."

Rubbing his chin in mock consideration, Troy stated, "Shit, I bet you even had the hots for her when we were twelve and you used to tease her and pull her hair all the time. When I think about it, Kendrick and I could easily ignore Licia, but you never could. You had to always win where she was concerned. So, yes, dude, you owe me big time for this little trip."

"How did you know that Alicia was going to be at the *Source* Awards?" More than a little irritated by everything that Troy had said, the fact that he knew that Alicia was going to be in Miami irritated him more.

"When I told Sonya that we were going to Miami for the awards show, she said, 'Oh, you guys should find Licia while you're down there. She's going to be there with that rapper guy she took to my wedding.' And that's when I knew that one of my best friends was pulling the okey-doke on me. Imagine how hurt I was." Clutching his heart in fake pain, he grinned and polished off his champagne.

So, she decided to go anyway.

He knew that she would, but a part of him had hoped he would go to Miami and she wouldn't be there. Nothing with Alicia was easy.

It seemed as if she went out of her way to irritate him, even when he was playing nice and laying on the charm. Most women would have been impressed by his suave moves. Hell, he'd let Alicia get away with things he would never put up with in another woman. There were just too many of them to go around.

He didn't have to put up with attitude. In fact, because of who he was, women usually went out of their way to be nice to him. The sole heir to Whitman

Enterprises was quite the catch, and people usually did what he wanted them to do. He didn't have to tell them twice.

Alicia was determined not only to fight him, but also to fight her feelings for him, and he found that refreshing. Once he decided he was done playing Mr. Nice Guy, he knew that he was in for a struggle, but it was a struggle he was determined to win.

"Oh, you're crushed," Troy teased. "I thought you knew she would be there and that's why you wanted to go. I saw the way you were dancing with her at the wedding. I told you that you were going to have a hard time making Alicia come around when you were finally ready for her. If you were smarter, you would have played it a lot cooler when she was a kid and had that huge crush on you that summer."

"Shut up, Troy."

Darren could tell that Alicia had feelings for him. Hell, he knew that when she was fourteen. What he didn't know was how determined she was to fight those feelings, or how damn sexy he would find that determination.

So he was going to Miami with Troy so that Alicia could see exactly what she was dealing with. He was not the kind of man to stand idle while something he wanted escaped his grasp. The more he thought about it, he was more his father's son than he could have ever imagined.

"Don't get mad at me because you're just now realizing how fine she is." Troy leaned back in his chair.

Darren just glared.

"Hey, man, you know it's not like that with me and Licia, so don't even give me that look. She's like a kid sister to me. But you have never had feelings that pure where she was concerned. I'm just glad you're finally deciding to pursue them. I guess I'll be the best man at your wedding next?"

"Hell no, you won't. You beat me out for best man at Kendrick's wedding, and we both know that spot should have been mine. I'm still pissed about that," Darren snapped.

"Oh, so there is going to be a wedding between you and Alicia? Interesting, how are you going to pull that off?"

Realizing his slip, Darren glared at Troy. "Man, shut up. I didn't say that there was going to be a wedding. You're trying to put words in my mouth. Just shut up."

"Hey, I'm just saying that you should let me in on your plans, and maybe I can help you out. Licia *likes* me. Maybe I can put in a good word?" Troy grinned, but Darren could tell that his friend was sincere.

The pilot announced that they should fasten their seatbelts for landing.

"I don't need any help. Alicia will come around," he said more to himself than in response to Troy as he fastened his seatbelt and prepared for the upcoming struggle with Alicia.

Alicia stared at herself in the mirror and contemplated changing. The dress that seemed so perfect that she just had to have it now appeared a bit too revealing. It was a slinky number, one that showed way more skin than it covered and put out more sex appeal than she remembered.

The taupe raw silk dress sloped very low in the back and the front. The v-shaped slits in it meant she had to tape her breasts so that she wouldn't spill out and have one of those wardrobe malfunctions that Janet Jackson made famous.

The dress came so far above her knees that it stopped just under her behind. She decided that she would forgo stockings for the glimmering shea butter lotion that left the exposed parts of her body glossy and shimmering with flecks of gold.

The natural look went better with the gold and taupe strapped sandals she wore. Giving herself a once over, she decided that she didn't *exactly* resemble a hoochie mama, and it was way too late to change. So she left her suite in Flex's beach house and got into the huge SUV-style limo where Flex waited.

"Damn, Shorty, you trying to hurt a brother with that dress. You look good, Ma, real good." Flex gave her a quick peck on the lips.

"Oh, this old thing. You like it? It's just something I threw together last minute. You know how I do it." She smiled and batted her eyes.

"Yeah, I hear you. It's all good. Definitely all good from where I'm sitting. You're going to blow them away on the red carpet, Shorty."

"Isn't that why you invited me?" Soaking in the compliments, she smiled again. She'd have to do some major feminist penance for her less-than-politically-correct reactions.

"No, I invited you because you're cool people. You're fun to hang out with, and I know you aren't interested in anything I can't offer you." He rubbed his hand across his chin as he eyed her legs.

"That's because I know you're not trying to offer anything."

"You wouldn't be interested if I did," Flex countered.

She just smiled.

"That's cool. My ego's not crushed because I like you, and that's okay for now." Brushing something non-existent off the shoulder of his casual but clearly tailored dress coat, he gave her a wink.

"Cool with me." Crossing her legs, she sat back to enjoy the ride.

The beauty of Miami was nothing short of breath-taking, especially the contrast between the water, palm trees, and the city line. She loved cities at night when they were all lit up and pretty.

The limo came to a stop, and the driver opened the door. Flex stepped out. What seemed like a million lights went off at the same time. The glare of the public was in full force. Taking the hand Flex offered, she stepped down from the limo. More cameras flashed as she walked arm-in-arm with Flex down the red carpet.

"So, Flex, this is the fourth time we've seen you and Alicia Taylor out in public together. Is there something we should know about? Are the two of you an item?" A red-headed reporter yelled out from the sidelines.

Screaming women reached out to touch Flex's arm, leg, any piece of him they could. He simply smiled and held on to Alicia's arm as they kept moving down the red carpet into the Historic Olympia Theater.

Soon, the people were screaming and snapping pictures of whoever had arrived after them. Flex's entourage cleared the path in front of them, and they also brought up the rear. Sure that she would never get used to that much public attention, Alicia didn't know how Flex did it.

She marveled at the amount of celebrities standing around chatting, posing and profiling. No matter how many of these events she attended, she would never get used to it.

The beautiful people were definitely in attendance, and they were in rare form. Most of the men were casually dressed, and she noted everything from designer sweat suits to leather get-ups to sharp, brightly colored suits and matching gator shoes.

The women were more formally attired, if you called the kind of sexy, skin revealing dress that she was wearing formal attire. No, the hip-hop awards show was not the Academy Awards or the Golden Globes for that matter; it had a style all its own.

The people started to blend together after a while. Then she saw what was arguably the most beautiful woman there, besides herself of course. This woman was not wearing anything particularly revealing. She wore an elegant pantsuit made of silk that most women would kill to have hug their curves the way it hugged hers. The rich mocha brown of the pantsuit contrasted nicely with the light brown of her hair and the golden highlights that ran through it. The woman turned around, and Alicia's jaw dropped when she saw that it was one of her favorite rappers, Sweet Dee. She appeared very different than she had back in the day.

She noticed a stillness come over Flex, who stopped mid-sentence in the conversation he was having with his bodyguard. He had obviously noticed his former love, and it had an impact on him.

Alicia's intrigue grew even more when she watched the play of emotions that went over Sweet Dee's face. Her light brown eyes went from panic to concerned to just a blank stare in a matter of seconds. She walked over to them and smiled.

"Hello, Fredrick. It's nice to see you. You look well." Her smile seemed forced to Alicia.

For the first time since she'd known him, Flex actually seemed at a loss for words. Soon, he managed to say, "Hi, Sweetness. Long time no see."

Sweet Dee glanced at Alicia, and what passed for a smile crossed her face.

Flex followed Sweet Dee's glance and suddenly became aware that Alicia was standing there. "Oh, where are my manners? Alicia, this is Sweet Dee; Sweet Dee, this is Alicia Taylor."

Sweet Dee held out her hand, and Alicia shook it. "Please call me Deidre. No one has called me Sweet Dee in ages."

"It's so nice to meet you, Sweet Dee, I mean Deidre. I'm a huge fan. I used to rap along with your lyrics in my bedroom whenever my parents weren't home. My mom hated your music, and that made me love you even more," she babbled.

That fake smile crossed Deidre's face again, and her light brown eyes flashed. "Well, your parents were right not to let you listen to my music. You couldn't have been more than ten years old at the time."

"Oh, I think I was more like twelve or thirteen," she answered before she realized where Deidre was going with her comment, clearly making a dig at Flex about her youth.

She started to tell her what she could do with that fake condescending smile, when she figured that given the history between Flex and Sweet Dee, Deidre was more than entitled to make snide remarks to the young girl who he appeared to be dating.

Knowing what it was like to carry a torch for someone for years, Alicia thought that both Flex and Deidre fit the bill. In fact, judging by the tension that seemed to engulf the area around them, they had it worse than she and Darren did.

Darren? Now where did that come from?

She tried to focus on the two lovers in denial in front of her. It was hard. For a moment she actually thought that she caught a glimpse of Darren walking into the theater. Baffled, she shrugged it off because he wouldn't be caught dead at a hip-hop awards show. Clearly, she had Darren on the brain. *Shake it off, girl. Refocus.* Imagining him in public places was yet another reason to stay away from him. Things were going too fast and getting out of hand.

"So what are you doing here, Sweetness?" Flex asked in what Alicia was sure he thought was a nonchalant manner but was really the farthest thing from it. "You haven't been to anything in years. What made you show up tonight?"

"Oh, they asked me to present the award for Outstanding Female Rapper of the Year, and they also want to give me some kind of pioneering award. Oh and you know how Lil' Niece and Sexy T sampled my voice in their cover of my song *'Take 'em Out'*—"

A dam of excitement burst inside Alicia and she couldn't help but cut in. "Oooo, I loved that song. They didn't do nearly as good a job with that song as you did. That was my jam back in the day!"

"Well, anyway," Deidre cut her eyes at Alicia, "the girls thought it would be cool if I performed with them. Even though it has been years, I thought, 'what the hell.'"

"That's nice. It will be good to see you perform again, Sweetness."

"It will be great!" Alicia said. "I can't wait. Bring wreck, girl!"

Flex and Deidre gave Alicia perplexed stares.

"Anyway, I'm going to go backstage and get ready. Lil' Niece and Sexy T are performing early in the show, and I have to get ready for the performance."

"Cool, I guess I'll catch you around now that you have resurfaced and decided to come back into the limelight?" Flex's voice was *way* too hopeful in Alicia's opinion. He would have to work on that if he was going to get anywhere with Deidre. She was a tough one.

"Actually, you probably won't see me around. This is a one-time thing. I'm quite happy with my life the way it is, and that doesn't include all the glitz, glamour, and hoochie mamas." Cutting Alicia a final glance, she walked off before Alicia could respond.

"I am not a hoochie mama. See what you did, Flex? I finally meet my favorite rapper, and she hates me because she's still in love with you." Her tone was lighthearted, and she expected it to lighten the mood and the uneasy tension that circled the air.

Flex shook his head as if he was coming out of a daze. Pulling his gaze away from Deidre's retreating backside, he mumbled, "No, she doesn't love me. She made that clear a long time ago."

"Well somebody should send the memo to both of your hearts, because from what I just witnessed, you both have it bad. Now let's go and take our seats because I don't want to miss the return of Sweet Dee." She placed her arm in Flex's, and they walked in.

Their seats were fairly close to the stage. Alicia marveled at the perks of being arm candy for a day. She was attending the *Source* Awards, a hip-hop lover's dream. She had on her best public picture-ready smile and stared around indifferently as Flex shook hands with various rappers and other stars.

Her smile quickly changed when they finally reached their seats and she saw Darren and Troy sitting in the seats next to theirs. Troy got up and stepped toward her while Darren just glowered at her with a piercing gaze that she couldn't read.

"Damn, baby girl! Who are you trying to hurt with that dress? You're looking fine as hell." Troy hugged her, and she returned the hug.

"Troy, what are you doing here? I didn't know you would be here. You remember Flex from the wedding, don't you?" Making the introduction in a forced pleasant voice, she spared a glance at Darren.

Flex and Troy shook hands. "Flex, you remember Darren. Troy and Darren are best friends with my cousin Kendrick."

Flex held out his hand to shake hands with Darren who eyed Flex's hand for several seconds before grudgingly shaking it.

"Well, Alicia, I have to say, I wasn't expecting to see you here either." Darren's voice was clipped, his eyes were piercing, and she was finally able to read his expression—pissed.

CHAPTER 10

It was all Darren could do to sit through the awards show and not make a scene by dragging Alicia out of there in that non-dress she was wearing.

The dress was shorter than anything he had ever seen her wear. It exposed all of her back, and he was not even going to think about her breasts.

What the hell is she thinking?

Then there was Towns who had his arm draped around her as if he owned her. Boiling, Darren shot Troy a glare because he seemed to be enjoying every minute of it. Well, at least Alicia finally had enough sense to be worried. A nervous flicker swept across her hazel eyes once she realized how upset he was.

He caught her trying to sneak a glance in his direction, and he frowned at her. The expression she gave in response would have stopped a less-pissed-off man. Once she saw that he couldn't be scared off, she turned her attention back to the stage.

Darren tried to focus on the show, but he had no interest in who won the Best Rap Single of the Year or Best Rapper or Best Producer. Well, he knew who he didn't want to win Best Producer, Flex Towns.

Glancing at Town's arm draped over Alicia's shoulder and all the diamonds, or *bling* as the rappers called it, which covered his watch and fingers, Darren wondered how much money it would take to buy Flex's distributor and put him out of business. A smile crossed his lips for the first time that evening.

Maybe I can just threaten to put him out of business unless he agrees to never see Alicia again.

He almost smiled again until he realized how much he sounded like his father.

Alicia leaned over and whispered something in Flex's ear, and Flex laughed.

Frowning, Darren turned away from the giggling couple and found that Troy was watching him watch them. "What the hell are you looking at?"

"You. Why don't you just enjoy the show and relax? Damn, whatever happened to 'never let them see you sweat?' You are bordering on pathetic. If I was Alicia, I'd pick Towns, too."

"She didn't pick Towns," Darren said between clenched teeth.

"Whatever, man. All I'm saying is just chill."

Darren counted to ten and kept his eyes focused on the stage. They had just introduced two women rappers, Lil' Niece and Sexy T. Apparently, they used to hate each other but came together to do a song to promote peace in hip-hop.

As far as Darren was concerned, the clothing they wore, or rather the lack of clothing, made them comparable to glorified strippers. It was hard to concentrate on what they were saying when they were barely covered. Enjoying the perform-ance, Alicia rapped along with them.

The crowd went wild when another woman joined them on stage. Even Alicia jumped out of her seat and started dancing as well as rapping along with the woman. Unlike the other young women on the stage, this woman was slightly older. Though she exuded sexiness, she was completely covered.

The only thing overtly raunchy was her lyrics. While shocked that Alicia knew all the words and was saying them with such feeling, Darren found Flex's behavior a little more interesting. Flex was completely mesmerized by the woman rapper, and Darren wondered if Alicia knew that her *friend* had the hots for another woman.

Peeved, he didn't think he could sit through one more award acceptance speech or hear one more rapper thank God and their momma for their success. In spite of all the negative energy he sent out, Flex *still* won the Producer of the Year award. He almost lost it when Towns brushed his lips across Alicia's before he got up to accept his award. When the night was finally over, he couldn't get out of the theater fast enough. First, he had to say a few words to Alicia.

Alicia thought twice about walking over to Darren when he motioned for her. Not in the mood to hear whatever he had to say, she folded her arms across her chest and walked over to him.

"What do you want, Darren? And why are you here?" She bit the words out in a harsh whisper,, because she didn't want anyone around them to hear. People were leaving the auditorium, but there were still plenty of folk around.

"I could ask you the same questions, Alicia. What do *you* want? Why are *you* here?" The words were clipped and angry, but eerily soft, almost chilling.

"I told you that I made a promise to a friend, and I was not going to back out just because—"

"Just because we had sex?"

Glancing around and leaning closer, Alicia snapped softly, "Listen, Darren, I don't want to talk about this now."

"When would you like to talk about it?"

"Not now, Darren."

Troy, Flex, and his entourage came over just as Darren opened his mouth to respond.

"Hey, man, Flex just invited us to the after-party his label is hosting at Club Mirage. I told him we didn't have any plans, and we'd be happy to hang out in the VIP room. Licia, you're going to be there, right?"

"Well actually, Shorty usually doesn't hang out. She usually studies after these things. Every once in a while she'll hang out and let loose, but for the most part, she's focused on her studies. But you all know her better than I do." Flex put his arm around her.

The beginnings of a snarl formed on Darren's face.

Laughing, Troy responded, "Yeah, we know Licia very well, and I know that she wouldn't miss a chance to hang out with her boys. Would she?"

"Actually, Troy, I do have a lot of studying to do. I was planning to go back and study a bit—" she started.

"Oh come on, Licia, we're in Miami, the party city of the country. We have to go out and party. Darren and I will meet you guys there. You'll put us on the list right, Flex?" Troy said, not giving her a chance to back out and escape.

"Sure, we'll catch up with you guys later." Flex gave Troy a pound and did not attempt to connect with Darren at all.

Darren watched as Flex and Alicia left surrounded by his entourage. "What the hell was that about? I don't want to go to his after-party. I definitely don't want to hang out in his VIP room," he snapped.

"Well, I figured it would give you some time with Alicia. I was looking out for you. Besides, it didn't seem like you were getting anywhere with her. Just a hint man—most girls don't dig the brooding angry glares, especially when they are the targets of them.

Try spreading a little charm. I know you have better skills than that. I've seen you in action," Troy said.

"Yeah, well Alicia doesn't like charm. Come on. Let's go to this after-party."

The club was packed, and the VIP room was like a miniature version of what was happening down-stairs. They were enclosed behind glass walls, and they could see the action downstairs. The same music played, but the VIP room also had unlimited cham-pagne and lots of food. Flex made his rounds while Alicia sat and talked to an up-and-coming rapper on his label.

Although she didn't want to be rude, she could barely concentrate on what he was saying because she was too busy watching the door for Darren and Troy. Half-hoping that they wouldn't show up, then half-hoping that they would, when they finally walked in, her breath stopped.

Darren still seemed upset with her, and that irri-tated her. The fact that he took it upon himself to show up in Miami bothered her.

Troy spotted her, and they came over to where she was sitting with the young rapper.

"Hey, baby girl." Troy squeezed down in the plush sofa next to her. Darren just stood there.

"Hey, Troy, glad you guys made it. This is, I'm sorry, what was your name again?" Alicia asked.

"Road Rage," the young rapper said.

"This is Road Rage. He's a new rapper on Flex's label."

"Oh yeah, I read about you. Didn't you have some lines in the *Source's* 'Unsigned Hype?'" Troy's chocolate brown eyes gleamed with interest.

Perking up considerably at the prospect of talking to someone who had actually heard of him, Road Rage responded, "Yeah, man, you saw that? That was last year. Flex signed me, and we been working on my album all year. It's gonna be hot."

"All right, can't wait to get it. I'll be watching out for it. So, Licia, I didn't get a chance to dance with you at all during the wedding reception. So what do you say we hit the floor for a bit now?" Standing, Troy held out his hand for her.

Glad for the opportunity to get away from Darren, Alicia knew that the best way for her to take out her aggravation was on the dance floor.

After dancing for the better part of an hour, she was tempted to take off her strapped sandals, which were clearly not made for dancing. If she didn't have any cares about being tacky, she would have removed the dreaded shoes.

Cool and easy-going, Troy didn't seem to notice that her feet were killing her, and he didn't seem winded in the least bit. He was tall and shared the same "more cream than coffee" complexion as his sister. His brown hair was a few shades darker than Sonya's, and he kept it cropped close to his head. His brown eyes resembled chocolate drops and shimmered with mischief.

Why didn't I fall for him when I was fourteen?

While handsome and fun loving, he was also a player. Even though she once thought Darren was the biggest player in the group, when she really thought about it, Troy had Darren and Kendrick beat in the player department. No, unofficial big brother status was the only role he could ever play in her heart.

A slow and sexy reggae tune started playing, and neither she nor Troy missed a beat switching into reggae mode. The tune was a throwback to the old-school rockers-style reggae. She had visited enough reggae clubs with Jazz to know what you did with rockers.

"Okay, baby girl, when did you learn to rubba-dub?" Troy spoke in a fake Caribbean accent and placed his arms around her waist. They slowly wound their hips to the music.

"I should be asking you the same question. I always knew you were a good dancer, bro, but dang," she said while laughing. "No wonder you have to beat the ladies off with a stick."

"Yeah," Troy said, glancing over his shoulder. "Well, I might have to beat my best friend off with a stick if we don't take a break after this dance. Darren seems mad enough to spit nails. What's the deal, Licia? You guys obviously have something going on that's more than the dance you shared at Sonya and Kendrick's wedding."

Feigning nonchalance, Alicia shrugged. "It's no big deal. I don't know why he's tripping. I don't know why he's even here. They have anti-stalking laws, you know."

"Oh so it's like that? Can't you tell Darren really likes you? Or do you realize that he likes you, and you're just giving him a hard time for the hell of it?" Troy's usually smiling face formed a frown.

"What are you, a talk show host? You'd give Maury Povich a run for his money the way you're getting all in my business."

"I'm just looking out for two people I care about. So why don't you just tell me? Do you like Darren or don't you? If you really don't want to be bothered with him, I'll let him know, and I'll make him leave you alone. If you like him, cut a brother some slack. You're playing with fire, you know? You have got to stop seeing Flex."

"Flex is my friend." Stepping away from Troy, she kept moving to the music.

"I get that. But, Licia—" Troy was interrupted by a thugged out gold-toothed young man in a denim suit tapping his shoulder.

"Scuse me partner, I was wonderin' if I could holla at Shorty for a moment. I'd like to dance wit her." Bold, Mr. Gold-Teeth held his head up unflinchingly, determined to have his dance.

"Sorry, man, she's dancing with—" Troy started.

Dismissing Troy with her eyes, she turned and smiled at the other man. "I can decide who I dance with. Thanks, Troy. I enjoyed dancing with you. I'd like to dance with him. I'll catch up with you later."

Troy let go of her waist and stepped aside. "I hope you know what you're doing, baby girl."

"I'm dancing. I'll catch you later." Alicia's voice was overly bright as she stepped over to the denim-clad man just as the DJ switched the music to a slow jam. *Oh great,* she sighed internally.

Mr. Gold-Teeth, actually known as G-Spot, was a wanna-be rapper, and he was also an octopus. She was about to knock his hand off her behind for the seventh time in less than a minute when Darren walked up and tapped him on the shoulder.

"Naw, partner, we dancing here." Giving Darren an irritated glance, G-Spot made a slurping sound and pushed up his gold-fronts with his tongue. "I'm handlin' this. It's plenty of ladies here tonight. Go find yourself one, Son."

"I don't think you understand. *She is mine,* and I think she's had enough dancing for tonight. So if you don't want any problems, I suggest you step." Darren's deep voice had even more bass than usual.

Speechless, she didn't know whether to insist that she was fine with finishing her dance with G-Spot or be thankful that Darren interrupted. She didn't have time to do either.

"Oh, my bad, man. I didn't know she was taken. She rolled in here with Flex, and then she was dancing close with that other dude. My bad. I misunderstood." G-Spot looked her up and down as if he were surveying a piece of meat and walked away without so much as a second glance.

"Let's go, Licia." Darren's voice remained low.

"I'm not going anywhere, Darren. Or did you forget, I didn't come here with you," she snapped as she started to walk away.

Grabbing her elbow, Darren pulled her close so that he could whisper in her ear. There was nothing sexy about it. "You can either walk out, or I can carry you out? Have it your way."

Glancing at the arm on her elbow before looking into the eyes of the man holding her, she paused. His eyes were two pieces of coal. Eerily expressionless, they made her long for the pissed expression he'd had earlier that evening.

"Well, I have to tell Flex that I'm leaving with you. I'll be right back." She started to walk away, but Darren still held on to her arm, and he jerked her back.

"No, let's go. Now. Walk or be carried." Darren motioned for Troy to come over, and he did. "You ready? We're leaving." His tone was flat and just as expressionless as his eyes.

Confused, Troy glanced from Darren to Alicia before he spoke. "Sure man, I'm ready whenever you are. Licia, are you leaving with us?"

"I guess I am. Troy, can you do me a favor and tell Flex that I'm leaving with you guys?" Trying to snatch her arm away from Darren, she huffed when he held it even tighter. Nerves frayed, she realized that she had better leave before both she and Darren ended up making a huge scene.

"I'll be right back, Darren." Troy glanced at Darren and turned to find Flex.

"We'll be in the limo. Let's go." Darren led her out of the VIP room, out of the club, and into the limo, without another word.

Gritting her teeth so tightly that her jaw actually hurt, she followed.

Darren tried counting to ten, then twenty, then thirty. He had made it all the way to three hundred, and didn't feel any calmer. The night had gone from bad to worse in a matter of minutes. Maybe Alicia was right and he shouldn't have come. All of that was null and void when he saw her dancing with that fool; he would be damned if he was going to let some rough-neck put his paws all over her like that. Even Troy had tread on very thin ice by dancing with Alicia for so long and so close.

"Flex said he'd catch up with you later, Shorty," Troy said as he got in the limo.

Alicia simply nodded and sighed.

Why does Flex call her Shorty anyway? She was far from short. It was probably some stupid hip-hop slang. He counted to ten, again.

"What hotel are you staying in, Licia?" he finally managed to ask once he'd calmed down a little.

"I'm staying at Flex's beach house," Alicia mumbled.

Flex's beach house! Like hell!

"What's the address?" Darren managed to get the question out. Alicia gave him the address.

Darren put down the partition between them and the driver and gave the driver the address.

"You can go and get your things and come back to our hotel."

"What? Thanks, but no thanks. I'm not staying anywhere near you, Darren." Her voice epitomized outrage.

"Yes, you are. If you would like your things, I suggest you don't argue about it. I can just as easily have the driver take us directly to the Intercontinental Hotel, and you can do without your things."

When she started to open her mouth, Darren prepared himself for the coming barrage. But she closed her mouth just as quickly. Troy made a snickering sound, and Darren simply kept his gaze honed on Alicia. Her eyes narrowed, and she pursed her lips before she turned her attention to the passing scenery.

When they pulled up to Flex's beach house, she seemed to perk up. "Well, I guess I'll go get my things." She stepped out of the limo, and he followed her.

"You don't have to follow me, Darren. I know how to get my things," Alicia snapped.

"Yes, but do you know how to come back?"

"Good grief! I am not a child, Darren. Would you please stop this? You are pissing me off."

Darren simply gestured toward the door. Tired of the back-and-forth, he only wanted to gather her things and return to his hotel.

Alicia took a deep breath and entered the house. He followed her in, up the stairs, and to her room.

Well, at least they don't appear to be sharing a room.

Throwing her clothing in the little red suitcase, she didn't say a word. Silent during the limo ride as well, she didn't even say a word in the elevator ride up to the penthouse suite. Her silence must have been contagious because neither he nor Troy said a word either.

Once inside the suite, she snapped, "How dare you treat me like I'm a child? You do not have the right to treat me like that, Darren Whitman. You do not have the right to tell me what to do. I did not give you that right!" Alicia's eyes were blazing, and the flecks of green and brown danced in anger.

Startled by the suddenness of her rant, he took a step back. They had barely closed the door, and he figured that she would not want to have the discussion in front of Troy who was standing there with an expression that was perplexed and intrigued.

It didn't take Darren long to realize that he was the one who should be upset, not Alicia. Since he felt himself to be the measure of restraint, she should have been glad that he was able to contain himself for as long as he did.

"Why don't you just calm down, and we can discuss this like adults?" he said to pacify her anger.

"I will not calm down. And I will not be discussing anything with you until you change your controlling, condescending attitude. In fact, you don't have to worry about me talking to you ever again, Darren." Turning to leave, she quickly spun back around. "Who do you think you are anyway?"

"Licia, let's just calm down," he said and glanced at Troy. "Can you excuse us for moment, Troy? Alicia and I have some things to discuss."

"No, Troy, you don't have to leave. I'm not discussing anything with this…this…bully!" Alicia's eyes glistened with angry unshed tears.

He reached out to touch her cheek, and she smacked his hand away. Taking a deep breath, she squinted her eyes in what appeared to be an effort to hold back her tears before she backed away.

"I'm going to bed. I hope this place has more than two bedrooms because I don't want you anywhere near me." Alicia stormed into the nearest bedroom, which just happened to be one of the two bedrooms in the suite, and the one that Darren picked for himself.

Standing in silence for a moment, they soon heard the sounds of her muffled sobs.

"She's crying," Troy stated, and Darren wondered why Troy's penchant for stating the glaringly obvious never bothered him before.

"Maybe I should go and see if she's okay," Troy said as he walked toward the bedroom door.

"No, she's pissed at me. I'll go see if she's okay."

Rubbing his chin and glancing from Darren to the door, Troy asked, "You sure?"

"I'm sure."

"I mean, because she said she didn't want you anywhere near her. And she sounded pretty certain about that. You know you're my best friend and all. But that's baby girl in there crying, and from what I can tell, you're the cause." Troy appeared to be torn.

Darren let out an exasperated sigh. "Listen, man, I appreciate the fact that you are concerned about Licia. Just trust me to handle this. Go to bed or go hang out, whatever. I got this, man."

"Cool. I'll go catch some zzz's, but try to keep it down. All that yelling and screaming has given me a headache."

Ignoring the last of Troy's comments, he walked into the bedroom. In bed and under the covers, Alicia was still crying. Darren felt as if something had pierced his heart. It was one thing to hear the muffled crying on the other side of the door. It was quite another to see her balled up and crying into the pillow.

He remembered the times he'd seen his mother crying after some stupid thing that his father had said or done, and he suddenly felt ashamed. He never wanted to make a woman cry, and he especially didn't want to make Alicia cry.

Alicia had managed to take off her dress and put on her nightgown, all the while biting back the sobs that came out in gulps despite her attempts. Scolding herself that Darren was not worth her tears and that she shouldn't waste one moment crying over him, she cried nonetheless. Besides, she figured, she wasn't sad. No, pissed was a far better descriptor.

If she was pissed, then they were righteous tears that deserved to be shed. If she had to cry, she would do it into her pillow, and at least she wouldn't have to worry about Darren and Troy hearing her. Thus, she let loose and found that she was crying a mixture of sad and angry tears, and that was okay with her.

Once she reached a point when she was nicely spent, she realized that she wasn't alone. Darren was in the room, sitting on the edge of the bed. She could feel him, smell him, and sense him. "Get out, Darren."

"I'd like to talk, Alicia."

"The only thing you can say to me is an apology." Trying to keep her voice from shaking, she was having a hard time. She still hadn't looked up from the pillow.

"Okay. I'm sorry that I tried to tell you what to do. I'm sorry that I came down to Miami. I'm sorry that I strong-armed you out of the club and into my hotel. I'm sorry. Could you please stop crying?"

Gulping, she responded, "I'm not crying. And stop telling me what to do!"

"Fine, I'm sorry. Listen, Licia, could you come here please?"

"No. Could you leave please?"

Darren sighed and stood up.

Good, he's leaving. Don't let the doorknob hit ya!

She removed her head from the pillow to watch him leave the room only to come face to face with him. Leaning over her, he actually pulled her up the rest of the way so that she was sitting upright.

"What are you doing?"

Darren used his thumb to wipe what was left of her tears away and sat on the bed. He stared at her for what seemed like an eternity. Finally, she couldn't take it anymore.

"All right, Darren, you can leave now. I accept your apology. Just don't let it happen again."

He let out an exasperated sigh and kissed her.

That she so easily responded to the kiss unnerved her. When he finished she found herself voicing what she was feeling and not quite ready to share. "I feel so out-of-control," she mumbled breathlessly.

Touching her cheek, Darren sighed. "If it makes any difference to you at all, I'm feeling pretty out-of-control myself."

They sat in silence for a moment.

"I don't like it when people boss me around and tell me what to do." Her voice sounded like a whisper, and she wasn't sure that he heard her.

"I don't like bossing people around or telling them what to do. I just couldn't stand the thought of you spending the night with Towns." Darren's voice was low.

Alicia let out a shaky laugh. "For someone who doesn't like to boss people around and tell them what to do, you are pretty good at it."

He laughed. "That bad, huh?"

She wiped away her tears and laughed again. "Yeah, Mr. 'walk or be carried.'"

"Well, I'll try to keep my bossiness under control if you can try to push my buttons a little less." Holding out his hand he whispered, "Truce?"

A shaky, tentative smile crossed her lips as she shook his hand. "Truce."

Darren kissed her, and she felt the rest of her anger dissipate. When he stopped kissing her and reached for protection, she knew that, like it or not, she was headed into uncharted territory with Darren Whitman, and she hoped that her heart would be able to hang.

The next morning they decided to spend a little time in Miami sightseeing before Darren returned home and she returned to school. Breakfast in the hotel's version of a Mexican restaurant turned out to be a perfect date. The food's lack of spice and taste left a lot to be desired, but Alicia relished the company all the same.

Sure, the fact that he went all cave man in the club and strong-armed her into leaving her ocean view suite at Flex's beach house still left a bad taste in her mouth, but he was adequately apologetic, and that suited her for the time being.

Frowning at what was left of what was supposed to pass for huevos rancheros, Darren turned his attention to her and smiled. "So what are you planning to do when you graduate?"

After he smiled, she could have sworn she felt her heart do a flip-flop. *Get a grip, girl. It is just breakfast with a cute guy.* She took a sip of her orange juice, the one thing in the meal that actually tasted the way it was supposed to. "Graduate school, and I hope to get on at Taylor Publishing and eventually run it."

"*Of course.* Well, if anybody can make it happen, I know you can."

While Alicia couldn't tell if Darren was being sincere or sarcastic, she decided to give him the benefit of the doubt since the morning was going so well. "I'll take that as a compliment coming from Mr. Black Enterprise. What was it—'Top Thirty Under Thirty?' What number were you? Umm, let me see, number one!"

Thinking back to how proud she was when she saw that issue of *Black Enterprise* with him on the cover, she smiled, even though at the time it horrified her that she was actually showing genuine happiness for Darren Whitman. *Funny how things change...*

The twinkle in his eyes sparkled even more, and her heart really did flip-flop. She barely heard him when he acknowledged, "So we're both driven."

Swallowing because her throat was suddenly dry, she concurred. "I guess we have that in common."

"Oh, I think we have a lot more in common than that."

"Really? I can't think of anything," she said as she feigned nonchalance. The lump in her chest was pulsating, and the air seemed to suddenly thicken.

Taking a sip of his coffee, he studied her for a moment with an intense gaze. "What's your favorite basketball team?"

"The Pacers."

"The Pacers? What kind of self-respecting Detroit girl is a Pacers fan?"

"I like rooting for the underdog, and I became a Pacers fan a long time ago when they used to go up against the Bulls. What?"

"All the more reason to root for the home team! How long have the Pistons been the underdogs?"

Having never really liked the Pistons, she really couldn't say. "Well at least we both like basketball, if not the same team. Okay, I have one, which was the better album, *Illmatic* or *Reasonable Doubt*?" This question would tell her who he felt was the best male rapper.

He twisted his lips and frowned before shrugging. "What and what?"

Dang. Guess we don't like the same kind of music. "Never mind, fill in the blank, women have the right to do *blank.*"

Without hesitation, he responded, "Anything they want to do. Well, except commit murder I suppose, but then they have the right to the death penalty just like any other murderer."

Hearing the first part of his response, she started to smile, which turned quickly to a frown once he finished talking. "You believe in the death penalty?"

"You don't?"

She shook her head and sighed. "I'm going to let that slide because I liked part of your answer for the fill in the blank. However, we will definitely have to revisit this topic in the future."

Taking another sip of coffee, he leaned back in his chair for a moment before leaning forward again. "Okay, who is your favorite artist?"

"I think it would depend on what kind of mood I'm in. When I'm feeling particularly political, I'd have to say Frida Kahlo. And when I'm feeling free and whimsical, I *love* me some Varnette P. Honeywood."

Shaking his head appreciatively, he said, "That's quite a range."

"You're familiar with their work?"

"Yes. When I have time, I love checking out art museums."

Piqued and very impressed, she confessed, "Me, too."

"That's what we'll do today. Check out the local art scene. Since Miami is known as the Gateway to the Americas, I'm sure we'll be able to take in quite a bit. Are you finished with your breakfast?"

"Are you kidding me? This food was gross, but the company was nice. We'll have to get some real food later. Let's go. This should be fun."

A day with Darren in Miami checking out art was about as perfect a day as she could have imagined at that moment.

CHAPTER 11

Alicia pulled her rental car into the wrought-iron gate of her family's home and parked in the driveway.

She left her suitcase in the car and came in through the side of the house. Stepping into the recently remodeled kitchen, she saw her mother, Karen Taylor, sitting at the green marbled countertop sipping a cup of tea. Karen smiled, put down her tea, and got up to greet her.

Reciprocating Karen's tight embrace, Alicia reluctantly let go after a few seconds. Karen ran her fingers through Alicia's hair, then sat back down and patted the cherry wood barstool next to the one she was sitting on.

Karen was a tall woman with a model's figure who appeared to be ten years younger than she was. She'd recently cut her long, curly black hair—against her husband's wishes—into a short shoulder-length bob. The new haircut made her appear even younger. Her rich, dark skin was a couple of shades darker than her daughter's was, and her eyes were a deep dark brown. Other than the difference in complexions and eye color, the two women shared the same almond-shaped eyes, button noses, and lush lips. The resemblance between them was striking.

"So how were your visits? Have you decided which school you're going to attend in the fall?" Watching Alicia intently, Karen picked up her tea and took a sip.

Alicia had spent her spring break visiting three of the universities she'd been accepted to for graduate school. She spent the first part of the week visiting New York University, the middle of the week in Oxford, Ohio visiting Miami University, and the last part of the week visiting the University of Michigan-Ann Arbor. After visiting all three schools, she was sure she wasn't going to Miami of Ohio.

The cornfields and the small isolated college town were not the least bit appealing. Their Technical Writing Master's program seemed really good, but after spending her undergraduate at Mount Holyoke, she'd had her fill of small, quaint college towns. Thinking her distaste for small college towns would cancel out Ann Arbor as well; she was surprised when it didn't.

After she pulled out the stool, she sat down. "I don't know, Mom. I really liked Michigan for some reason." Absently twirling her finger through her hair, she considered what attending Michigan would mean.

The Ann Arbor visit went better than she'd expected. Impressed that they graduated more black students with graduate degrees than any other university in the country, she found them the most in-line with her own politics. Even with all the anti-affirmative action drama and Supreme Court cases, they still seemed committed to providing access for students of color, and Alicia found that commendable.

"I was sure that I would love NYU. It wasn't that I hated it or anything. I just really liked Michigan." Alicia let go of the curl she was twirling, sighed, and tapped her hands on the cool marble.

"Well, Michigan is a great school. From what you've told me, the program is excellent and would provide you with the flexibility to do a lot of things." Setting down her cup, Karen turned completely to face Alicia. Hesitating a moment, she seemed deep in thought.

"And they are offering you a full fellowship the first year and a TA-ship the second. Miami University is offering you a full ride as well. NYU is the only school out of all the schools that isn't offering you any kind of assistance. You don't need the aid, but you've worked hard and you've earned the support. Those aren't bad options to have," Karen noted.

"I know, and it would be so good not to have to get money from Daddy to pay for graduate school. I want to do this totally on my own."

"It would be nice to have you closer to home."

Eyes glazed and staring off, Karen had the expression of a woman making plans. That those plans involved Alicia at Michigan and Karen knee-deep in her business became clearer to Alicia with the wide grin that came across her mother's face.

Her parents would smother her if she were within driving distance, showing up unannounced, expecting her to come home on the weekends. They would expect to see her in church on Sunday mornings. Just the thought of spontaneous Saturday brunches and mandatory Sunday dinners made her cringe. None of that changed the fact that she really did miss her family when she was away. Even when they showed up unannounced, she was happy. Liking the attention and feeling loved, however, did not mean she wouldn't have to set some ground rules in place so that she could have a life of her own, especially now that she was sort of seeing Darren.

No doubt realizing that she needed to work on her game face, Karen quickly added, "I'm not saying that we'd be at your doorstep every day. But it would be nice to know that if you had time, you could come here or I could go there, and we could spend the day together." Her voice had a tentative tone, but Alicia knew there was nothing tentative about her mother's plans.

Keeping the frown fixed on her face, Alicia arched her eyebrow for good measure.

Her mother shrugged and pretended to let it go. Then she played her trump card. "Well, don't let that influence your decision. Because as you know from how frequently your father and I visited South Hadley, distance will not save you."

"I know," she said wryly. "At least when you had to fly, you called before you showed up. Well, most of the time."

Laughing, Karen added, "You know, I have tried not to interfere in your decision-making, and I've tried to give you space to make your own decisions and your own mistakes." She rested her hand on Alicia's shoulder. "But I want you to pick a school that is going to offer you a substantial package."

"Why, Mom? Do you think that Dad won't help me if I need it?"

A pensive expression crossed Karen's face, and she paused slightly. Her lips moved from one side to the other as she considered her words. "I think that the best way for you to have control of your life is to walk through life with your own things. You broke tradition and went to Mount Holyoke even when your father refused to pay."

Alicia laughed, remembering her father's fury and mother's determination that Alicia go wherever she wanted to go. Also an alumnus of Howard, Karen had wanted her daughter to go to school there and pledge Delta there, but she fought hard for Alicia to attend the college of her choice.

"Yeah, but you helped, and you made sure that Dad eventually came around."

"I know. I'd do it again. I want you to know that you always have choices, no matter what. You life is your own." Karen stressed each word firmly, but she put extra emphasis on the word choices.

The conversation had picked up an almost somber tone, and Alicia didn't know what to make of it. "I know that, Mom. Believe me, if I didn't learn anything else, I learned that. I also learned I need to maintain control of my life through my choices." Pausing for a moment, she studied her mother. "What I don't know is why you felt it was so important for me to know and live that and not you?"

She always wondered if Karen resented not working outside of the home. She had a college degree, and she'd worked as an assistant buyer for a major department store up until Alicia was three years old.

Giving up her career to be at home with Alicia and to do the kinds of things that the wife of a man like Kyle Taylor needed to do always struck Alicia as bogus. Thinking her mom gave up her own dreams and goals to be at home with her always concerned Alicia, so she vowed not to attend or plan dinners and parties, meet with society women, and devote herself to public service because of some antiquated image of what the wife of a powerful man is supposed to do.

Since her mother gave up everything to stay at home and raise her, she would have the life and career that would make Karen's sacrifice worth it.

What she couldn't understand was why Karen made that choice to stay at home and yet instilled in her the desire to go out and do and be whatever she wanted.

Karen Taylor's eyes squinted, and her eyebrows furrowed. "What do you mean?"

"Well, you had a life and a career, and you gave it all up for what? Love? To help Daddy's career? To raise me?"

A knowing smile creep across Karen's face, and she shook her head. "What you should know is that I don't have any regrets, honey. I decided to stay at home with you because I wanted to give you the sense of self that I knew you would need in this world. Each time you stand up for yourself and make your own decisions, I know I made the right decision. I did what I wanted to do. Make no mistake about it."

"Didn't you think you could have had it all and still done all that?"

"Who says I didn't have it all? I made all my own choices, and I wouldn't change a thing. I don't have any regrets." Karen got up, hugged her, and planted a kiss on the top of her head. "I love your father, and I love you. And believe it or not, I love my life—the life I chose—just the way it is. What I want more than anything is for you to have a life that you choose. So remember, you always have a choice."

Returning the hug, she sighed. "I know that, Mom."

"So what do you want for dinner tonight?"

"Oh, I'm going downtown to meet Darren at his office. We're going to have a bite to eat." She tried to sound nonchalant so that her mom wouldn't jump into twenty-one-questions mode.

Pausing momentarily, Karen held her at arms-length, and studied her. "So, you're meeting Darren. Darren Whitman?"

"Yes, Darren Whitman."

"Do you like him?"

"I don't know, I guess I do. Yes. But I don't want to talk about it right now." Smiling shyly, she turned away from Karen.

She more than liked him, and she had no desire to have a conversation with her mother of all people. Also, she wasn't ready to label it.

Darren had a problem with her hesitation and wanted her to concede that they were involved, exclusive. They talked about it at length, and she felt that they were going too fast. She needed to slow down before she got caught up.

She was still getting used to the fact that they were intimate. He called her daily, and he'd visited her twice since they left Miami. The day they spent in

Miami checking out the local art scene was perfect. They attended a basketball game in Boston, Celtics versus the Pistons, and he was able to woo her into rooting for the Pistons, at least when they weren't playing the Pacers. They also spent time eating carryout and hanging out in her apartment. Even with all of that, she still thought labeling what they seemed to be doing and calling it a relationship might bring in a new set of issues, and Darren already took way too many liberties as far as she was concerned.

If they were in a relationship, then the fact that she planned to spend a large part of this weekend with him would be taken to mean that she really cared about him. Even though she cared about him more than a little bit, she was scared to own it. A part of her was still waiting for the other shoe to drop and Darren the player to pop up. It was safer if she at least tried to monitor her feelings and hold a little bit back. That way, if he did break her heart, maybe it wouldn't be so earth shattering. *Yeah, right. Good luck with that*, she thought to herself, because she knew she was already too far gone.

"Well, I guess if you didn't like him, you wouldn't be spending time with him that you could be spending with your dear sweet saint of a mother."

Karen's words pulled her out of her musings about Darren. "Oh brother, give me a break. Stop fishing."

"What? I just want to know if you like the man. I have to say that the way the two of you went at it as kids was a sight. I don't know how many times I had to come and settle an argument or something." Laughing, Karen shook her head at the memories.

"That's because he was a jerk."

"I guess he's no longer a jerk if you're going to have dinner with him." Karen's face formed that all-knowing expression that mothers must have a patent on.

"Oh, I don't know if I'd go that far." She almost fell for her mother's ploy. "Stop fishing," she added when she realized her mom's tactics.

"Well, just remember, sweetie, you always have choices." A smile crossed Karen's face, and she brightened up considerably. "Anyway, do you think that Sonya and Kendrick are expecting yet? Momma called me this morning wanting to know if I was pregnant or if, God forbid, you were pregnant because she dreamed of fish last night." Karen sat back down and picked up her teacup, all the while keeping her eyes on Alicia.

Shaking her head in disbelief, she sputtered, "What? That's crazy."

"Well, you know the old folk and their superstitions. I told her that she was way off base with me." Squinting, Karen studied Alicia intently.

Alicia's eyes widened. "Well, she's way off base with me, too. Hey, are you fishing again, Mom? My goodness, sometimes you can be just as bad as Daddy. Stop trying to find out about my sex life."

"I'm not fishing. I'm just wondering if Momma's dream could have been about Sonya. I thought you would know since she is one of your best friends. What's this about a sex life?" Tilting her head and widening her eyes, Karen's expression was all too innocent.

"Well, tell Grandma it's *definitely* not me." Alicia walked out the door to get her bags.

CHAPTER 12

Darren tossed the report he was reading to the side and massaged his temples. As usual during the last half of the day, he found it hard to concentrate. The normal end-of-the-day distraction was multiplied, however, by his anticipation about seeing Alicia again and spending the whole weekend with her.

He still hadn't gotten her to admit that they were in a relationship, let alone that she had feelings for him. It really shouldn't have mattered to him, because he didn't have any concerns about her going off to be with others or anything like that. It just felt like her resistance toward labeling their relationship was her holding back a part of herself from him, and with his own feelings so firmly on the line, he wanted it all.

Resigned, he was willing to give her all the time she needed to come to terms with their relationship. Hell, if he was honest with himself, he'd had a whole lot more time to come to terms with the idea of the two of them together than she had, since she was not privy to the entire extent of things.

If he could keep Jonathan and Mr. Taylor at bay, maybe, just maybe, everyone would get what they wanted. Now ready to admit that he wanted Alicia, he just had to get her to admit that she wanted him.

Her guard was slowly coming down, and he couldn't wait for it to be completely down. Sure that he could get his father to agree on a long engagement, he knew he and Alicia would be able to fully explore their relationship while she finished graduate school.

He glanced at his watch, got up from the sleek leather office chair, and walked away from his desk. The huge mahogany desk was finally cleared of most of the papers he'd had to sign-off on, but still held several pending projects that he wanted to run by his father.

He never thought that he would get used to being second-in-command at Whitman Enterprises, but he'd grown into the position with relative ease. It was almost as if he really was born to do it. The thought gave him pause.

Taking over companies and turning over huge profits was fine, but in his heart he wanted to help build things, not tear them apart. The desire to do something else consumed him as he gazed out of his top-floor office window at the view of the Detroit River.

Caught up in the calm of the water, he didn't hear his father walk in.

"Daydreaming on the job is not productive."

He didn't turn around immediately. "It's the end of the day, the end of the week, and I'm done with being productive for now."

"If you want to stay on top, your work is never done, and you are certainly never done with being productive. Once you are, you're dead." Jonathan Whitman's serious tone bounced off the walls and echoed through the room.

Sighing, Darren turned around and thought that he was really going to have to get his secretary to understand that no one was allowed in his office unannounced, not even the great Jonathan Whitman. He walked back to his desk and stood behind it next to his leather chair.

"Alicia is on her way over. We're going out to dinner. She's in town for the weekend." He decided to throw Jonathan a bone.

"Oh." Interest piqued, Jonathan smiled broadly. "How are you coming along on that little project?"

"My relationship with Alicia is not a 'project,' Dad." He immediately regretted giving Jonathan any information.

"Oh, so you've moved to the relationship stage. That's impressive. I had no idea that you had made such significant progress since the wedding. In fact, I just saw a picture of her at yet another event with that rapper person. Surely, if the two of you are in a relationship, the photographs must have been from an earlier occasion."

Massaging his temples, Darren pulled out his leather chair and took a seat. Jonathan sat down in the chair in front of his desk.

"I must say that I'm rather disappointed that Kyle would allow his daughter to consort with such people. Surely he must have *some control* over the girl." Jonathan made a tsking sound with his teeth, and twisted his mouth as if he'd just tasted something either really sour or just plain nasty.

"The 'girl' is a twenty-year-old woman, and I think she is pretty much capable of deciding whom she should and whom she should not consort with." In an instance, he felt like a hypocrite voicing those words.

Didn't I try to tell Alicia who she should and should not be friends with?

"Well, I think that the Taylors have given her far too much flexibility and freedom. For example, why on earth is Kyle encouraging her to go to graduate school? Look at where she did her undergraduate studies. She's the first Taylor not to attend Howard in over seventy-plus years."

Jonathan frowned, swallowed as if he was taking bitter medicine, and tsked again. "Surely, Kyle must realize that the girl is out of control. You'd think he'd try to rein her in. I hope that you will have a better time of it once you're married."

Darren flinched. "I don't want to control her. Alicia has her own mind." Loving all of that about her, he didn't want to rein her in. At least he didn't think he did, not consciously.

Jonathan shook his head. "She really doesn't need her own mind now does she? All she needs to do is to produce the future heirs to Whitman Enterprise." Moving his head even more emphatically, he patted his hand firmly on the desk.

"No, really, Son, you will need to get her in-check fairly early on. The fact that the two of you are an item now could actually bode well for the merger. You have more time to work on her than if you had simply gotten married without this little courtship you've hatched."

Pleased with himself, Jonathan let out a sigh. "I really don't know what Kyle was thinking while he was bringing that girl up."

Darren stared at the ceiling and willed Jonathan out of his office. The intercom buzzed.

"Ms. Alicia Taylor is here to see you, sir," announced Pam, his secretary, her voice crisp and efficient.

Darren wondered why she could never seem to work the intercom whenever Jonathan Whitman decided to barge in unannounced.

"Thanks, Pam, send her in." Eying Jonathan wearily, he said a silent prayer that the man wouldn't use this encounter to let Alicia know his thoughts on her education or her decisions.

Alicia breezed into the office wearing a brown knit dress that hugged all her curves and stopped about five inches above her knees. Her legs were covered with brown cotton tights, thigh-high chocolate boots with stiletto heels, and she carried a matching leather jacket in her hands.

Jonathan followed Darren's gaze and stood. "Nice to see you again, Alicia. I hope that all is well. I hear you'll be graduating soon."

Alicia walked over and placed her jacket on the chair next to the one his father was now standing beside. "Yes. I spent spring break visiting graduate schools. I think I have it narrowed down to two schools." Alicia's eyes flashed, and she spoke in a hurried pace.

Darren could tell she was excited about her visits, and he couldn't wait to talk with her about them.

"Really...that's...nice. But I'm wondering why you even want to go to graduate school." Jonathan's tone was wry.

Darren turned and stared at Jonathan with an open mouth. Even when he cleared his throat suggestively, he knew there was no stopping Jonathan Whitman.

"One would think that you would be content with the BA and ready to settle down and start a family." Jonathan's deep bellow vibrated the room once again, and his gaze took on the condescending air that he was best known for.

"I'm *way* too young to be thinking about that right now. I'm only twenty." Laughing nervously, Alicia turned her gaze to Darren, and he read clearly, *what the hell is up with your dad?*

"Yes, but soon you'll be twenty-one and—"

"Dad, Alicia can make her own decisions. She doesn't need you to plot out her life for her." Giving Jonathan a pointed stare to make sure he got the double meaning he meant the statement to carry, he walked over to Alicia. "She's highly capable." Giving her a hug and a much too quick kiss that he fully intended to finish later, he picked up her coat and nodded at his dad.

"If you'll excuse us, Dad. We have plans for this evening. I'll see you on Monday."

"Aren't you going to come by on Sunday for brunch with your mother and me?"

Taking another glance at the way the dress hugged Alicia as he helped her with her jacket he responded, "No, I don't think so."

"Son, this is the third weekend in a row that you've missed." Jonathan obviously did not like not getting what he wanted.

"I'll see you Monday."

Darren and Alicia walked out.

After dinner, Darren didn't want the evening to end. They were driving back to the parking garage at Whitman Enterprise so that Alicia could pick up her rental car and go back to her parents, but he wanted to go back to his loft and unwind.

"So are you really tired from all those campus visits? Do you feel like hanging out a little longer?" Reaching over, he caressed Alicia's cheek.

Alicia smiled and tilted her head. "I don't know. What do you have in mind?"

He turned into the parking garage and pulled up next to the cherry red rental. "Well, let's see, you could get your car and follow me back to my loft for a little conversation and relaxation. Or, we could leave your car here, I can drive both of us to my loft, and I could bring you back for it in the morning?"

"Hmm, interesting choices. They each mysteriously involve the two of us at your loft." Alicia placed her finger on her chin in mock consideration.

"Yes, I guess they do. So what do you think?" Shaking his head, he pretended that he too was struck by the irony of the similarities between the two choices.

"Well, if those are my only options, I guess…I'll have to go with the first and follow you to your loft. I would hate to have to explain to Kyle Taylor why I didn't come home tonight." Alicia got out of the car and held the door open for a second. "I'll meet you at your place."

"That sounds good to me."

CHAPTER 13

"So where do you think you'll be attending graduate school in the fall?"

As they lounged in Darren's loft on his comfy leather sofa with her head on his lap and the TV providing white noise in the background, Alicia considered Darren's question. It was a simple enough question, and she could see why he would be interested, but she didn't want to discuss it with him because she didn't want him or what they were involved in to influence her decision.

Apparently, her silence lasted a second too long because Darren felt the need to add more. "Because if you want my opinion, out of the three—"

"Yeah, actually, I don't." She realized she sounded a little too flippant after the words came out.

"You don't?" he asked incredulously.

She could almost feel Darren's eyes peering down on the top of her head, so she kept her eyes on whatever was playing on the tube. "Yeah, I don't want anyone's opinion. I kind of want to make the best choice for me." Adding an air of finality to her voice, she hoped it would bring an end to that particular topic of conversation.

"Okay, but don't you even want to consider what might be the best choice for us?"

"No, not really, because if I did that, I'd be sacrificing my wants and needs for this…whatever we're doing…" She couldn't bring herself to say the word. It would have given the conversation more ammunition for the opposing side.

"This relationship? Could that be the elusive word you're searching for?"

Noting that Darren was past peeved and headed straight toward pissed; she decided to appeal to rationality and reason.

"No, because I wouldn't classify what we have as a relationship. I think we're still in the getting-to-know-each other stage. Feeling each other out, literally and figuratively." Pausing for effect, she added, "And I think that we should take it slow for a while. Hold off on the labels and see where this thing leads us."

"Well, suppose I said I need some clarity about where we are?"

She blinked. The conversation that she didn't want to have about her choice of graduate school had turned into the conversation she didn't want to have about the kind of relationship they were in. *Oh brother.*

Sitting up from her comfy position with her head on his lap, she sighed and hiked her dress so that she could comfortably straddle him. Clearly, reason and rationality were over-rated. She focused on taking off the tie he'd already partially loosened and started to unbutton his shirt. Tossing the red and navy striped silk tie aside and gently massaging his shoulders after opening his white shirt to reveal his perfectly rippled chest and washboard abs, she smiled tentatively.

Since he was not making any protest, she offered, "I would have to say that I think we are a lot clearer about where we stand right now than we were a few weeks ago."

Pausing, she let her hands play with the hairs on his chest. "I would also say that we at least know that I am perfectly willing to get to know you better and explore things between us more. A few weeks ago *that* was not the case."

Darren cleared his throat and pulled her closer to him. "No, that was not the case at all."

"So what do you say we just continue to get to know each other, and take it from there?" She wrapped her arms around his neck.

Darren paused for a moment before placing his mouth on hers. Tracing her lips with his tongue, he then probed every region of her mouth.

She moaned softly and ran her hand across his close-cut hair, teasing the waves she found there.

When he finally pulled away, she knew what it meant to be kissed senseless. She was tempted to agree to any label he wanted to give their union if it meant that he would start kissing her again.

Darren cleared his throat. "Well, I guess a lack of clarity will have to do for now. But after a while—"

Kissing was better than talking, she decided, and pulled his face to hers again.

Pulling away, he started, "We are going to have to have a serious talk soon about where we stand and—"

"Where are the condoms?" she whispered.

He closed his eyes and sighed.

"We'll talk soon. I promise." She kissed him again. "Just not now."

He mumbled, "Upstairs."

"What?"

"The condoms are upstairs."

CHAPTER 14

While home for Easter weekend, Alicia could barely contain the energy to keep her eyes open for long periods of time. If she could have found a way to nap every half-hour with her hectic schedule, she probably would have. It seemed like she couldn't get enough sleep lately. She thought it must have been because she was studying non-stop, maintaining the growing "r-word" between herself and Darren, and obsessing about starting graduate school in the fall.

She was just not getting enough sleep. She'd slept the entire plane ride home, went home and slept some more. If she hadn't promised Sonya that she would come over to hang out, she would have slept through the night.

Sonya wanted to have the entire gang over on Good Friday because everyone would be having separate family dinners on Easter. If Alicia had blown off the get-together, she would never have heard the end of it.

After driving around quite a bit because they lived in one of those new developments in West Bloomfield where all of the cul-de-sacs resembled each other, she finally parked her rental in the driveway of Kendrick and Sonya's brand new house.

Their home was red brick and had bold, brass accents. Everything from the mailbox to the lights to the handrail on the steps was made of brass. It looked huge from the outside, and she was sure, knowing Sonya and Kendrick, it was just as spacious on the inside.

She got out of the car and walked up the beautifully landscaped walkway to the front door. Sonya answered before she even got a chance to ring the bell. "Well, it's about time you made it. I thought you'd never get here. The guys are all here already." Sonya hugged her and held the door open for her to pass.

"Girl, you are lucky I woke up in time. I was dead tired. I slept all afternoon."

Giving Alicia the once over, Sonya agreed. "Wow, you do look kind of tired and haggard. What's up? Why are you so run down?"

Alicia surveyed her friend. She was dressed in what constituted casual wear for Sonya, a dressy skirt and blouse. She was perfectly made-up and had on her usual bright and bubbly face. Married life agreed with her, and she couldn't be happier for her friend. The bubbly personality, however, was a bit much, especially when she was so tired herself.

Alicia examined her own jeans and tennis shoes, and reasoned that she was in study mode, and she didn't have the time or inclination to dress up. She'd managed this trip home even though she had two papers to write and an Honors thesis to complete. Running on air, she'd lost at least five pounds that she could barely spare.

"Girl, shut up. I don't look that bad. It's just been rough finishing up my last semester." She followed Sonya into the living room.

"Well, you sure don't look as good as you normally do. You need to take some vitamins or something for energy." Sonya sounded like a walking advertisement for One-a-Day.

"What I need to do is get some friends who aren't player-haters." Alicia sat down on the couch, crossed her eyes and smiled.

"What you need is some gingko and a good multi-vitamin." Sonya sat down on the love seat across from her and started laughing.

"Where are the guys?" She kicked off her tennis shoes and relaxed on the floral Queen Anne-inspired sofa. It was clearly not made for lounging, but that didn't deter her from trying to make it into the bed she'd just left.

"They're downstairs trying out Kendrick's new pool table. So why are you so tired? All those late nights staying up talking to Darren?" Sonya said Darren really slowly, the way that girls did in grade school when they teased their friends about a boy they liked.

Ignoring her, she asked, "Anyway, what kind of snacks do you have? I'm hungry."

"Don't try to change the subject, spill. Troy told me that you and Darren are going pretty hot and heavy. He said that it was clear to him in Miami that the two of you had more going on than you were letting on." Sonya's voice picked up an indignant tone that made it clear she was not happy about having to hear about her best friend's love life from her brother of all people.

"Oh he did, did he? Well, I guess since you have heard all that from Troy, you don't need to hear anymore from me." Positioning the burgundy throw pillow behind her head, she tried to get a more comfortable fit.

"I'm your best friend. You should be ashamed that you haven't shared this with me already." Pointing her finger accusingly, Sonya literally started bouncing up and down in her seat. "This is big! You and Darren! I knew putting the two of you together would spark that old flame. And Kendrick said that I shouldn't have done it because you hated him. I knew better."

"You should have listened to your husband. All you've done is make my life way more complicated than it needs to be right now." Finding a nice niche of comfort in the sofa, she closed her eyes but kept talking.

"I was planning to remain uninvolved until I was done with graduate school and the editor of my own magazine. A sista had plans, and you being the player-hater you are had to throw salt in my game."

"What? Player-hater? See, you have been spending too much time with that rap producer. What's up with that by the way? You went from hardly dating to juggling two men. Troy told me that Flex had his arm around your shoulder the whole time at the awards show, and Darren was about to blow a gasket."

Wondering if becoming a housewife had turned her friend into one of those people who watched talk shows and soaps all day, because she was feeding off the sensational elements of Troy's gossip a little too much, Alicia decided to put her out of her misery and give her a little something.

"Girl, please, just one of the many reasons I don't want to be seriously involved with anyone. Darren came to Miami trying to regulate. He actually thought that because he told me not to go that I was going to back out on a friend."

"He told you not to go? Now what would make him think that he could tell you what to do?" Eyebrows furrowed and finger on chin, Sonya appeared to be seriously considering the questions before getting an "aha" expression on her face.

"Things must be far more serious between the two of you than you are letting on if he's taking that many liberties."

"Why does it have to be that? Why can't it just be that he is crazy and tripping?" The feeble attempt at diversion was wasted on Sonya, and Alicia knew it even as she spoke the words.

"Please, girl, we are talking about Darren. I went to college with that man. He has never tripped like that over any woman. He and my brother were of the love-them-and-leave-them variety." Sonya shook her head, clearly remembering the guys' college antics.

"They would never tell a woman they didn't care about not to go out with another guy. In fact, they ran from monogamy."

"Oh, that's sweet! This is the kind of guy who you scheme and conspire to hook your best friend up with." Shaking her head in mock disgust, Alicia's tone dripped with sarcasm.

"I would hardly call partnering the two of you at my wedding scheming and conspiring." Sonya defended her actions and brightened up considerably. "Anyway, you're missing the point. The point is that Darren is clearly *crazy* about you! I always knew he was! That's why he never really got serious with one girl in college. He went off to Howard with feelings for you." The bubbly personality frayed Alicia's already shot nerves.

"Girl, you have been reading too many romance novels. Anyway, if that's the case, what's Troy's excuse for not getting serious with anyone? Whom did he have feelings for?"

"Girl, please, Troy was just a big old slut puppy. He doesn't have an excuse. He's my brother and I love him to death, but that's just the way he is."

Alicia laughed. "So, how is married life? Is my big head cousin treating you right? Or do I have to go put my foot in his behind?" she teased. "And shouldn't they have their behinds up here already so we can get on with this little reunion?"

"Married life is lovely. I am so happy I could burst." Sonya placed her hands properly in her lap and grinned so hard she beamed. "I still can't believe that I'm a married woman."

Gush. Gush. Gush.

Alicia crossed her eyes and twisted up her face. "I'm happy for you, girl. However, I'm hungry and tired, so get those boys. Let's hop to it. I thought we were *all* hanging out, not the little ladies upstairs gossiping while the men-folk shoot pool."

"We are. Dinner has been done for a while." Still beaming, Sonya folded her arms on her lap. "I was waiting for you before I rounded everyone up."

"Well, round them up." Shifting the throw pillow, Alicia turned around to take a quick power nap while Sonya finished her preparations.

"I'll set the table, and you go round them up." Sonya got up from the loveseat and walked toward the kitchen.

Shoot, Alicia thought to herself as she reluctantly got up from the cozy little spot that she'd made for herself.

Darren tried to ignore the ribbing from his friends and concentrate on his pool game. He was doing a lousy job. Between Troy's jokes and Kendrick's glares, he couldn't seem to focus. Since he didn't like to lose, he finally stepped out and let Troy and Kendrick play one another while he watched.

Originally, he thought that if they were busy playing each other, they would leave him alone. He soon found that was not the case. No, they kept on with the smart remarks and constant questions.

"I knew I shouldn't have let Sonya put the two of you together at the wedding." Holding his pool stick to make a shot, Kendrick's lip formed an impressive snarl.

"Like you had a choice. Sonya was determined to help give *true love* a push." Troy leaned on the edge of the pool table and grinned.

"Darren doesn't love Alicia. Do you, Darren?" Kendrick still did not shoot.

Tempted to tell him to play the game and stay the hell out of his business, he opted for the sarcastic route instead. "Is it any of your business?"

"I'm making it my business. If you don't care about her and you're not going to be serious, then you need to leave her alone." Kendrick turned angrily and finally made a shot. It was a poor shot that made it easy for Troy to come and run the table.

Troy gladly took advantage of the opportunity, placing ball after ball in the pockets grinning the whole time.

"Well, since when did you become all holier than thou? Who are you to tell me how to handle my relationship with Alicia?" Indignant and in no mood for Kendrick's "leave my little cousin alone" routine, Darren folded his arms across his chest and narrowed his gaze at his childhood friend.

"Oh, so now you're in a relationship? When did that happen, in Miami or after?" Troy glanced up from his steady focus and missed his next shot as payment for being nosy.

"None of your business. My goodness, would the two of you cut me some slack?" Darren snapped a bit more harshly than he intended.

"No. By the way, if my cousin sheds anymore tears over you, I will personally deal with you." Posted again in his glaring stance and not taking his turn in the pool game, Kendrick's eyes held the threat of his words.

"Oh, this is rich." Darren turned and threw up his hands.

"Then I'll deal with you when he's done." Troy walked over and stood next to Kendrick.

The two of them made quite the menacing pair; however, Darren just shook his head in a manner meant to show his friends that he remained unfazed. "You too? Oh come on, you've got to be kidding me." He dismissed them with a glance, but then he turned back and eyed them cautiously.

"Do we look like we're joking?" Kendrick picked up the chalk and leaned against the table as he chalked his cube.

Darren couldn't imagine why he even bothered chalking; Kendrick wasn't playing the game.

"Yeah, if you're not serious about her, leave her alone." Troy echoed his two cents.

"Well, not that it's any of your business, but I am very serious about Alicia. She is very special to me. I love her!"

Whoa! Where did that come from?

Both Kendrick and Troy stopped and stared at him.

Recovering first, Troy joked. "Well she definitely doesn't love you. You should have seen her in Miami, man." The joke was followed by hysterical laughter.

Troy leaned against the pool table for support. "She was mad as hell at this guy."

"What do you mean? Are you kidding me? Alicia is just fighting her feelings. But I'm willing to bet my fortune that I can make her fall in love with me!"

Who is Troy to say that Alicia definitely isn't in love with me? She is, and I intend to prove it.

Contemplating the irony of his own words, he realized that he actually was betting his inheritance on Alicia's love, in a sense. If he couldn't get Alicia to love him, he wouldn't marry her, and if he didn't marry her, his father would disinherit him. *Am I really willing to give it all up for love?* Her father would lose Taylor Publishing. And Kendrick would lose his job.

A lot is riding on this, and now my heart is firmly at stake as well.

"Trust me. Alicia is already in love. She's just too damn stubborn to admit it." His voice was cockier than he actually felt given the pressure he was feeling. "She will admit it eventually. How can she not love a guy like me? I'm going to make her fall so deep in love that she won't be able to picture her life without me." His confidence took on a swagger that he hoped would make his boys back off.

"Why go through with all the trouble, man. You never had to work this hard for a woman before?" Unimpressed, Kendrick eyed him suspiciously.

He let go of his façade and simply came clean. "I've never met one more worth it before. I told you I love her."

"Another one bites the dust. Well, I'm not going down without a fight." Troy bowed his head in mock mourning. "Well, I guess it's up to me to keep up the good fight for all those fallen comrades lost to the demon of love." Shaking his head, Troy glanced up, grinning.

Kendrick gave Darren one last evil glance as he sunk the eight ball. "Man, shut up and rack 'em." He motioned at Troy, whose grin quickly soured to a deeply set frown.

What part of "tired" doesn't Sonya understand?

The last thing Alicia wanted to do was trek downstairs. She opened the door that led to the basement family room. The plush carpet felt lovely on her feet, and she forgot about her attitude long enough to be impressed with the carpet Sonya had picked out.

The guys were loudly arguing about something as she walked down the steps. She could barely hear her own footsteps on the stairs over their big mouths. Stopping three steps shy of the bottom, she listened, and her mouth fell open. Darren was bragging about how he was going to make her fall in love with him.

What a jerk! He actually made a *bet* about how he would make her fall in love.

He is playing a game! She bit her lower lip and clutched the stair rail before huffing back upstairs. She'd actually started to trust him, and was considering a commitment. Now she couldn't help but feel foolish. The only saving grace was she'd never agreed to a relationship, and she never told him she was falling in love with him. *Who the heck are you kidding, girl? You're already in love with the jerk!* It was a sobering thought, and she just hoped that she would be able to pull it together long enough to face him, let alone recover from it.

Once upstairs, she shut the door silently, even though she wanted to slam it. Barreling down the hall, she nearly knocked Sonya down when she entered the dining room.

Sonya caught her balance and frowned at her. "Girl, where are the guys?"

"They sounded like they were having so much fun, I couldn't bare to interrupt them," she mumbled sarcastically.

Perplexed, Sonya tilted her head and sighed. "Weren't you the one who said that you were hungry and wanted to eat? Girl! Let me go get these guys." Sonya headed off to round up the guys, and Alicia sat at the dining room table fuming.

Gazing around angrily, Alicia took in all the cherry wood surrounding her. Everything from the table and chairs to the buffet and hutch was Queen Anne-style. Sonya's passion for floral, Alicia would never understand, not to mention her frilly decor. Her frown deepened when Darren walked into the room.

Darren smiled when he walked into the dining room and saw Alicia sitting there. Walking over to her, he expected her to get up so that he could give her a hug; however, she just sat there.

"What's up, Licia? Don't you have a greeting for me?" Waiting for her to enter his embrace, he held out his arms.

Alicia barely glanced at him. "Hey."

The fact that she refused to look him in the eye and when she did she could only glare at him was not lost on Darren. He wondered if she'd had an argument with her dad or something. Reaching down, he took her arm, and pulled her up from the chair. Holding her tight, he kissed her. She loosened up momentarily, and he could feel whatever it was melting away.

Still holding her as he closed the kiss he gave her a curious glance, hoping she would share whatever it was that was bothering her. "Now that's what I call a greeting."

"Oh man! Get a room." Troy pretended to be disgusted, but he was smiling.

"Yeah, man, nobody wants to see that." Kendrick, on the other hand, was decidedly sincere in his disgust.

"I think it's romantic." Sonya beamed happiness and love.

"Oh brother. What's for dinner?" Kendrick addressed his wife and gave Darren and Alicia a pointed stare.

Alicia went cold again and pulled away from him.

He took the chair next to hers and sat down. Studying her carefully, he couldn't get a read.

"This is buffet-style, folks. I know you guys don't expect me to serve you." Sonya stepped to the side and motioned toward the kitchen.

"A good woman would," Troy joked, but quickly ducked when Sonya reached to hit him upside the head as he walked past her on his way to the kitchen.

"I'll tell you, they just don't make them the way they used to. That's why I'm remaining a bachelor for life," Troy yelled out from the kitchen.

Sonya rushed into the kitchen behind her brother. "If you keep it up, you are not going to get a taste of my food," she threatened playfully.

"Well, you might be doing me a favor. You never were that great a cook," Troy yelled back.

Soon, all they heard was Troy yelling "Ouch!" and screaming for help. Sonya was laying into him. It sounded like a dishtowel hitting skin.

"I'd better go and break that up." Kendrick glanced back at Darren and Alicia. "Are you guys getting any food?"

Not taking his eyes off Alicia, Darren responded, "I'll get some in a minute."

"I'm not really hungry anymore. I think I'm heading back home. I'm kind of tired." Alicia stifled a yawn and got up from her chair.

"Sonya will be upset. But you do look a little tired. Must be partying too hard there at Mount Holyoke." Kendrick eyed his cousin with concern.

"Please, try studying too hard and writing too many papers. Just tell Sonya that we can hang out on Saturday, and maybe I'll come by and watch a flick with the two of you on Saturday night if you don't mind a third wheel." The forced smile and fake pleasant voice did not fool Darren. He could tell that something was really bothering her.

"You know you're always welcome, Licia. I'll see you tomorrow." Kendrick offered as he left to join the others in the kitchen.

Once Kendrick left, Darren watched as Alicia stood to leave. He rose and followed her back to the living room. She put on her tennis shoes, grabbed her jacket and was heading for the door. Once he realized that she was seriously just going to leave without so much as a goodbye, he took off behind her, following her out of the living room and into the foyer.

"What the hell is going on? Are you just going to leave like that? What are you doing?"

"I'm going home. I'm not feeling well. I'm tired, and I want to go to sleep. Do you have a problem with that?"

"Yes, I do have a problem with that. What's the problem? What's wrong with you?"

She shrugged. "Can't I just be tired?"

"Well, what about you hanging out with Sonya tomorrow and watching a movie with them tomorrow night? Am I going to get a chance to see you at all tomorrow?" Feeling his skin prickle and the hairs stand up on his neck, he knew the trigger for his body's reaction had everything to do with the nonchalant tone of Alicia's voice.

"Oh, don't tell me, now I can't hang out with my cousin and his wife? What next, Darren? My parents?" Alicia's voice reeked of sarcasm.

"Ha, ha. You know that's not what I meant." His gaze narrowed, and he rubbed his hand along the back of his neck. "Fine. Your dad invited me to Easter dinner. So I guess I'll just have to wait and see you then."

"He what? He invited you to Easter dinner? Why would he do that? And why would you want to come?

Don't you usually have Easter dinner with your own family?" Alicia's eyes were wide, and she sounded more flustered than annoyed.

"Well, yes, I was thinking that we could go to brunch with my folks after service and have dinner at your folks. How does that sound?" He couldn't resist pulling her into his arms, even though she was starting to get on his nerves.

"I think that is the most ridiculous thing I've ever heard. I'm not going to brunch. I probably won't be at the service, and I suggest that you consider other options for your Easter dinner. My father shouldn't have invited you."

"Why not?" In his opinion his plans for their Easter were perfect, and more than that, he saw his plans as the start of their own Easter tradition for years to come.

Alicia hesitated only briefly; she raised her head. "I invited Flex to Easter dinner. He doesn't really get along with his dad, and he'll be in the area this week anyway. I invited him a while ago, and he wasn't sure he could make it. He called the other day and said he could."

Darren held Alicia at arm's length. "You what?"

"I invited Flex to Easter dinner." She tilted her head defiantly.

"Un-invite him then." Voice clipped, he wanted his message to be understood and firm.

"No." Alicia tilted her head a little higher.

"What?" He dropped his hold on Alicia and folded his arms across his chest.

"No, I don't want to." Pose unyielding, Alicia's voice was firm. Then she sighed. "Listen, Darren, I'm really tired, and I'm leaving. I guess I'll see you at Easter dinner or *not*." She walked to the door, opened it, and stepped into the crisp night air.

Following her outside, he played the only card he had left. "If I come over to your house on Easter and Flex is there, that's it. It's over between us, Alicia." He realized it was lame even as he said it; however, he was tired of the Flex Towns situation.

Shocked for a moment, Alicia bounced back with the speed of a cheetah. "Well, since it never really started, I guess that's all right. I mean it's not like we're *in love* or anything like that." She opened her car door.

Speak for yourself, Darren thought. "I mean it, Licia. Do not test me on this." Walking away, Darren went back into the house.

Alicia stared at Darren's retreating back and took deep calming breaths as she narrowed her eyes. She started to follow him and tell him that he had no right to tell her who she could and could not have over for Easter dinner, as well as a few other choice words;

however, her tiredness had taken its toll, making her feel physically and mentally drained. The "make her fall in love" situation had her feeling vulnerable. Realizing that she'd almost told Flex that he could no longer come to Easter dinner because she didn't want Darren to get the wrong idea, she banged her hand on the steering wheel. The fact that she'd almost cancelled on a friend while Darren was apparently playing games made her skin crawl. It also made her chest ache with a pain she hadn't felt since she was fourteen. In fact, it was much worse. That puppy love had nothing on what she felt for the betting playboy now. She had to focus and strategize, or she would lose more than the game Darren was apparently playing. She was well on the way to losing her heart.

CHAPTER 15

Alicia didn't hang out with Sonya and Kendrick on Saturday like she'd planned. Hoping against hope that she wasn't experiencing an onslaught of lovesickness, she spent the entire day in her pajamas, lounging around the house and napping frequently. When she got up on Easter morning, she thought she would have been well rested, but she felt like she could still sleep some more. She managed to convince her parents that she needed to study, so she didn't have to go to Easter church service with them. While she tried to study, she kept dozing off.

By the time her parents got back and started preparations for dinner, she had at least gotten dressed and felt somewhat coherent. The smells wafting through the house sparked her energy a bit, and she went downstairs to see if she could help out.

As soon as she walked into the dining room, Kyle Taylor frowned.

"Is that what you're wearing to Easter dinner?" Eying her red velour sweatpants and Delta crop T-shirt with distaste, his gaze moved to the ponytail sitting on top of her head.

"What's wrong with this?" She tried to tame her ponytail to no avail. She peered down at her outfit. "It's comfortable and gives me plenty of room to get nice and full."

She patted her non-existent tummy and tugged the elastic waistline of her pants to prove her point.

"Well, I've invited Darren Whitman to share dinner with us, and I think it would be nice if you dressed up a bit." Kyle said the words as if she was supposed to jump, run, and change clothes just because Darren Whitman was coming to dinner.

"I think she looks fine, Kyle. I think I might put on something a little more comfortable myself." Karen jumped in as usual to rein Kyle in.

He started to say something but paused. "I guess you're right. It will only be the four of us since Kendrick is having dinner across the street with Sonya's folks."

"Actually, there will be five of us. I'm sorry. I forgot to tell you that Flex is coming over for dinner." She pulled out one of the Shaker dining room chairs and sat down. Kyle and Karen usually had an open door policy when it came to friends of hers and friends of Kendrick's. An extra person at dinner shouldn't have been a problem, but Alicia did wish that she had remembered the open invitation that she'd extended to Flex and told her folks earlier.

"What? Well, Alicia, surely you could have remembered such a detail." Dumfounded, Kyle paced the floor and shook his head as he spoke. "If I'd known you had done such a thing, I would never have invited Darren over. What is he going to think?"

"Don't know. Don't care," Alicia lied. She knew exactly what he thought, and she cared a lot more than she was willing to admit.

Kyle didn't know how she felt about Darren, and it was starting to bother her that he continued to try and throw the two of them together even though for all he knew she couldn't stand the man.

Flustered, Kyle stopped pacing and ran his hand across his head before giving Alicia a pointed stare.

"What's the big deal, Dad? I mean really. It's not like I'm ready to be seriously involved with anyone right now. I'm about to go to graduate school. Good grief. Lighten up."

"She's right, Kyle. Give it a rest. I, for one, am going to take this opportunity to check out both of the young men who have an interest in my child and make my suggestions based on informed interaction." Karen took on the expression of a plotting woman.

Alicia might have laughed if she didn't know that Karen was dead serious. "Oh God. I don't know which one of you is worse. You two are going to make me rethink the decision I made about graduate school," she threatened mildly.

"You've made a decision? What did you decide?" Karen's face lit up, and Kyle was strangely silent.

"I decided to accept the University of Michigan's offer. Michigan has offered me a fellowship for the first year and a TA-ship for the second year, Dad. So I won't need any financial help. I'll be on my own."

"That's nice, dear. It's… really nice." He squeezed her shoulder.

"It's more than nice. It's fantastic. That news makes this a celebration." Karen walked over and ran her hands through the curls in Alicia's ponytail.

"Thanks, Mom." At least one of her parents was happy about her decision.

The doorbell rang, signaling that one of their two guests had arrived. Alicia went to let him in. Flex stood at the door with a bouquet of peach and yellow roses.

"Oh my, are those for me?" she said as she reached for the flowers.

Holding them out of her reach, he replied, "Nope, they're for your mother. I was raised to always bring a gift for the lady of the house."

Putting on her best fake pout, she broke into a wide grin. "That's fine. Mom will love them." She hugged Flex, and he gave her a peck on the lips. Just as she was about to shut the door, she noticed Darren coming up the walk. Clearly having seen the hug and the brief encounter of their lips, he didn't appear to be too happy.

"Flex, you can head to the dining room and give those to my mom. She'll find a vase for them. The dining room is the third door to your right down the hall." She turned to greet Darren.

Darren was also carrying a bouquet of roses, pink with sprigs of baby's breath. Eying the flowers her eyebrows arched in question mode.

"For Mrs. Taylor," Darren said shortly. He walked in and headed toward the dining room, without attempting to say hello or greet her in any way.

Darren told himself that he would be able to get through the dinner, and when he left, he would be done with Alicia Taylor.

No woman is worth all this drama!

If she couldn't commit and admit that she loved him as he loved her, he'd have to risk losing his inheritance. While he would no longer be rich and have the world at his disposal, he wouldn't be desolate. He had a healthy portfolio from the small trust fund he inherited from his maternal grandparents. It wasn't a lot, and life as he knew it would never be the same. The thought of giving it all up still gave him pause. He loved Alicia and knew that without a doubt. What he did doubt was the feasibility of making it in the world without the trappings of being the heir to Whitman Enterprise.

Love. He was able to admit he was in love with Alicia, but she was clearly not in love with him. Tired of all the uncertainty, he made a pact with himself to get on with his life. When he left the Taylor's house today, he would do so with at least some of his dignity in tact.

To say that his feelings for Alicia had taken him to places he never thought he would go would have been a huge understatement; however, if she wanted to be free to have whatever friends she wanted, free she would be.

Flex Towns really wasn't a bad guy. In fact, if they had met under different circumstances, Darren figured he might even find that he and Towns hit it off. He could almost see why Alicia would become friends with Towns. He just wasn't in the mood to admit any of that.

Shaking his head, he tried to focus on the conversation that was going on. Mrs. Taylor engaged both him and Flex equally in conversation during the whole dinner. The more questions she asked of the two of them, the more obvious it appeared that she was trying to gauge which man was better suited for her daughter. Darren wondered if she knew about the little deal her husband made with his dad, and he also wondered if that knowledge would influence her judgment.

Mrs. Taylor had asked Flex what made him go into the recording business. Flex was giving some long, drawn-out answer about how much he loved music and how he also wanted to do something different from what his father did. It turned out that Flex's father was a prominent attorney and was now a well-respected judge.

Mrs. Taylor perked up, and Mr. Taylor even became interested in the conversation.

"So you went into the music business as some sort of rebellion? Because you didn't want to follow in your father's esteemed footsteps?" Mr. Taylor shook his head and frowned.

"Partly, yes, but partly, no. I had my rebellious streak, no doubt. I'd been kicked out of every boarding school imagined. When I graduated from Teaneck High School by the skin of my teeth and went to Morehouse College just like my dad and his dad before him, I was really trying to follow the path my dad had chosen for me. I just realized that I couldn't do that and be true to myself. Being the son of Fredrick Towns II is something I'm just now getting a handle on."

"Fredrick Towns II?" Mr. Taylor glanced at Darren for the first time that afternoon.

Since Mr. Taylor had been hesitant to make eye contact, Darren figured it was because he was thrown for a loop by Alicia's decision to invite a guest of her own.

"Isn't Fredrick Towns II the Grand Polemarch of the fraternity?" Mr. Taylor asked.

"Yes, he his."

Darren eyed Flex Towns incredulously.

Mr. Taylor gazed at Flex with renewed interest. Even Alicia, who had been half listening to the conversation and picking at her food, perked up.

"So, did you manage to pledge while you were at Morehouse?" Mr. Taylor asked Flex.

Flex smiled a knowing smile. "Yes, I pledged, but I didn't pledge Dad's fraternity. I couldn't see myself as a Kappa. I pledged Sigma sophomore year."

Mr. Taylor took a sip of his drink as if he was trying to get a bad taste out of his mouth. "Do you mean to tell me that your father is one of the highest ranking Kappas in the country, and you pledged Sigma?"

"Yep. Can you please pass the potato salad?" Shrugging, Flex motioned toward the rapidly disappearing dish.

"That's cool, Flex. I never knew that about you." Alicia passed Flex the potato salad and grinned at Mr. Taylor.

"Yeah, Flex, no wonder Alicia likes you so much. The two of you have a lot in common." Darren's voice was clipped and sounded harsh, even to his own ears. He could no longer hold in the smart comment that had been sitting on the tip of his tongue throughout the whole conversation.

Although she didn't say a word in response to him, Alicia's eyes narrowed and her mouth hung open for a moment. Swallowing, she turned to Mrs. Taylor. "See what a good child I am? I could have pledged one of the other sororities, then what would you have done?"

Mrs. Taylor shuddered briefly in mock horror and laughed. She focused her attention on Darren. "So Darren, how are things going at Whitman Enterprises? I've been keeping up on all the articles about you in the press. Everyone is talking about how you've made your own mark in the company."

"Things are great. I think people are finally realizing that I am more than the boss's son, and they are taking my assets and contributions seriously. I guess I really didn't have a problem following in my dad's footsteps." He relished the chance to talk about something else besides Flex Towns.

Flex's head turned at Darren's remark. He simply nodded and whispered something in Alicia's ear. Frowning at first, she started to giggle.

Darren felt the heat rise from his neck to his cheeks.

Mrs. Taylor noticed and smiled. "You know, I remember when you were a kid and you boys used to play here in the summer. I had to break up so many fights between you and Alicia I lost count. I never thought the two of you would learn how to get along. You were like oil and water. If you said red, she said blue. Do you remember those days?"

Darren noticed that Alicia stopped giggling. Neither he nor she said a word in response to Mrs. Taylor's lighthearted trip down memory lane.

"Umm, umm, umm." Mrs. Taylor studied them both carefully and shook her head. "Anybody save room for dessert?"

Alicia could see that Darren had a serious attitude. Even her father had come around and was open to at least talking to Flex, but not Darren. She knew that once her folks got to know Flex, they would like him. Darren's attitude was his problem. Especially since she found out that this had all been a game to him, and, once again, he really wasn't interested in her. Having Flex around made it easier to salvage what was left of her pride and her heart.

Darren seemed to get even angrier when Flex whispered in her ear. She tried not to react, but the thought of what Flex said made her giggle.

He said that Darren was in love with her and that she had better stop playing with the dude before he exploded. Imagining Darren exploding in front of her parents at Easter dinner caused her to giggle uncontrollably.

She thought about what Flex had said and wondered if it was true.

No. I heard him with my own ears again. It is just a bet, just a game. He doesn't want me. He doesn't really care.

Karen had two desserts, a red velvet cake and a coconut cake. Coconut cake was Alicia's favorite, but she found she didn't have nearly the appetite she thought she had. She opted for a cup of herbal tea instead.

She sipped it slowly as she half listened to the conversations going on around her, just wanting to get through with the meal. Once the meal was over, she wouldn't have to see Darren anymore. As she listened to Flex and her father haggle over sports, she was surprised when even Darren grudgingly joined the conversation.

When she glanced up, she found Karen watching her, and they smiled at one another. Surprised at how comforting the exchange was, she reasoned she might just make it through her stay at the heartbreak hotel after all, eventually.

"Do you want to help me clear the table?" Karen asked her.

Knowing her mother, Alicia figured it was a ploy to get her into the kitchen so she could get the dirt on Darren's sour mood, but she took the lifeline to get out of Darren's presence anyway. "I don't want to, but I will." When she started to get up, she found that Kyle had a surprise in store for everyone.

"No, Karen, let me do that. You sit and relax."

Dad is actually offering to do housework. Wonders never cease.

"I'll help you, Mr. Taylor," Flex offered.

"I'm actually going to head over to my folks. Thanks for inviting me, Mr. Taylor. I really enjoyed the meal, Mrs. Taylor. Flex, it was good seeing you again. Take care." Darren gave Karen a hug and shook hands with Flex and Kyle. He didn't even give Alicia a backward glance.

He is ignoring me!

Fine! I don't care! She knew all about his little plan to make her fall in love now, so his attitude didn't matter, at least not as much as the lump in her chest.

Karen went to let Darren out. When she returned to the dining room, Alicia was contemplating her feelings for Darren and his plans for her.

Flex came back to collect more plates and food to bring into the kitchen, and Karen stopped him. "Why don't I help Kyle with the rest of this while the two of you catch up? Go relax in the den, listen to some music, whatever. Kyle and I can handle the rest of this."

"Are you sure?" Flex hesitated.

"Yes, go on." Shooing them both away, Karen started to remove the dishes herself.

Alicia spent the rest of the afternoon and early evening hanging out with Flex and her parents. When Flex left for the airport to take his jet back to New York, Alicia allowed herself to ponder what he had said to her earlier about Darren.

She didn't know if Darren loved her or not, but she was determined to find out for sure why he made a bet about making her fall in love.

When she stormed past her parents who were sitting comfortably in the kitchen having tea and seconds on dessert, Kyle's eyebrows arched in concern.

"Hey, princess, where are you going? Don't you want to sit down and have some dessert with us? You ate like a bird today." Kyle's concern was touching; however, she was a woman on a mission.

Determined to get her to stay in, Kyle continued. "And with all the sleeping you've been doing this weekend, I'm afraid you might be coming down with something. Maybe you should stay in."

Karen simply sipped her tea and eyed her suspiciously.

Good grief!

"I'm fine, Daddy. I'm just going to take a little ride. I'll be back later." Kissing him on the cheek, she raced out the door in order to head off the second round of persuasion.

She was out the side door and closing it when she heard him yell, "Well, don't forget you have an early flight back to school tomorrow."

Letting the door close, she smiled. "Thanks, Dad. I know. Love you. Bye. Don't wait up."

CHAPTER 16

Darren was almost tempted to tell the doorman not to let Alicia up. It was the principle of the thing. Even though he could tell after being around Flex that he and Alicia were indeed just friends, she should have enough respect for his feelings not to rub their friendship in his face. It was an ego thing.

Determined to see her directly out, he opened the door to let her in. As soon as he opened the door, she brushed past him and stormed into the loft.

He closed the door and followed her in. "Listen, Alicia, I don't know why you're here. I'm not in the mood for this. I told you Friday night that if Flex came to your house for dinner on Easter, I'd be done. He was there. I'm done."

Alicia spun around, and her eyes were like green daggers. "Good for you. Bravo! You're done. Well, I'm not done. I'm going to have my say."

Walking over to him, she pointed her French-manicured finger in his chest. "First of all, Flex is just a friend, and nobody tells me who I can be friends with. I thought you understood that. Apparently, you have a hard time grasping things."

He grabbed her hand and held it. When she tried to pull it away, he held it tighter. "I don't have a problem with you having friends, Alicia. I do have a problem with your lack of respect for me."

Tilting her head to the side, she narrowed her gaze before she broke out in a sarcastic laugh. "Are you serious? You wouldn't know respect if it smacked you in the face. If you did, you would respect me enough not to make bets with your friends about how you're going to make me fall in love with you. What else did you bet on? How quickly you could get me into bed?" She snatched her hand away with so much force she almost tumbled backwards.

Catching her, he held her close. "What are you talking about?"

Alicia tried to pull away, but he made sure his hold was firm. "Oh, don't play dumb. I heard you bragging to Kendrick and Troy about how you could make me fall in love, how you would bet your inheritance on it. I heard you!"

Shaking his head, he gazed at her with all the amazement he felt, because she was truly unbelievable. "Your eavesdropping is going to get you in trouble one day. What else did you hear?"

"I heard enough. And I was not eavesdropping! I came downstairs to get you guys for dinner, and I heard you talking about me. It's not eavesdropping if you walk up and accidentally hear people talking about you." Still trying to wiggle free, she huffed and finally stopped for a moment, only to start again.

He didn't care what rationale she came up with; she eavesdropped.

"Did you hear me tell Troy and Kendrick that I love you?" He moved one of her wild curls from in front of her face with one hand and still maintained his hold.

Flustered, she sputtered, "You what?"

"I love you. I love you, Alicia. But I will not continue the way we have been going. So either you admit how you feel and commit to us. Or you can leave." Loosening his hold, he released her.

"You love me?" Not taking advantage of her newfound mobility, Alicia just stood there, close. Placing her index finger in her mouth, she eyed him cautiously.

"For someone who is supposed to be so smart, you seem to have trouble with comprehension," he commented wryly. "It's on you, Licia. What's it going to be? Are you going to come clean, or are you going to keep lying to yourself and me?"

"How do I know this isn't a part of your master plan to get me to say I love you?" Her eyes narrowed, and she took a step back.

Taking her face in his hands, he sighed. "Does it seem like I'm lying to you? Look me in the eyes and tell me you don't believe that I love you."

Alicia studied him carefully, and he could feel her softening. She stepped even closer to him and placed her arms around his neck. She pulled his head to hers, and despite his resolve, he kissed her. They kissed for several minutes before he could gather the strength to pull away.

"No, not so fast, Licia. I need to hear three things from you."

Alicia sighed and pulled herself closer to him. He could feel the soft cushion of her breasts against his chest, and he temporarily forgot his train of thought.

"Can't we talk later?" Her fingers seductively fingered the back of his neck, and he felt goose bumps throughout his entire body. It was all he could do not to give in.

"No, Alicia. I need to hear this from you before we go any further. Do you believe that I love you?"

She shook her head yes.

"I need to hear you say it, Licia."

"Yes."

"Do you love me?"

When she started to shake her head again, Darren frowned.

"Okay. Yes. I love you. Are you satisfied?"

"Good, one more thing. Will you commit to a relationship with me? The two of us, a couple, monogamous, no more awards shows and red carpets, unless you're with me?"

"I will commit to a relationship if you agree not to try and run my life and tell me who I can be friends with." Alicia put her hands on her hips. "I will continue to be friends with Flex, and if I get other friends who happen to be men, that's fine. Just because we're a couple does not mean that I have to stop having friends."

"That's fine. I can deal with that. So, I need to hear you say it." He eyed the hips that her hands rested on and licked his lips.

"Okay. I want to be with you and only you. I want to be in a relationship with you. Are you happy?" With her arms folded across her chest and her head tilted defiantly, Darren couldn't help but admire her spunk. She held out until the end, and she didn't go down without a fight.

Feeling his heart beating wildly, he realized how happy he really was just to hear her say the words. "That wasn't so hard was it?" Walking over to her, he took her hand and led her upstairs to his bedroom.

Once upstairs, he simply stared at her for a while before helping remove her leather jacket. He would have felt more than a little self conscious if she were not staring at him as well and he didn't see the love that he knew without a doubt he felt echoed in her gaze.

"Let's get rid of these clothes, shall we?" he whispered in her ear.

Finished helping her with her jacket, he couldn't resist running his hand under her cropped T-shirt, caressing her belly and moving slowly to her back. The shudder that passed from her to him made his heart stop.

"You like that, don't you?" Lifting her arms, he removed the T-shirt, allowing his fingers to linger and trail her soft skin as he did.

Swallowing, she closed her eyes. "Umm hmm."

As he removed the rest of her clothing, he thought of how special what they were about to share was. They loved each other. Just that morning, he never thought he would hear a sentence such as that in regard to the two of them, and yet there they were. Closing his eyes, he paused, composing himself.

Lowering Alicia and himself to the bed, he started kissing her neck with soft pecks at first before moving on to teasing nibbles. He unclasped the front of her bra and tasted her left nipple. His tongue circled until her nipple formed a tight, aroused point, and then he tasted the other. He used one hand to tend to the abandoned nipple and the other to explore the sweet spot below her waist. His finger found her slick and wet. He added another finger and stroked her pleasure spot with his thumb.

"Umm, baby, you're nice and ready for me, aren't you?" Darren murmured as he went back to the other nipple with his mouth. "I love you, Licia."

As she caressed his back, she gazed deeply in his eyes and responded with the words he realized he would never tire of her saying, "I love you, too, so much, baby."

Darren reached up and removed the scrunchie that held her hair on top of her head. The curls fell and spread across the bed, and he brought his mouth down to hers and kissed her. His heart filled with so much emotion that he thought his heart would burst.

He undressed, opened the nightstand and took out a condom.

As he moved down toward her, she instinctively moved up to take him. He entered her with one deep thrust, and she pulled his head to her, hungrily taking his tongue in her mouth as she pulled him deeper and deeper inside of her.

Alicia had never felt more connected to anyone in her life. The closeness she felt to Darren at the moment of penetration overwhelmed her. It was all she could do not to cry out with the joy she felt. Naively, she'd thought that the lovemaking between them couldn't get any better, but she quickly realized just how wrong she was. *Love made everything better.* The lump that resided in her chest for so long was gone, set free by love. Suddenly struck by a need to give the man she loved as much pleasure as he was giving her, she wrapped her arms around his neck, pulled him close, and gazed into his eyes.

"Me on top." She was awed by the breathless boldness of her voice.

"So you want to control this." Darren thrust deeply inside of her, and she shivered.

Alicia sighed and nodded her head in the affirmative at first because she temporarily lost the ability to speak.

Finally, she managed to voice her desires. "Yes, I'd liked to be in control."

"You sure that you can handle all that power?" Darren went deep again and teased her neck with his tongue.

This time Alicia met his thrust with one of her own. "Oh, I'm very sure."

Darren rolled over, never breaking the connection between them. Alicia took a minute to get used to the new position.

She moved slowly at first, getting used the way he filled her with her on top. Intrigued by the way her own movement controlled her pleasure; she was even more amazed by Darren. Watching him as she moved up and down and rocked back and forth, her heart swelled. His face was a reflection of his pleasure, pleasure that she was giving him, pleasure that was a reflection of their love. Seeing it gave her a vigorous energy.

She ran her hands across his chest, and he moaned. "So you like that, huh? Is that good to you?" She bent to lick his chest as she continued to work her hips, and he sucked in a deep breath.

"This is nice. A girl could get used to all this power." She rose and arched her back. Before she could come back down, Darren reached up and grabbed her waist.

He pulled her down and claimed her lips with his own. He moved his hands down her back, stopping at her behind, and grabbed it as he lifted to meet her with a tremendous thrust. She felt a surge and met the rest of his thrusts with her own.

She broke away from their kiss and trailed his neck with her tongue. He flipped her over on her back and spread her legs further apart. His head bent down in pursuit of her breasts.

Darren moved from her breasts to her neck, all the while maintaining his powerful thrusts. She found herself on the verge of climax, and she could tell that Darren sensed how ready she was. She wrapped her arms around his waist, and he surged deeper inside of her.

"Oh, God, don't stop." Alicia barely recognized her own voice.

Darren smiled. "I couldn't even if I wanted to. Are you ready, baby?"

"Yes."

She lost all sense of reality as Darren moved inside of her. She could feel herself moving to meet him. But it was as if only her body was in control. She heard what sounded like her own voice scream out, and felt Darren shudder as they simultaneously reached fulfillment. Then she could feel Darren cuddling her in his arms and planting kisses on her face, lips, and neck. She wondered if this was what love felt like, and if so, she liked it very much.

CHAPTER 17

Returning to school with a newfound desire to finish, Alicia couldn't wait for graduation in two weeks and the start of her new life in graduate school. She had accepted Michigan's offer, and soon she'd be in Ann Arbor, in driving distance to the man she loved.

I love Darren.

It didn't feel weird when she said it. Instead, she felt oddly secure and at peace.

On the Tuesday of finals week, she woke up sick to her stomach. It couldn't have been anything she'd eaten because she hadn't had much of an appetite for the past few weeks. Chalking it up to stress, she continued trying to get all the things done that she needed to accomplish before graduation.

Between graduation, the new relationship, and pending graduate study, she figured it was only natural for her body to act weird. Though not as tired as she had been during Easter weekend, she still found herself sleeping more than usual.

Before she knew it, she was in the bathroom gagging and dry heaving, again.

"Girl, are you okay?" Jazz walked into the bathroom without even knocking.

"Do you need some help?"

Alicia moved over to the sink, rinsed her mouth out with water, moved the yellow polka dot shower curtain, and sat down on the edge of the tub. "I'm fine."

"You don't look fine. You look like death warmed over." Jazz leaned against the doorframe and eyed her curiously.

"Thanks a lot. Have I told you lately how much I appreciate your friendship?" Placing her head between her legs, she hoped that the position would help the nausea.

"Seriously, girl, this is like the third time this morning you've been in here puking your brains out. Are you pregnant?"

"Are you crazy?" she mumbled.

"Don't get smart, missy. You're showing all the signs. When was the last time you had your period?"

"I am not showing any signs. This is just a little stomach virus. I have been losing weight, not gaining weight. So I'm not pregnant." She lifted her head long enough to shoot daggers at Jazz with her eyes.

"My cousin Sheila lost close to fifteen pounds when she first got pregnant. She didn't have an appetite, and she couldn't keep anything down." Jazz crossed her arms and smirked. "When was the last time you had your period?"

Sighing, Alicia responded, "You know I'm not regular anyway. Plus, I always skip a period or two when I'm stressed. These have been some very stressful times. So please, stop tripping."

"Alicia, you're sexually active now. I don't have to tell you how much that changes things. You could be pregnant."

Lifting her head, Alicia tried to wrap her mind around the viability of what Jazz was saying. She and Darren had used protection every time but the first time, and even though she knew it only took *one* time, she refused to believe that she was pregnant.

"How could I be pregnant?" she mumbled more to herself than to Jazz.

"I pray that's a rhetorical question." Jazz was still smirking.

Glaring at Jazz, she tried to stand up but felt a sudden wave of dizziness that she contributed to missed meals. She quickly sat back down.

Jazz moved to help Alicia and stopped once she saw that Alicia was settled. "I'm just saying you *are* about to graduate from college. I know you know about the birds and the bees."

"But we did use protection, after that first time. Oh God! I cannot be pregnant! This is not my life. Pregnancy is nowhere in my plans." She ran her fingers quickly through her hair and massaged her temples.

"Nothing is one-hundred percent, Alicia. What do you mean you didn't use protection the first time? Why didn't you take the morning-after pill?"

Groaning, Alicia pulled her hair over her face. After a few seconds, she lifted her head and turned to Jazz. "Do you have a pregnancy test?"

"What am I, a drug store? No, but I can go get one. Do you want me to?"

"Yes," she mumbled.

She returned to her bedroom and sat on the bed. She had several things on her to-do list for that day, and taking a pregnancy test was not one of them. Everything was going to have to wait until she did that.

She had to make the final revisions on her Honors Thesis and hand that in by four p.m. the next day. She had to be fitted for her graduation gown. While she'd planned to study for the one class that required a final exam instead of a paper, all she could do was stare into space.

All the while, she wondered how she went from not dealing with guys and staying focused on her goals to being in a relationship, feeling out of control, and nervous about the possibility of being pregnant in a matter of months.

This is definitely not my life.

By the time Jazz came back from the drug store, Alicia had effectively ruined her manicure by picking at her nails. Surveying the damage she'd done, she added "Make a nail appointment" to her growing list of things to do.

"So are you ready? I got four just in case." Jazz held up a plastic drug store bag filled with pregnancy tests.

"Four? Why would we need four?" One pregnancy test should surely put her in the clear to go on with her nicely planned life.

"Well, I figured we could take one, and then we'd want to test the accuracy of that one with another. Better safe than sorry, right?" Jazz laughed nervously. "Well, I guess that's not a good saying in this situation, but you know what I mean."

She snatched the bag from Jazz. "Ha, ha, ha."

Taking the test was the easy part—waiting five minutes for the result was the killer. Dying repeatedly, she waiting another five minutes and another, and another, because she just refused to believe what each of the four tests told her.

Each one read positive.

I am pregnant.

She couldn't even blame the company for putting out a series of defective tests because Jazz, in all her wisdom, had purchased tests from four different companies.

Toying with the idea that she just happened to get the four defective tests from each of those companies, she realized how far-fetched that was.

I'm going to have a baby.

"What are you going to do?" Jazz sat next to her on the sleigh bed with her arm around her. They sat in silence for about twenty minutes.

I'm going to have a baby.

Strangely, even though she just found out she was pregnant, she knew that she wanted her baby. As for the rest, she had no clue. She was somewhat shocked that her mothering instinct kicked in so quickly. Wondering if being a stay-at-home mom was something she would one day consider, she started to bite her lower lip all the while picking off what was left of her French manicure.

"Are you going to call Darren and tell him?" Jazz was a whiz at bringing things that she didn't want to face to her attention.

Still in shock, she hadn't even thought about the prospect of telling Darren. She didn't know how she felt about telling him. Reasoning that he had a right to know, she also reasoned that he didn't need to know yet. What if he didn't want her to keep the baby?

I want my baby.

Darren was supportive of her other plans and goals, and she'd even told him about her plans for her own magazine and how she wanted to eventually take on a leadership role at Taylor Publishing. He would more than likely support her in this.

Even though he really wanted to spend time with her during the weeks leading up to her graduation, he respected her need to focus and study, and he settled, instead, for their nightly phone calls.

He was coming to her graduation, and Alicia couldn't wait to see him. It would give them a chance to tell her parents about their involvement.

Even though Alicia was sure that Darren was just the kind of man her father would approve of and handpick for her if he could, she didn't mind. Whoever said that you couldn't help whom you fell in love with sure knew what they were talking about. Even with all of that, she wasn't sure she was ready to tell him that she was pregnant. She didn't know if she could handle it if he didn't want the baby as much as she did.

"I probably won't tell him yet." She forced a light-hearted tone. "I want to wait. I need to process this and think about how it'll change my life, you know?"

"Well, it would change his life, too. If you decided to have it, he'd be a dad. If you decided to abort, he would miss a chance to be a dad."

I would never abort my baby. Alicia forced the snarl from her face. "In theory I get that, but right now, I need to deal with this in my own way."

"Okay, just know I'm here for you. Whatever you need, if I can do it, it's yours." Jazz squeezed her shoulder.

"Thanks, Jazz. Right now, I have a million and one things to do while I'm not feeling sick to my stomach. I guess I need to take full advantage of every minute that I'm not throwing up or dead-on-my-feet tired." Walking over to her computer, she began to finish the revisions on her thesis.

CHAPTER 18

Darren was on the way to the elevator, ready to meet Troy and Kendrick for a couple of drinks and a game of pool, when his father stopped him.

"Son, glad I caught you. I was on my way to your office." Jonathan Whitman barreled down the hall toward Darren.

Sighing, Darren let the elevator close. There was no use telling his father that he was on his way to meet his friends so that he could unwind after a long and stressful day. Jonathan would not understand nor would he care. "My office or yours?"

"We can talk in my office. I see you're heading out early today." The slightly disapproving expression on Jonathan's face spoke volumes.

Though well after seven in the evening, Darren gathered that given the late hours they had spent during the past week carrying out a hostile takeover of an urban clothing company, seven was early. Therefore, he decided to let Jonathan's comment pass.

Once they were in Jonathan's office, Darren took off his overcoat and sat down. His father sat behind his desk and pulled out his box of Cubans. Darren detested the habit, so instead of offering him one, he simply lit up.

Loosening his tie, Darren settled in for the long haul. If Jonathan was taking the time to enjoy a cigar, he more than likely was going to take a while.

"So what's up, Dad?" Darren leaned forward for the eye-to-eye advantage.

"How is your little plan going with Alicia?" Jonathan chuckled. "Is she in love with you yet? Is she ready to become your wife?"

"You know, I really don't feel comfortable talking with you about my relationship like this. What goes on between Alicia and me is between us. I would like you to respect that." Unflinching, Darren sat up straight in his chair.

Jonathan took a pull from the cigar and studied it briefly before exhaling. "You don't have much time. If you're not making progress, we need to move on to another method."

"If it doesn't work my way, it won't work. If she doesn't want to be with me on her own accord, I won't be with her at all."

"Then you will no longer be the heir to Whitman Enterprises." Jonathan stared Darren in the eyes.

His heart skipped, and he paused before responding. "So be it. I'm standing my ground on this."

"You would give it all up for what? *Love*?" Saying the word love like it was a dirty word, Jonathan pursed his lips into a bitter frown.

Would I give it all up for love? Darren wasn't totally sure, but he knew that he loved Alicia, and he wanted his relationship with her to be based on that. "Yes."

Jonathan laughed. "I know I did not raise a fool. You will come around. I know that you think love is important, but trust me, you can live without it."

"Like you did?" Holding Jonathan's stare, Darren searched for some sign of regret or even caring from the man.

"What? What…what do you mean?" The great Jonathan Whitman stumbled over his words. "I love your mother in my own way. And I think she loves me in hers. We both love you. It works for us."

"Yeah well, I still won't discuss Alicia with you." Darren moved to leave.

"Then I will just have to take that to mean that you haven't made any significant progress, and we will need to move to another method." Calling Darren's bluff, Jonathan placed the cigar on the gold ashtray that sat on his marble desk. "Perhaps it's time for Kyle to have a talk with his daughter."

"No, it's not! I am handling this, Dad. Alicia and I are very close. We are in a relationship." The last thing he wanted was for Alicia to feel that she had to be with him out of some obligation to her family's business.

While he knew she loved him and he loved her, and he was sure he had found the woman he one day wanted to marry, he didn't want her to feel like she had to marry him for any other reason than she loved him. Call it ego. Call it pride. Whatever. Anything less was unacceptable.

"Okay. When are you planning to ask her to marry you?"

"Huh?" he sputtered.

"I'm assuming that you'll want to spend this year engaged and plan a wedding for next spring."

"Huh?" Darren struggled to find words to combat Jonathan's bulldozer approach to his love life.

"What do you mean *huh*? You did realize that the wedding would have to take place eventually?" Jonathan's stern voice was a mixture between annoyed and mildly amused.

"Well, I was thinking that as long as we were involved I could ask her when the time was right, and we would get married when *we decided* to do so." He emphasized his words even as he realized it didn't make a bit of difference. "I thought that as long as I was making progress, you guys would lay off and let Alicia and me naturally go where we needed to go."

"Well, that won't work, Son."

"Why not?" Darren gritted his teeth and clutched the leather armrest until his knuckles ached.

"Because deals have been made, and it is time for them to come to fruition." Picking up his cigar, Jonathan spoke in a matter-of-fact tone before taking a pull from his cigar, savoring it and exhaling.

"Besides, if we gave you guys the option of a prolonged courtship and engagement, Alicia would probably go off to get her Ph.D. or decide she doesn't want to be married at all."

"Oh come on," Darren snapped. *What is wrong with Alicia having her own mind and doing what she wants to do?*

He didn't mind that about her. In fact, that's what made her love all the more sweet. She made up her own willful, stubborn mind—with a little help from him—to give into her feelings.

"No, Son, I suggest you float the idea past Alicia. You never know, if she's as serious about you as you are leading me to believe, she might just jump at the chance to be Mrs. Darren Whitman."

Darren laughed at the prospect of Alicia jumping at the chance to be his wife. "Dad, I have to take things slowly with her. I just got her to agree to call what we have a relationship. I don't think she will jump at the chance to be married to anyone, even me."

"Nonsense. Ask her. If she is not willing, work your magic and make her willing." Jonathan stood, and Darren took that as the signal that he was being dismissed.

CHAPTER 19

Darren showed up in South Hadley two days before Alicia's graduation, carrying an engagement ring and his hopes that what he felt for Alicia and what she felt for him were strong enough to stop her from bolting for the door the moment he proposed.

He'd talked to her enough to realize she probably didn't envision marriage or any of its trappings as a part of her short-term future. *When would she find the time between running her own magazine and taking over Taylor Publishing?*

She also didn't want to fall in love, and now that she was, he hoped it would be enough for her to see that accepting him wouldn't mean losing her dreams.

As he hiked up the three flights of stairs to her attic apartment and knocked on the door, he hoped someone was home since he didn't let her know that he was coming early. The past two weeks without seeing her were hell and made him realize even more how much he wanted and needed to have her in his life. So, he'd made an appointment with the jeweler, and he was going to propose.

Even though he told himself that his father's not-so-subtle threat had nothing to do with his decision—that he was going to ask her eventually anyway—in the back of his mind, he wondered if that was truly the case.

While his father had certainly forced his hand, Darren was proposing because he loved Alicia. All he wanted was for her to marry him because she loved him—not because she felt obligated to save Taylor Publishing.

He was about to knock on the door again when Alicia answered it. She appeared surprised to see him, not pleasantly surprised, just genuinely shocked.

"Darren, what are you doing here?" She rubbed the sleep out of her eyes and leaned against the door. Wearing a pair of sweats and a long T-shirt, she looked like she was just waking up, and it was well after one in the afternoon.

"I thought I'd come a little early to celebrate with you alone before all your folks get here." He stepped into the apartment and gave Alicia a hug. She felt so soft; he barely wanted to let go.

"So did you have a late night? Did I wake you?" Reluctantly, he let go of her softness.

"No. I was just napping and lost track of time. It's been a hectic couple of weeks. I guess it all just came down on me at once." Alicia wrapped her arms around herself and started walking toward her bedroom.

"Yeah, I remember those days." He followed her back into her bedroom where they took a seat on the comfy sleigh bed.

"So, what kind of celebration did you have in mind?" Toying with the hole in the knee of her sweatpants and making it bigger than it already was, she barely spared him a glance as she spoke. The sweatpants seemed as if they'd seen better days.

Darren placed his hand over hers and brought his mouth down to hers. His tongue had a mind of its own as it roamed over the crevices in her mouth. She opened to his kiss and leaned into him. His hand moved from her knee and started to trail up her T-shirt. *No bra*, he thought and silently thanked God as he gently squeezed her breast.

Alicia winced and went stiff in his arms.

"What's wrong?"

"Nothing, I'm just a little sore." Sliding away from him on the bed, she pulled her knees to her chest and stretched out the already misshapen T-shirt to cover her knees.

Repeating the question because his gut told him she was not being forthright, he asked, "What's wrong?"

"Can't you just take my word that it is nothing?" Alicia pulled the T-shirt even further over her knees.

There was no way that shirt would ever regain its shape.

Okay, let's try another approach. "Let me tell you about the evening I have planned for you. First, we're going to take a nice, relaxing limo ride to Boston. Then, we're going to have a nice, romantic candlelight dinner."

Edging closer to her on the bed, he brought his voice down to a seductive whisper. "Then we're going to spend the night in the Westin at Copley and reminisce on old memories while making some new ones."

"Oh really." Alicia stretched out her legs, and the T-shirt surprisingly bounced into shape somewhat.

"Yes, really. So how soon can you pack an overnight bag and be ready to go?" Stopping just shy of the middle of her thigh, he ran his hand across her legs.

"Wow, Darren, this all sounds lovely, and I wish I could go, but I can't." Alicia started to fiddle with the hole in the knee of her sweatpants again.

"Why not? You've finished your exams. You've handed in your Honors Thesis. What's stopping you?" He studied her face carefully for some sign of what was going on with her.

"I just can't. I made plans to rest so that I'm relaxed for graduation and dealing with family." Alicia concentrated on the hole and wouldn't look up.

"It's one night, Licia. I promise I'll let you get some rest." Edging closer, he gave her his most wholesome smile.

Tentative, Alicia glanced up and smiled as she stifled a soft yawn. "Do we have to go to Boston? Can't we just stay here? I'm just not up for that long car ride."

"Fine, whatever you want." Things were not going as he'd planned. The more he thought of it, he wouldn't expect anything less from Alicia. If she made this easy for him, he would suspect that the body snatchers had invaded her. *On to plan B.*

"I'm sorry, Darren, I can tell you put a lot of thought into the celebration. I'm really glad you came down early. We could hang out here, maybe order in, I don't know." She started fussing with that darn hole in her sweatpants again.

Realizing that it really was fine as long as he was with her, he placed his hand over hers. "That's fine. I'll make some calls and some arrangements for our romantic celebratory evening."

He flashed a smile. "Will Jazz be joining us this evening?"

Alicia tilted her head and grinned. "No, she went home after her last final exam, and she's making a special trip back on graduation day. We have the place to ourselves."

Feigning disappointment, he slapped his palm on his leg in mock dismay. "Oh, and I was so looking forward to chatting with her again."

Alicia twisted her lips in a sardonic manner and shook her head. "Liar. Go make the arrangements while I shower and freshen up."

Darren watched as Alicia walked out of the bedroom. Even in those raggedy sweats and T-shirt, she still looked good. He blinked to break his daze and picked up his cell phone in order to have the perfect evening brought to them.

Alicia closed the door to the bathroom. *What in the world is Darren doing here early?*

She'd planned to use the few days reprieve she had from Jazz and school to figure out how she would go to school and take care of her baby. Granted, she spent most of that time in bed.

Just about ready to start making some plans, she even considered calling Darren and telling him. She turned on the shower, pulled off her clothing, and stepped in. When the time was right, she would tell Darren about the pregnancy. Until then, she would just go with the flow and hope that she didn't have another attack of nausea.

As she rubbed the soaped sponge over her achy, tender breasts, she hoped to God that Darren didn't have an urge to touch them or squeeze them before she was ready to tell him. They were so sensitive these days that she was sure they would hurt if he so much as blew on them.

Once she was done in the shower, she walked back into the bedroom wrapped in a bath sheet. Darren had taken off his red tie and his gray pin-stripped suit jacket, which were now lying across the chair in front of her desk. He was lounging on her bed in his gray silk shirt and pin-stripped slacks. The top three buttons of his shirt were loose, and he was talking on the cell phone, ordering flowers.

When he glanced up at her and smiled, she almost melted. That smile had done something to her heart when she was fourteen, and the feelings sparked back, then never really went anywhere. She had fallen in love with him the very first time he smiled at her.

Once finished with his call, he walked over to her, removed her towel and pulled her to him.

She sucked in her breath as her tender breasts crushed against his hard chest. Still damp from the shower, her wetness went right through his silk shirt.

"Darren, I'm still wet. Let me dry off at least."

"You're not nearly as wet as you're going to be."

A shiver ran down her back, and she felt herself clinch and release in anticipation as Darren picked her up and placed her on the bed. *He is certainly telling the*

truth, she thought as she felt herself getting wetter by
the second.

Darren ordered in Italian and filled the room with
roses and candlelight. After spending the better part
of the afternoon and the evening in bed, it was time
to get to the real reason he was there early—to ask the
woman he loved to become his wife.

If she would only say yes, she could have as long
an engagement as she wanted. He would fight his
father on that. She could finish graduate school and
do whatever else she felt she needed to do. If his father
didn't agree to whatever kind of engagement Alicia
wanted, he would have to figure out a way to make
him understand. All he wanted was for her to agree
that at some point she would be his wife.

The ring would be a symbol, a token of how much
she meant to him and how committed he was to
her—to them.

Surely, she should be able to see the logic in that.

He watched her fiddle with her chicken marsala,
barely touching it. Also, she didn't drink any of her
wine.

"Well, I know you're not officially legal, but surely
you can have a sip of wine to celebrate your graduation and your future graduate studies," he joked as he

took a sip of wine. "And you haven't touched your food."

"Yes, I have. I'm full, that's all." Alicia touched her stomach as if touching it would prove her point.

"Well, I don't know whether to be insulted or not. If you're not famished and starving after this afternoon, I obviously haven't done my job." He wanted to keep the evening lighthearted. So if she didn't want to eat, he wouldn't make a big deal out of it. It wasn't extremely noticeable, but it did seem as if she'd lost a few pounds.

Alicia smirked. "Oh, you've done your job just fine. In fact, if you come near me again tonight, I might have to run for help. Now I know what it feels like to be worn out. Thank you very much."

"Well, I try to provide the very best."

"That you do."

It was as good a time as any to go for it and take the leap. "So, Licia, can you see this going on in your future?"

"See what? Being worn out by your sexual appetite and made love to until I could barely stand, or even finish my dinner?" she teased.

Smiling wickedly at the thought, Darren continued, "That and other things. I think we're good together, and I would like us to take this to the next level."

"What level would that be, Darren? We're already in a relationship. That's been a bit of a whirlwind process, don't you think?" Alicia eyed him in consideration. "I mean we only just met up again in February. Here it is May, and we're in a committed relationship. What other level could we possibly take it to?"

He walked over, knelt in front of Alicia, reached in his pocket, and pulled out the ring.

"Licia, I'm in love with you, and I would like for you to be my wife. We can have as long or as short of an engagement as you want." He paused and watched her face. The expression on her face could only be described as deep and utter shock.

"I know that you have plans, and you want to complete your graduate studies. I fully support that. I just want to make it known in the best and most basic way I know that I love you, and I envision spending the rest of my life with you."

Alicia simply stared at him with her mouth hanging open. Her gaze went from him to the jewelry box in his hand. Peering at the ring, her mouth fell open even wider.

Returning her gaze to his face, she glanced back at the ring, and her eyes narrowed ever so slightly. "Five carets, emerald cut, flawless. Oh. My. God." She closed her mouth and turned away.

"Darren, this is just way too soon. We barely know each other really. I mean, I love you too, but this is way too soon. We're going too fast."

"Alicia, I have known you for most of your life. And if I'm really honest with myself, I've loved you for most of that time." He ran his hand across his jaw, remembering just how long he'd known her.

"Even when we kids and I used to tease you and pull your hair, I think I was acting out because I liked you so much and I couldn't stand it. Honey, I love you. All I need you to do is believe in our love enough to take the leap and become engaged."

"Darren, I…I don't know what to say." Alicia pushed her chair away from the table and ran into the bedroom.

The proposal didn't go nearly as smoothly as he had planned. He expected some hesitation, but not a fifty-yard dash. Flustered, he followed her into her bedroom.

"You are hell on a guy's ego, Licia," he offered wryly.

"I'm sorry. I don't mean to be. Just when I think I have a handle on things, you throw me a curve. I just wasn't expecting this." Sheepish, Alicia spared him a glance and chewing on her bottom lip.

Since she didn't seem dead-set against marriage, just a little nervous, Darren thought there might still be room for persuasion.

"Do you love me?"

"You know I do. That's not the point. I just don't think I'm ready to be anyone's wife." Her voice was hesitant at first, but picked up a decided firmness.

"I know I'm not ready to be Mrs. Darren Whitman. I don't think I want to be Mrs. Anybody. I always envisioned keeping my name and just remaining *Ms.* Alicia Taylor—if and when I ever decided to get married."

"That's fine with me. You can certainly keep your name. I want you. I really don't care what you call yourself. I mean, sure I would probably prefer it if you hyphenated, but it's not that big of a deal."

"Yeah, right! I can see your father now. *What do you mean she's not taking your name?*" Alicia did a damn good impersonation of Jonathan Whitman, and he had to laugh.

"Our marriage wouldn't be about my father or your father for that matter. It would be about us. You and me and our love for one another." Reaching for her left hand, he pulled the ring from the box and slipped it on her ring finger. "Look at that, Licia. It's a perfect fit. We are meant to be together. I know it. Just say yes."

Alicia stared down at the ring. It was beautiful. It fit perfectly, and strangely, she couldn't think of anything she would rather do at that moment than become engaged to Darren. Chewing on her lower lip, she contemplated what being engaged to Darren would mean, especially given the recent events. While she would have been against him marrying her because she was pregnant, he was asking her before he knew. *So, that must mean he loves me and really wants to marry me. Right?* While she knew without a doubt that she loved him, he didn't know about the baby yet. Glancing at him, she bit her lip again. *What about my goals?* Would he change his mind about her going to school once he found out she was pregnant? Could she really trust him? Trust their love? She was ready to say yes when her face went hot and the little dinner she managed to get down decided to come back up.

She leaped from the bed and ran to the bathroom. She knelt in time to give the little bit of chicken marsala she managed to eat to the toilet. Darren stood in the doorway, watching her and frowning.

"Does the thought of becoming my wife make you physically ill?" Darren spoke in a strained voice. "I don't know how much more my ego can take. First you bolt when I propose, now you puke when I put the ring on."

Alicia slowly rose from her knees, flushed the toilet, rinsed her mouth, and splashed water on her face. Not able to face Darren yet, she put down the toilet seat cover and sat.

For some reason the phrase "shit or get off the pot" came to her mind, and she decided to come clean with Darren about her pregnancy. Glancing up at him she said, "I'm pregnant."

"You're pregnant?"

"Yes. I'm pregnant."

"When did you find out?"

"A little over a week ago."

"You've known for a little over a week?"

"Are you going to echo all of my statements with a question?" Shaking her head, she turned away.

Darren pulled her up from the toilet and turned her to face him. "Well, pardon me, Alicia. I'm having a hard time comprehending why, if you knew you were pregnant with my child, you didn't call me and apprise me of it immediately. When the hell were you going to tell me?"

Diverting her gaze downward, she sighed. She didn't need him making her feel any guiltier than she already felt.

He placed his hand under her chin and lifted her face. "You were going to tell me weren't you, Alicia?"

Her shoulder sagged just a little.

"You weren't going to go and have an abortion or something without telling me were you?"

"No. I'm not having an abortion." She tilted her head defiantly. "But if I were, it would be my choice. My body, my choice."

"Oh don't start that women's lib bullshit with me, Licia." Darren ran his hand across his head in frustration. "I believe that you have the right to do just about anything your heart desires. But that is my child, and I'll be damned if I won't have a say in this."

Wishing that she could crawl in her bed and hide, she responded, "You can have a say. I planned on telling you eventually. I just needed to figure out what I wanted to do, how I can juggle motherhood and going to school. I've decided to keep it and raise it myself as a single mom."

Saying it aloud didn't sound scary at all.

"You are truly nuts, aren't you?" Darren shook his head in amazement. "Listen to me and listen well, Licia, because I'm only going to say this once. You will not be raising my child as a single mother. I won't allow it. You have my ring on your finger, and although you haven't said yes, that hardly matters now." Stopping, he stared at her as if to check that she was getting every word.

"You are going to marry me, and we are going to raise our child together. If you don't agree with those plans, the only single parent will be me, because I fully intend to be a full-time parent in my child's life."

Her eyes narrowed to a menacing squint. "Are you threatening me?"

"I don't make threats, Alicia. I don't have to."

"You can't make me marry you."

"No, I can't. You have a choice. You can either marry the man you love and are about to have a child with. Or—"

"Or what, Darren? Let you sue me for custody? Let you take my child?" Two seconds away from kicking him out of her apartment, she crossed her arms and tapped her foot on the linoleum floor as she waited for his response.

"Our child, Alicia." Darren ran his hand across his head again. "I'm sure we can work something amicable out."

She tried to brush past him. The bathroom walls were closing in. Air, that's what she needed. Her whole world was changing so fast, and she couldn't get a grip.

Darren would not let her pass, and he blocked her exit from the door. Pulling her into an embrace, he ran his fingers through her hair.

"Why are you making this harder than it needs to be?" He lifted her chin and gazed deeply into her eyes.

"Licia, I love you, and I want to marry you. The fact that our child is growing inside of you right now has nothing to do with the way I feel. It does make me want to speed things up a bit. I was willing to have as long an engagement as you needed. Now I think that we should get married as soon as possible."

Darren pulled her close and whispered in her ear. "Don't worry about graduate school or your plans. I'll be there for you. I'll commute from Ann Arbor, and we can hire help once the baby comes. Things will work out. Trust me. I love you."

The sincerity and love in Darren's eyes over-whelmed her. She wanted to believe him, to trust him, to trust them. It wasn't too good to be true; it was just right, perfect, the way it should be. She exhaled, snuggled in the warm security of his embrace, and believed that everything would work out just like he said it would.

"Okay, Darren. Yes, I'll marry you."

Darren let out a sigh of relief and covered her mouth with his.

CHAPTER 20

Graduation went by in a blur. Caught up in the celebratory wave of family and friends and the knowledge of her impending marriage to Darren, she felt like someone had taken her nicely planned life and substituted it for a life that felt right but still made her a little nervous and uneasy.

If only her mother would go with the flow and not question her seemingly quick decision to get married. From the time she and Darren broke the news to her parents, Karen wanted to know why she decided to get engaged and why she wanted to plan a wedding so soon after graduation. Kyle, on the other hand, appeared surprisingly calm about it and even tried to halt Karen's non-stop questions. Determined to get to the bottom of it, Karen Taylor refused to be sidetracked and hammered away.

Karen started up again at the small lunch between the four of them before they headed back to Detroit.

"I just think it's rather sudden. I mean, the two of you just started officially dating, and it seems rather foolish to rush into marriage." Karen's eyes narrowed in, first on Alicia and then Darren.

"Karen, leave them be. They are grown-ups; they can make up their own minds. They're in love. They want to be together. We should support that. At least they're not talking about shacking up." Grinning, Kyle took a sip of his water.

Alicia watched as Karen gave Kyle a glare that could have melted the ice in his glass.

"We got engaged right after college. I don't see what the big deal is," Kyle mumbled before turning his attention to his club sandwich.

"The big deal is that Alicia has plans. I would hate to see her put them aside because she feels like she has to get married now. Why can't you two just start with a commitment ring of some sort and then move to a proper, *long* engagement in a year or so. Perhaps once Alicia has finished graduate school?" Karen's voice picked up a pleading tone toward the end.

"Mrs. Taylor, Alicia is still going to go to graduate school. I plan to commute from Ann Arbor. I won't stand in the way of her plans. I just want to help her."

Alicia knew that line was not going to fly with Karen Taylor.

Karen shot Darren a pointed stare before speaking through somewhat clenched teeth. "Well, she has miraculously made it this far without your help, Darren. So I imagine she will be able to make it a little further."

"Mother!" She knew that Karen wasn't going to be nice, but that was harsh.

"What? Alicia, I really don't understand this, and I am *trying*. You need to make this plain for me. Because I am not buying all this bull about how much you love each other and want to be together. You're only twenty, and this is your first serious boyfriend. So forgive me if I have some doubts." Karen folded her arms across her chest and stared pointedly at them both again.

"Karen," Kyle said quietly.

There was only one way to put an end to the conversation. "Fine. Mom, I'm pregnant. We're rushing the wedding because I got knocked up. Is that what you want to hear?"

Darren's jaw went slack, and his eyes widened, but he recovered quickly. "That's not totally true. I asked you to marry me before you told me that you were pregnant. Mr. and Mrs. Taylor, I love your daughter, and I want to spend the rest of my life with her. I came here ready to make that commitment, and the fact that she is having my child only makes me more determined to make her my wife."

"Well, now we're getting at the truth." Uncrossing her arms, Karen almost appeared pleased. "Alicia, you don't have to get married because you are pregnant. You have choices." Karen shrugged. "You can still have your dreams. Your father and I will help. We'll take care of the child while you finish school. So, you don't have to feel pressured into marriage."

"Mom, I know that you and daddy would help me. But I've made my choice. I want to marry Darren. I love him. I would want to marry him even if I wasn't pregnant. I've wanted to marry him ever since I was fourteen. The pregnancy just has us moving a little quicker. That's all." She stared at Karen intently so that she could see that this was indeed her choice.

Kyle frowned. "Well, I have to say that I'm a bit disappointed in the two of you. In this day and age, you should have taken precautions." Shaking his head, he suddenly brightened. "I'm still behind you in whatever you decide, Princess. Of course, we'll pay for the wedding. We'll have to get on the ball. Honey, do you think we can make the necessary arrangements on this short notice? Get all the proper invitations out and get the venues booked?"

"I don't want a big wedding, Daddy. I only want family and my close friends. I don't want a big society wedding."

"Well, Alicia, that's not the way these kinds of things are done." Kyle turned to Darren for backup. "Darren, surely you realize that with a wedding such as this, there are expectations?"

Unwilling to be dismissed when it came to her own wedding, Alicia's voice raised just a notch, and she made sure to enunciate her words clearly so that there would be no mistake. "I *don't* want a big wedding. If this is going to be a problem, we will go to Vegas and let Elvis perform the ceremony."

"Darren, surely you understand..." Kyle had an air of urgency in his voice.

Darren shook his head before Kyle could even finish. "Alicia can have whatever kind of wedding she wants. This is not going to be a matter of stress and aggravation for her."

Karen smiled at Darren, and Alicia breathed a sigh of relief. *Two down, two to go*, she thought.

Darren eyed his parents wearily. Kyle and Karen Taylor were a piece of cake compared to his parents.

They were at the Whitman mansion waiting for Alicia to join them for lunch. He and Alicia would announce their engagement and the fact that it was going to be a very short one.

He expected all the same arguments that the Taylors had put forth in addition to others. Jonathan Whitman would not buckle as easily as Mr. Taylor did when it came to not having a big society wedding. Darren figured he could keep everyone at bay long enough to make the announcement and get the hell out of there.

Jonathan wasn't used to not getting his way. Knowing this, Darren was sure he would try and bully them to wait and have a proper wedding. Darren prayed Alicia didn't get as frustrated as she did with him and her own parents and blurt out that she was pregnant. *I should have prepped her. But knowing Alicia, she would do and say what she felt like regardless.* If his parents knew that she was pregnant, it would make his parents see the need for a speedy wedding, but he was sure it wouldn't be a pretty conversation.

Jonathan eyed his watch. "Looks like Alicia is running a bit late."

"She'll be here."

"Well, I should hope so. I don't like to be kept waiting. I am a busy man. What was so important that you called this lunch anyway?"

"I'll wait for Alicia to get here to tell you the news." Darren glanced at his own watch and hoped that would be soon.

No sooner than he said the words, the family butler, Harold, led Alicia to the formal dining room where they were all waiting for her.

"Sorry, I'm late." Alicia sat down in the chair next to Darren's without making any other excuse for her tardiness.

Jonathan frowned and nodded. Patricia simply sighed and signaled for Harold to begin bringing in the first course of the lunch.

"So, Alicia, I hear congratulations are in order. You must be delighted to be done with school." Trying to lighten the air, Patricia spoke in her usual polite manner.

"Well, yes, until the fall when I start graduate school." Alicia smiled graciously. "I'm glad to have the undergraduate degree under my belt."

"Right, so lovely." Patricia smiled and took a sip of water.

"In any case, shall we hear this news you want to share with us?" Jonathan's voice reeked of impatience.

"Well, Mom, Dad, I've asked Alicia to marry me, and she's said yes. We plan to get married in two weeks."

"Two weeks!" Frantic was the word that best described Patricia's demeanor at that moment. Her eyes popped open, and she was literally bouncing in her chair. "Well, there's no time to plan a proper wedding in two weeks. How can I possibly plan a proper wedding in two weeks?

"Oh, you don't have to, Mrs. Whitman. I have it all planned. My mom and friends are going to help me." Alicia tried to calm his mother, quickly adding, "You're welcomed to help us as well. I've already picked out the chapel, Stony Chapel in Hickory Grove. And Reverend Richardson has agreed to perform the ceremony. We plan to have a small number of guests, very intimate, only close family and friends."

"Well, what about all of our other friends and business relationships? The members of the Links and your father's country club? My sorority sisters? Oh my, there are so many people that *really* do need to be invited." Patricia's eyes went wider, and she took deep breaths between words.

"This simply will not do at all. I will not accept it. There will be a proper wedding. Anything less is unacceptable." Jonathan waved his hand in dismissal, as if with one stroke of his hand he could banish all talk of small intimate weddings in chapels.

"This is the kind of wedding that Alicia wants, Dad. Since we all know that the wedding day is about the bride, it's best that she gets the kind of wedding she wants." He tried to reason with his dad, even though he knew no amount of talking would help Jonathan Whitman see their line of reasoning.

"I don't care what she wants. There are appearances to keep in mind, Darren. We are a very important family as are the Taylors. Alicia *should* know better." Jonathan cut Alicia a piercing stare.

Alicia leaned forward in her seat and pursed her lips.

"Dad, it's our wedding, and we'll have the kind of wedding we want. We hope that you and Mom will join us on our special day, but we'll be getting married in a couple of weeks at Stony Chapel." He knew Jonathan would be unreasonable, but he didn't expect him to be so hostile toward Alicia. In Darren's opinion, Jonathan needed to calm down, and quick.

"Why two weeks? What will people think with the two of you rushing off and marrying so quickly?" Voice strained to a stilted whisper, Patricia's eyes pleaded with him.

"Well, if they think that I'm pregnant, they'll be right." Alicia leaned back in her chair and folded her arms across her chest.

"Oh my God!" Patricia gave the startled outburst, reached for her handkerchief and fanned her face.

"Alicia, you have got to get better with dropping that information on people," Darren said wryly.

"Sorry, but they left me no choice." Alicia's voice hinted that she was anything but sorry.

"Well, this is interesting news to say the least. Tell me, Son, are you sure the baby is yours?" Dropping the accusatory words as nonchalantly as if he had just said "Pass the salt," Jonathan raised his eyebrow ever so slightly.

"Dad!" He couldn't believe it. That was over the top, even for Jonathan. Darren had to hold himself in his seat and take deep breaths.

"Well, she was seen around quite a bit with that hip-hopper. People will speculate. I am only voicing what others will no doubt wonder once the two of you marry after such a brief courtship and a practically nonexistent engagement." He crossed his arms and turned his gaze from Darren to Alicia.

"Oh my," Patricia worked her handkerchief even more vigorously.

Fuming, Darren threw his napkin on the table. He couldn't believe Jonathan could be so rude and tactless. He was about to tell his father what he thought of him when Alicia defended herself.

"You know what, Mr. Whitman? Not that it's any of your business, but who I'm pregnant by hardly seems to be the point." Alicia's eyes blazed with defiance. "What is the point is that Darren and I are getting married in two weeks. We are going to have the kind of wedding we want to have, and you can either come or not." She paused for effect. "Frankly, I don't care. But I think your son would like you to be there. So I'm here putting up with your insufferable rudeness because I love him."

"You should watch your tone, young lady. I know that your father did not raise you to behave so badly with your elders and as a guest in their home, no less," Jonathan chastised.

Hardly rebuked, she calmed herself with some effort before responding. "No, he didn't. He also did not raise me to sit idly while someone insults my character.

"For the record, I did not want to get married, but Darren has made me see that raising our child without both of its parents would be unfair, especially when we love each other and can be happy together. So I am going to do this with him and not by myself like I planned. But I will continue to make my own choices, and that begins with the kind of wedding we'll have. If you want the whole world to be privy to it, take pictures and send them to *Jet*, because we are having a small wedding!"

"Well, Alicia surely you can see that there are proper ways to go about having an event such as this?" Patricia pointed out.

"Well, Alicia," Jonathan Whitman gave her a pointed stare before continuing. "Since you are deter- mined to have the wedding in a *little chapel* with only friends and family—and, given your condition, stalling the wedding is not an option—I have to insist that we have a formal reception with the proper guest list. The reception will take place the day after your *little chapel* wedding, and I will get my people working on it. We will have it at the country club, of course."

"Well, of course. Will we be able to get the club in such short notice?" Practically glowing, Patricia stopped fanning.

"I'm Jonathan Whitman. We will get the club." Jonathan dashed his hand through the air, and his voice was a mixture of firm and nonchalant.

"I don't want a big formal wedding reception. Haven't you heard a word I've said?" Alicia leaned forward in her seat and glared.

"I heard you. You can have your wedding exactly as you choose. And, you full well will get married as soon as you possibly can. I am in full agreement with that. An illegitimate Whitman would not do at all." Something that passed for a smile crossed Jonathan's lips. "But we will have a proper wedding reception at the club."

"That would be Taylor-Whitman." Alicia squinted her eyes and crossed her arms.

"What?" Jonathan turned slightly.

"Since I'm keeping my last name, the children will have their last name hyphenated, Taylor-Whitman," Alicia said smugly.

"Oh my Lord." Fanning herself again, Patricia's eyes rolled toward the ceiling.

"Well, why don't we wait for the child to be born before we start haggling about names?" Darren was putting an end to the fireworks before they did irreparable damage—before he said something to his parents he could never take back. "Right now we need to just agree that Alicia and I will have our wedding at the chapel and a reception with a modest number of guests—nothing outrageous Dad—at the club."

"I don't want a reception." Alicia almost pouted.

"Baby, I know that, but can we make a small compromise on this so that we can go about planning our wedding and starting our lives?" Each person had to give a little, or they would never come to an agreement.

Alicia's eyes darted toward Jonathan before she turned her gaze to Darren. She must have seen and felt how strained Darren was, because she softened a little.

He took a deep breath. "Alicia, you will still get the wedding of your dreams. I promise you that, okay?"

Alicia spared Jonathan an evil glance; Jonathan, in turn, raised his glass to her.

"Fine, we'll have the reception," Alicia huffed.

"Now that that is settled…" Barging ahead, Jonathan set down his glass. "Just what are you planning to do about this graduate school foolishness? Surely you don't still intend to go? You will need to focus your attentions on my grandchild."

"Dad, *do not* start. Alicia is still going to graduate school. We will live in Ann Arbor, and I'll commute from there to Detroit for work. It will work out fine. The graduate program is only two years."

"The first years of a child's life are very important. Darren, surely I don't have to tell you that. Alicia, have you thought seriously about how hard it will be to be a mother, wife, and a student? Something will no doubt suffer." Jonathan actually wagged his finger at Alicia.

"Jonathan, this hardly seems our place." Always the etiquette queen, Patricia tried to intervene.

"Patricia, do not tell me my place in my own home." Jonathan's eyes narrowed in on Patricia, and his lips formed a sneer as she bristled.

Darren had had more than enough. "This lunch is over; come on, Alicia. Let's go."

"Darren, do not leave here. We need to talk about this. How can you expect to do all you need to do for Whitman Enterprise spending so much time on the road traveling from Ann Arbor?"

Jonathan did not know when to stop. That might work in the business world, but it made interpersonal relationships next to impossible. Darren had no more patience for the man. The way his father behaved toward Alicia was deplorable in Darren's mind.

Darren inhaled and exhaled sharply. "It's only for two years, and frankly, Dad, the other option is not an option."

"What do you mean?"

"He means that I will not get married if it means I have to put all my plans and goals on hold. Your grandchild would be born illegitimate. I will raise it alone as a graduate student in Ann Arbor." Alicia arched her left eye, twisted her lips, and crossed her arms in battle pose.

"Oh my God!" Patricia renewed her vigorous fanning.

Alicia eyed them all wearily. "God, maybe this was a bad idea." She got up from the table.

"Alicia, don't go." Darren reached for her arm.

She snatched it away. "I have to get out of here."

Darren gave Jonathan a disgusted glare and bolted after Alicia. He caught her in the huge foyer entrance and grabbed her before she could make her way to the door. She turned around and started to take off her engagement ring.

"What are you doing?" Darren grabbed her hands and stopped her. "Don't do that."

"I'm leaving. This won't work. I'm sure we can work out a visitation arrangement. I'm perfectly willing to have some sort of shared parenting. But I *will not* sacrifice myself to fit your father's ideas of a proper wife." Alicia's voice was shaky but firm.

"Did I ask you to do that?" He pulled her close.

"No, you didn't. But I can tell that your father and I will never see eye-to-eye." Alicia almost hissed that last sentence.

"You don't have to see eye-to-eye with him."

"I barely see eye-to-eye with you," Alicia noted wryly.

"We see eye-to-eye on the important things. Number one being we love each other, and there is no way I am letting you out of this engagement. And number two, our child is going to have both of us in its life." He lifted her chin.

"This is too hard."

"I never promised you it was going to be easy." He laughed. "After chasing after you the past few months, I know things with us will never be easy. I've come to like that."

"Oh you have, have you?"

"Somewhat."

"Hmm, well if you can deal with me and my difficult self, I guess I can deal with your arrogant, obstinate jerk of a father." She shrugged her shoulders in a haughty gesture.

"Okay. But take it easy, he is my father." Darren was starting to agree with what she was saying, but he was raised to "honor thy father and thy mother."

"Sorry," Alicia said in a way that made it obvious she was anything but.

"It's okay. I understand." He shook his head and wondered what the next two weeks would bring.

CHAPTER 21

Waiting for the rest of the guests to arrive for the rehearsal dinner that Patricia Whitman swore they had to have, Alicia glanced around the dining room of the country club and frowned.

With the addition of the reception and rehearsal dinner, it seemed as if everyone had taken her desire for a small intimate wedding and trashed it.

The only thing she felt sure about was she wanted to marry Darren. By the night of the rehearsal dinner, she just didn't want to have a wedding.

The funny thing was, she didn't regret anything. Feeling more at peace than she had ever felt in her life, she was sure everything was happening the way it was supposed to happen. When she watched Darren, she saw the man she wanted to spend the rest of her life with.

That thought alone would have scared her a few months ago. As she sat waiting for her family and friends to show up for the rehearsal dinner, she was not the least bit afraid.

There early because she wanted to get herself composed for what she was sure would be a night of constant disagreement with Mr. Whitman, she took another calming breath. The man was a throwback from the Ice Age. Controlling and overbearing, he made Kyle Taylor look like a teddy bear.

As if the saying "speak of the devil" were true, Jonathan Whitman burst into the room with Mrs. Whitman trailing behind him. Surveying the room with a glance, his eyes rested on Alicia.

She took a deep breath. *All the breathing in the world won't calm me enough to put up with this man.*

"Well, you're here early for someone who didn't want a rehearsal dinner." Mr. Whitman was his usual charming self.

"Well, since we didn't have a rehearsal, I just thought it was sort of dumb to have a rehearsal dinner," she snapped. Her gaze narrowed slightly. Then she remembered the rehearsal dinner was Mrs. Whitman's idea, and she felt bad.

"Oh, but its tradition, Alicia. It's a time for the families and friends to get together and celebrate the couple and their future." Mrs. Whitman seemed pleasantly oblivious to any possible hint of insult.

"Oh, I thought that was the wedding and the reception." *What is she anyway? A Stepford wife?*

"Well, those too. But, we want to take every opportunity to celebrate you, Darren, and your marriage." Mrs. Whitman was so bubbly and happy it was irritating. Then, she did have a little sassy streak and could cut you in that way only the highly prissy could.

"This is really a happy time. Try to be a little more pleasant this evening, dear. You're about to be a bride!" Mrs. Whitman offered advice in a friendly voice that smacked of condescension.

Alicia fought the urge to roll her eyes because she really didn't think that Mrs. Whitman was *that* bad—at least not compared to Mr. Whitman. Mrs. Whitman seemed genuinely excited about the wedding. Well, once she got over the shock and horror of the pregnancy and the shotgun nature of the whole thing.

When Kyle walked in followed by Karen and Darren, Alicia couldn't help but smile. *My backup is here. Bring it on, Mr. Whitman.*

Karen must have noticed the air of tension in the room. "Baby, come with me to the car. I want to show you something."

Taking a deep breath, Alicia walked out, head held high.

She followed Karen into the parking lot, and Karen put her arm around Alicia.

"Alicia, are you okay?"

"I'm fine, Mom. I just…that man just irritates me to no end. I swear if I didn't love Darren, I wouldn't put up with him."

"Do you love Darren?" Karen watched her carefully.

"Yes, I do. You know, I think I've loved him ever since I was fourteen. Even though I told myself I hated him. I guess I never really got over him."

"So that crush was a little more than a crush? Interesting." Karen ran her fingers through Alicia's hair and rubbed Alicia's arm in gentle, loving strokes.

Surprised by her mother's statement, her eyes widened and her mouth fell open. "So you knew I had a crush on Darren back then?"

"Yes, how could I not know? I caught you gazing at him when you thought no one was looking." Karen laughed at the memory. "And I also caught him watching you when he thought no one was looking. I just kept praying that he wouldn't act on his desires and that you were not brave enough, or should I say hot in the pants enough, to go after yours. Believe me, I said many a prayer."

"So your prayers were the reasons we didn't connect that summer. You gotta give it to prayers and divine intervention." Alicia laughed.

It felt weird laughing about that summer, especially when she spent so much time remembering it as the summer her heart was broken. "I was so ga-ga over him."

"I know. Could you imagine my fear? What with the teenage pregnancy rate so alarmingly high? I just prayed you wouldn't end up another statistic before you got a chance to spread your wings and make something out of your life." Karen's tone sobered considerably.

"I'm still going to do everything I planned, Mom." Alicia promised more to herself than to Karen.

"I know you will, baby. I know you will." The faith and belief that she heard in Karen's voice lifted her confidence and her spirit.

Darren motioned for Jonathan to follow him to the other side of the room, and Jonathan Whitman went grudgingly. It was obvious that he didn't like his son telling him what to do.

"What is it, Son? Can't this wait until after the dinner?"

"Lay off Alicia." Staring Jonathan in the eye, Darren did not flinch.

"What do you mean? I haven't done anything to the girl, not one thing that Kyle shouldn't have done some time ago." Jonathan pointed his finger and scolded. "The girl is out of control. She needs a firmer hand. You heard the way she spoke to me. No respect, that one."

"She's the one you picked for me, and more importantly, she's the one I've picked for myself." Ignoring Jonathan's wagging finger, Darren continued, "So, you will leave her alone so we can get through this wedding and have our child. Everyone will get what they want."

"Yes, I suppose they will." Jonathan stopped wagging and touched his hand to his chin, giving Darren an appreciative once over.

"Brilliant plan, by the way. I admit it was a bit risky. But you carried it off wonderfully. You took bold action. Just the way I taught you in business. You showed us that you could carry off what you promised us in February."

"What are you talking about?" Darren's eyes squinted as he tried to figure Jonathan out.

"I'm talking about the pregnancy, of course. It was a bold move that ended up well." Still nodding with appreciation, Jonathan reached to pat Darren on the back.

Stepping back out of reach, Darren simply stared at Jonathan. "What?"

"Well, she is marrying you. You get the wife who loves you. You get to keep your inheritance." Jonathan's tone was matter-of-fact, and Darren stood dumbstruck for a second. Torn between wanting to punch his own father for the first time in his life and just walking away, he opted for the more respectful route.

Finally, he threw his arms up in disgust and walked away from Jonathan. It was hard to believe that the man was serious. Did he really believe that Darren would deliberately get Alicia pregnant so that she would have to marry him?

What kind of a man does he think I am?

Darren was still brooding when Alicia walked up to him. It amazed him that she managed to put a smile on his face just by walking in the room.

"It's not too late; we could always go to Vegas and have the blue suede shoe wedding special." Alicia's voice was joking, but her expression was serious.

He pulled her into his arms and kissed her. "Don't tempt me. I'm about ready to do just that."

"I know. We just have to get through with this fake rehearsal dinner, our wonderful wedding, our wonderful wedding night, and that god-awful reception the next day. Then we can be done with them in our business, trying to tell us what to do." Eyes wide and full of hope, she made a bright and cheery picture.

So happy and hopeful, he hated to burst her bubble. "Do you really see my folks not having a say in the Christening and what school the baby will go to and—"

"Oh, you are a killjoy! Let me live in denial for a minute." Alicia put her arms around his neck.

"Okay, after the wedding we'll banish our parents from our business." He decided to humor her.

"Yeah," Alicia smiled and snuggled closer.

"If any one of them dares to step over the boundaries we have firmly put in place, then we'll put them in a state of purgatory from which their only hope of escape would be penance and a promise never to forsake our boundaries again." He put an extra bit of bass in his voice.

"Yeah!" Alicia pecked him on the lips.

Savoring the brief contact, he smiled at her. "Does that make you feel better?"

"Oh, yeah. Thanks, you know just how to please me," Alicia teased.

"If you think that's something, wait until our wedding night."

"Ooo, oh my." Her voice sultry, she wiggled just a little.

Much to her surprise, Mr. Whitman actually calmed down a bit during dinner and wasn't on her case as much as he was earlier. As long as the subject of her going to graduate school or keeping her own last name didn't come up, they could get through the god-awful dinner without her burning *too* many bridges with her new in-laws.

Seeing all her friends and family around the table almost made the rehearsal dinner worth it. Jazz had flown in, and Kendrick and Sonya were there along with Troy.

She didn't understand Mr. Whitman, and she definitely didn't know why he felt the need to offer his opinion about her life choices. She did know that if she didn't let her own father tell her what to do, she certainly wouldn't let Jonathan Whitman tell her what to do.

Darren, on the other hand, was another story. She knew she had to be very careful where he was concerned. Falling in love had made her vulnerable in ways she'd never intended to be, and it made her susceptible to the will of another in ways that still frightened her. After the misunderstandings and her other failed attempts at relationships, she was stepping out on faith. She only hoped she was doing the right thing and could really trust Darren with her heart.

Little conversations were going on all around her as she sat there in her own thoughts, not really paying attention to any one conversation, but thinking about the fact that, by the next evening, Darren would be her husband.

"Alicia, do you hear me talking to you?" Kyle interrupted her thoughts.

"Sorry, Daddy. What were you saying?"

"I wanted to know if you decided what your plans were for the summer. You've been interning at various magazines every summer, and you haven't spent any time at Taylor Publishing." Kyle's tone was almost accusing.

What is that about? Is he asking me to work for Taylor Publishing this summer? Alicia realized that she was sitting there with her mouth open, and she tried to think of something to say.

"I hadn't made any plans for this summer. I was so busy finishing things so that I could graduate early and apply to graduate schools that I didn't apply for any internships."

"Well, you should work with your old man this summer so I can show you the ropes." Kyle tried to sound as if it didn't matter to him one way or the other, but she could tell it mattered, and he really wanted her at Taylor Publishing. Resisting the urge to pinch herself, she mused, *marrying Darren, working at Taylor Publishing with Daddy—all of my dreams are coming true!*

"That would be great, Licia! It would be cool to have you around." Kendrick got so excited. She found it contagious.

"Okay, I'll do that. It would be nice to learn more about Taylor Publishing." She smiled at Kyle, and he let out a sigh of relief.

"Well, it's settled then. You'll start when you get back from your honeymoon." Kyle nodded. Seeing what could only be pride in his eyes, she swallowed, took a deep breath and touched her hand to her chest.

"Won't you be busy this summer setting up house and getting ready for the baby?" Mrs. Whitman,

always the pillar of propriety, had to offer her
thoughts. "I mean, the way you two are rushing into
this wedding, you haven't even had time to pick out
your china or your linens."

Oh brother. If it isn't one Whitman, it's the other.

"Well, Mrs. Whitman, I really don't see myself
picking out linen just yet. While I'm sure one day I'll
feel the need, right now, china isn't really high on my
priority list." She made her voice extra sweet, but her
eyes said "back off."

"Well, what are you going to do for dinner parties?
I'm sure now that Darren is married, he will be
hosting business-related dinner parties and such."
There she was with the pleasant advice that reeked of
condescension.

How ever does she do that?

Mrs. Whitman carried on. "You'll need fine china,
and you'll need to spend the summer setting up your
home. You know, doing all the things that you would
normally be doing before the wedding, dear."

Alicia cleared her throat and took a sip of her
sparkling cider. Counting to ten, she tried to calm
herself for the impending confrontation, but before
she could get her thoughts into words, Mr. Whitman
chimed in.

"Have the two of you even found a house yet?"

Mr. Whitman would *always* annoy her, Alicia
decided. There was just no way around it.

"Well, we will live in Darren's loft this summer, and we'll search for a home in Ann Arbor to move into in the fall." She was talking through her teeth, but she couldn't help it. It was the only way she could keep her tight smile plastered on her face.

"Yes, that's right." Mr. Whitman feigned recollection when she knew good and well he remembered everything.

"I'm still not sure it's a good idea for you guys to live in Ann Arbor. Darren will be so busy at Whitman Enterprises. The commute would cut back on valuable time that could be spent in the office making deals. Have you thought about commuting from Detroit?" Mr. Whitman asked in a way that sounded more like he was telling her exactly what to do.

Done with being nice, Alicia sat up in her chair and narrowed her gaze in on Mr. Whitman. Luckily, Darren jumped in before she could respond.

"Dad, she's not going to be up and down the highway pregnant. I'll commute." Darren glared at Mr. Whitman in warning.

Mr. Whitman gave his son a pointed stare for a moment but kept right along. "Have you thought about deferring graduate school for a year? That way, you won't have to commute pregnant." Again, he asked her in a way that was more a statement or suggestion than a question.

"I won't have to commute, because Darren will."

"What's the big deal? It's not that far of a commute, and it's only for two years. Darren will be fine commuting." Karen was about to go mama lion on Mr. Whitman, and Alicia almost hoped that she wouldn't, wanting instead to take care of him herself.

"Karen—"

You would think Dad would know when to lay off and let Mom go off, but you gotta love him for trying.

"What, Kyle? I'm just giving my opinion since everyone else feels that they want to have some input on where these two *grown* people want to live." Voice laced with sarcasm, Karen gestured toward Alicia and Darren with her hand before giving Mr. Whitman and Mrs. Whitman a scathing glare.

Alicia decided she was more than cool with letting her mother fight her battles this one time.

"Well, Karen, you must admit that since Darren will be the breadwinner, his job should take priority." Still pleasant, Mrs. Whitman's tone held a condescending air, and Alicia almost felt sorry for the woman.

Patricia Whitman clearly had never seen Karen Taylor when she was in "I'm protecting my child mode." *Poor thing.*

"Well, *Patricia*, actually, I don't. I think that Alicia is building a career of her own and that the two of them should be able to decide together what will take priority. That is a decision that they will make. If

Darren is willing to commute from Ann Arbor while she finishes her degree, fine. Let him. End of discussion." Karen's voice snapped and shut Mrs. Whitman right up.

"I agree, I think it's wonderful that things worked out so they can be together while she's in school. If she had decided to go to NYU, this would be a very different conversation." Almost as if purposely defusing a potentially explosive situation, Jazz chimed in her opinion, and Alicia was grateful for good girl-friends.

"Yes, I think that it'll work out lovely. I'm already planning to visit often. They have such quaint little shops there in Ann Arbor." Wistful and always positive, Sonya added her response, and Alicia wondered what she did to get such wonderful friends and family.

"Well, yes and the intellectual community is thriving, and there are such interesting artistic venues," Mrs. Whitman added, albeit with some hesitancy.

Yes! They even got Mrs. Whitman to see the light, she thought.

"All of this is irrelevant to the main point! Fine, commute from Ann Arbor." Mr. Whitman waved his hand in a dismissive manner.

Unable to help herself, Alicia responded, "Oh, thanks so very much for your permission." It was going to be hard to make nice with the likes of Jonathan Whitman.

CHAPTER 22

Alicia stood in front of the full-length mirror in the choir dressing room of the chapel. Her wedding dress was just the way she'd always imagined it. It was slightly off-white—to Mrs. Whitman's horror and dismay—and it was strapless. The hem was just above her knees, and the dress had a detachable train on the back that stopped at the heels of her shoes. It was made of raw silk and was very simple. She wore matching gloves that stopped just past her elbow and a pillbox hat with a veil that covered everything but her smile. Her hair was in an elaborate French-twist, and her makeup was applied to reveal her natural radiant beauty.

The bridesmaids' gowns she'd picked for Jazz and Sonya were also very simple. Similar to her, they wore raw silk; but their gowns were a deep taupe, and the dresses had off-the-shoulder short sleeves and modest necklines. They looked beautiful. Seeing them all made Alicia pause as she tried to think about sports, the weather, anything that wouldn't cause her to break down crying and ruin her makeup. That they were all there to help her get ready and share the evening with her meant more to her than she could have ever imagined.

"You look so pretty, Alicia." Karen came and stood behind her in the mirror.

"Thanks, Mom."

"That dress is gorgeous. It really didn't seem like much on the hanger. Once you put it on, wow!" Sonya added.

"Well, I think that it looked wonderful on the hanger and off," Jazz said. "It really captures the simple elegance that you wanted for the evening."

"The chapel is wonderful, honey. The candles are flickering, and everything is so peaceful. This is just going to be the perfect wedding." Karen touched her hands to her chest and smiled as she gazed at Alicia.

"Yeah, too bad we can't just leave for our honeymoon tonight. We have to stick around for the reception tomorrow night." She turned away from the mirror to face her mother and friends.

"Well, I'm glad you guys are going to have a reception. So many people want to wish you happiness. If you weren't going to have the big wedding, you at least had to give people a chance to wish you well at the reception." Syrupy sweet and matter-of-fact, Sonya and Mrs. Whitman no doubt attended the same finishing school.

"Well, we could have done that after the honeymoon," Alicia said grudgingly. It wasn't that she didn't want to give people the chance to wish them well. She just didn't think they needed a big overdone party to do so. The only people who truly mattered were family and the small group of friends they had invited to share the wedding. The people coming to the reception were people she hardly knew, if she knew them at all.

What about simply sending a nice card? She thought ruefully.

"Well, just think, after the honeymoon, you'll be able to start your new life with your husband without being bothered." Karen voiced everything Alicia wanted to believe.

"Yeah, right." She knew her entry into the Whitman family would come with a lot of bothering and aggravation, especially where Mr. Whitman was concerned.

"It'll be fine, Alicia." Jazz straightened out Alicia's train. "Besides, you're about to marry a rich hunk—a fine rich hunk who loves your stinky drawers. So please, just have a good time at the reception and stop complaining."

A good girlfriend will always tell it like it is, Alicia thought, realizing Jazz was right—she had nothing to complain about. She was about to marry the man she loved. Even though she had initially resisted him and his advances in order to protect her heart, she was wide open and willing now. The lump in her chest that used to ache with wanting him was gone. She decided then and there to take Jazz's advice and stop complaining. Her life really couldn't get any better.

Calmly waiting for Alicia at the front of the chapel, Darren examined the audience. His parents were sitting up front, and the other guests were all seated and waiting. Darren bristled just a little when he saw Flex Towns walk in.

It would take him a minute to get used to his wife being such good friends with the guy. He was willing to try for the sake of peace in their relationship and out of respect for her choices. *Guess I have grown a little these past months.*

Mrs. Taylor was escorted in, and the music started playing softly. The pianist played the tune of Pure Soul's "We Must Be in Love." Kendrick and Sonya walked in arm-in-arm, followed by Troy and Jazz.

The candles flickered all around them and gave off a reflective mood. The lighting made everything appear magical. After Kendrick and Troy took their places at his side and Jazz and Sonya awaited Alicia, the pianist started playing "Here Comes the Bride." The few heads gathered in the small chapel turned and watched Alicia walk in, escorted by her father.

Darren had never seen anyone more beautiful in all of his life. She held on to Mr. Taylor's arm and seemed to glide toward him. He swallowed.

Her dress wasn't elaborate like most wedding gowns he'd seen. It didn't have any of the frills, sequins, or glitter, but it sparkled nonetheless.

How can something so simple be so beautiful?

She wasn't wearing a full veil, just a half veil, and he could see her smile. She was smiling as she walked toward him. He felt his chest swell, and he cleared his throat in an effort to compose himself. A tear slid down his cheek, but he didn't bother wiping it away.

He noticed Troy smirking at him out of the corner of his eyes, and he didn't even care that his friends would clown on him for some time to come about this day. He was marrying the woman he loved, and she loved him. That was all that mattered.

When they finally reached him, he took Alicia's hand with eagerness.

Alicia felt a tremor of electricity when Darren took her hand. She thought she must surely appear to be a grinning fool, but she couldn't stop smiling. Seeing her family and friends gathered to share in this special moment made her heart full. When she gazed down the aisle and saw Darren standing there, she was glad that the chapel was so small, and it wouldn't take her long to reach him.

He stared at her as if she was the most beautiful woman in the world, and she couldn't wait to start their lives together.

She heard Reverend Richardson talking, and she answered at all the right times, but she couldn't take her eyes off Darren. Handsome in his black tuxedo, his eyes were sparkling, almost glistening. He gazed at her through the whole ceremony, and she was happy for the veil because seeing his intense loving stare brought tears of love to her eyes.

She meant it when she said that she would love, honor, and obey the man standing next to her and holding her hands so lovingly in his. Even though she had argued intensely with the Reverend about changing the word "obey" or leaving it out entirely, it didn't matter in the moment when she made her final commitment to Darren.

When the Reverend finally said, "You may now kiss the bride," she felt an instant surge of urgency overcome her. Darren lifted her veil and gazed at her for a moment that felt like an eternity before he kissed her. Brushing her lips with his thumb, and cupping her chin in his hand, he wrapped his arm around her and covered her mouth with his own.

Lost in the power of his kiss, she didn't notice anything else around her. When they finally became aware of everyone else around them, all she could hear were loud applause, whistling, and clapping.

Reverend Richardson cleared his throat. She pulled her eyes away from Darren to pay attention to the reverend.

"Brothers and sisters, I present to you, Mr. and Mrs. Darren Whitman," Reverend Richardson proclaimed in his deep "take 'em to church" preaching voice.

Although she thought about correcting him and letting him know that she would be keeping her last name and would continue to be Ms. Alicia Taylor, watching Darren and feeling the love that filled her, she decided it wasn't important at that moment.

Darren put his arm around her and whispered in her ear, "So are you ready to make our trip down the aisle as a married couple, Ms. Taylor?"

Unable to speak, she smiled and shook her head yes. The phrase, *I love this man*, kept running through her head.

Alicia almost objected to Darren's carrying her over the threshold, but she didn't. It was romantic in a prehistoric sort of way.

Darren actually carried her all the way upstairs to the bedroom before he stood her on her own two feet. Then, he pulled her into his arms and kissed her.

At that moment, she realized she never stood a chance. She never would have been able to ignore him and stay away from him once he started to woo her. She didn't know that being loved by him—really loved by him—would be intoxicating.

Leaning into his embrace, she kissed him with all that was in her.

"So, how are you feeling?" Darren eyed her with concern.

"I'm feeling fine."

She had figured out how to curb her nausea. She didn't want to be sick on the day of her wedding or on her wedding night. She wanted to be fully functioning.

If she ate a little food every couple of hours, she was fine. It helped her to keep everything in, most of the time.

Standing in her husband's arms, she grinned a big smile because she'd remembered to keep stashes of fruits and vegetables, as well as cheese and crackers, to nibble on throughout the day.

"You're certainly looking fine. Have I told you how beautiful you are?"

Pretending to think about it for a minute, she tilted her head. "No, I don't think you have."

"Oh well, pardon me. I have been remiss. You're the most beautiful woman I have ever seen. I'm glad you married me, Ms. Alicia Taylor."

She smiled. "Are you sure you're cool with me keeping my last name?"

"Yes, I'm more than cool with it. As long as I get to come home to you everyday and make love to you every night, you can call yourself the Queen of Sheba for all I care." Darren held her close and nibbled on her ear.

Shivering, she gave him a saucy stare. "Hmm… I think I prefer Queen of the world."

"How about Queen of my heart?"

"That works."

Darren kissed her, and she felt his hands searching for her zipper before finally pulling it down. Her wedding dress dropped to the floor, and she stood in front of him in her white lace strapless bra, matching thong panties, thigh-high stockings, and garter-belt. She watched as her husband tried to gain his composure and catch his breath.

"I take it you like this?" She stepped away from the dress at her feet and spun around.

Although Darren said nothing, she found herself trying to catch her own breath when he once again lifted her off her feet and carried her over to the bed.

CHAPTER 23

Darren woke up the next morning fully satisfied. Alicia was in his arms sleeping so peacefully, curled up next to him and smiling. He didn't want to get out of the bed and wake her, so he watched her sleep.

He couldn't believe everything had worked out, and he had prevented their fathers from telling Alicia about that stupid arranged marriage plan of theirs. Things were better this way.

Watching her sleep and seeing the happiness on her face was proof to him that he had done the right thing. She may not have thought she wanted to get married so soon, but she was happy. He could tell.

He was almost tempted to share his knowledge about their fathers' plans with her. She might even get a kick out of the fact that the two men had gone to such lengths to try and control their children's lives.

Given Alicia's track record with her father and how she went out of her way to do the opposite of what he wanted her to do, he couldn't trust that she wouldn't ask for a divorce just because he happened to be the man her father picked for her. That wouldn't be good at all.

No. She can never know.

It was for the best. It was bad enough he knew.

Now that he was married to the woman he loved, he wasn't worried about the inheritance his father threatened to take away. A part of him almost wanted to tell his father he could keep the inheritance. Then, he and Alicia could start fresh with his small trust fund. Things would be tight, but they would be free. If he could denounce his inheritance without her questioning why and having to tell her all about the arranged marriage, he would. It was bad enough he would always have that little cloud of questions about his own actions because of the knowledge he had. No, it was best that Alicia didn't know.

Alicia woke up, smiled and snuggled closer. "What are you looking at?"

"My beautiful wife."

"I don't think your wife is very beautiful in the morning after just waking up." She raised her hand to her mouth to cover her yawn.

"Well, she is beautiful when she's sleeping and quiet and peaceful," he joked.

Alicia frowned. "Hmmm, I don't think that was a compliment."

"Of course it was." Brushing his lips against hers, he eased her lips open with his tongue. He never could get enough of kissing her. "So would you like breakfast in bed?"

"You're going to cook breakfast?" Alicia twisted her lips and squinted suspiciously.

"It's the one meal I can actually prepare. If you don't mind eggs, microwave bacon, and toast, and I have a bunch of fresh fruit, including *strawberries*."

"And whipped cream?" Alicia asked with a hint of seduction.

"Lots of whipped cream." He smiled wickedly.

"Well, in that case, breakfast in bed sounds like a lovely idea. Besides, if I don't get something in my stomach soon, I'll be sick all day."

"Want me to bring you up some warm ginger ale and saltines before I get started on your feast?" He got out of the bed.

"I knew there was a reason why I married you. You know just the right things to do to make a girl happy." Stretching, she looked so sexy that he contemplated getting back in bed. Common sense won out. The last thing he wanted was his wife puking all day.

"I'll be right back."

He headed downstairs, but first he grabbed his robe and put it on.

"Oh, you're obstructing my view." Alicia pouted.

"Don't worry; you'll be seeing a whole lot more of this later."

They were late to the reception. Things got a little out-of-hand during the day after the breakfast in bed, the strawberries and whip cream.

Who would have thought that a romantic cliché like that could be so much fun? thought Alicia.

Darren promised they would make an appearance at the reception for a couple of hours, do the customary father/daughter, and mother/son dance, greet their guests, thank everyone for coming, then discreetly disappear. People would understand that they were newlyweds and had other things they wanted to be doing.

She had to admit that after the night she and Darren shared and the morning and afternoon, she really did have a number of other things she would rather be doing.

When they entered the country club, they split up to search for their parents so they could start the traditional dances and get that portion of the evening out of the way. She couldn't find Kyle anywhere in the ballroom. After asking around, she found out that he was with Mr. Whitman in the cigar room. On a mission to get back into Darren's arms within the next two hours, she went downstairs to the cigar room to pull Kyle away from that arrogant, pompous, Mr. Whitman.

The door was cracked, and she could hear Mr. Whitman's loud voice as she walked up.

Condescending as usual, she thought wryly. She really couldn't fathom why her father remained friends with the man, let alone why he didn't just take a moment and give him a good telling off.

About to open the door and barge in, she heard something that gave her pause.

"Well, Kyle, you must admit that were it not for my son, you would be losing Taylor Publishing right now. He saved your family's company and his inheritance by stepping up to the plate and taking care of business. I have to admit, when he told us back in February at your nephew's wedding he could make Alicia fall in love with him, I had my doubts. But he pulled it off."

"I wasn't sure he would be able to pull it off either. Alicia didn't seem to like him very much. Even when they were children, they didn't get along. I was beginning to think we made a mistake arranging their marriage all those years ago."

"Rubbish, there is no such thing as a mistake. The merger between our families was an excellent idea. We can thank my savvy son for pulling off what you were unable to do." Mr. Whitman paused and made a tsking sound. "Honestly, Kyle, you really should have told the girl of her obligations years ago. You should have done a better job reining in that mouth of hers. Darren is going to have a time controlling her. Based on the way he has handled things so far, I have no doubt he will be able to eventually rein in her tendencies."

"Well, I hardly call knocking Alicia up savvy. He really could have handled the whole courtship thing a little better."

"Kyle, in the business world, we call that a hostile takeover. Yes, he used extreme measures, and there were numerous risks. The risk of losing his inheritance was greater." Mr. Whitman chuckled.

"I'm sure that my son, with the business mind he has, weighed all his options. Because he did, you will come out the better. They are married, and there will be an heir. You will have controlling interest of Taylor Publishing back in your hands in no time. Since you do not have controlling interests as of yet, there is the matter of Alicia's working there over the summer."

"What about it? She'll be an asset to the company. She's worked hard, and the internships with other magazines gave her a wealth of knowledge she can bring to breathe new life into our publications."

On any other occasion, Alicia would have been beaming to hear those words coming from her father's mouth. She'd waited her whole life to hear them it seemed. Now, they hollowed in her ear.

"I'm telling you, I've watched her over the years, and I am proud of her. She has proven she is serious about her career."

"That's all fine and well, but should we be encouraging her to think so much about a career when we both know it will take a lot of time to just be a wife and mother?" Mr. Whitman tsked again.

"Never mind, given the way Darren has gone about things so far, I have every confidence my son will prevail and get these crazy career ideas out of her head. He can't do it alone. I suggest you change your offer of employment for Alicia at Taylor Publishing."

Backing away from the door, Alicia went upstairs, careful to hold on tightly to the rails because she didn't trust her legs to hold her up. The ground felt uneven below her, and she now knew what it felt like to have your world shake apart and fall from underneath you.

She had to get out of there, and she had to get out of there quickly. Her chest constricted, and the sound of her heart pounding was so loud there were moments when she couldn't hear anything else.

Her eyes were getting blurry. She could see people laughing, dancing, and talking, but she couldn't hear anything but the beating of her heart. It didn't sound normal to her, especially since she couldn't *feel* it anymore.

She felt numb. Her face was wet, but she literally could not feel anything. She stopped to lean against the wall when she was partway between the ballroom and the exit.

If she could just will her legs to carry her out of the door without collapsing on the floor and bringing out all the emotions she was numbing herself from, she would be okay. She just had to make it out the door.

Walking again, the shakiness in her own steps gave her alarm. She took a deep breath that sounded like a sob in her ears. It made her walk all the more quickly toward the door. She was almost out, almost out of the country club, when she heard Darren call her.

She turned around in spite of the voice telling her to keep moving and get the hell out of there. She could see him, handsome in his tuxedo, and she willed herself not to throw up.

She couldn't get sick here—not here and not now. She turned back around and kept heading for the door. The hallway was closing in around her, and she had to leave, had to get out of there. *I need air.*

Darren came running up behind her, and she felt his hands on her shoulder.

"Licia, what's wrong? Are you okay?" He seemed so concerned.

Not able to turn and face him, she tried to keep walking because she didn't trust herself to talk, and she didn't want Darren to see what she knew were tears sliding down her face. That would be too much defeat for one night, and she couldn't bare another blow.

Despite her efforts, Darren's hold on her shoulder was firm, and he managed to turn her around.

"What's wrong? What happened? Why are you crying? Is it the baby?" He tried to hold her.

The hypocrisy of it was too much for her, and that he would dare to mention her child was the final straw. She wiped her hands across her face, not caring she was probably smearing her makeup and she probably resembled an ad for a horror movie. She took a deep breath, and that's when she began to feel it. Her chest constricted, and she felt a pain so deep it startled her for a moment. The lump in her chest was back, only this time it felt like a boulder. Her heart was broken.

"Alicia, you're scaring me. Please tell me what's wrong. What happened? Are you okay? Is the baby okay?" The urgency in his voice made her let out a hysterical laugh.

"I'm fine, Darren, and my child is fine. You do not have to worry about us."

"What are you talking about? Where are you going? Why are you leaving the reception?"

She couldn't believe he had the nerve to sound aggravated. With more conviction than she felt, she finally managed to speak. "I'm leaving because this whole reception, like our wedding, like our so-called marriage, is a sham. It's a lie, Darren, and so are you. I never want to see you again."

"What do you mean? Why are you talking so crazy? What is wrong with you?"

"Oh, I guess I am crazy. No, change that. I was crazy, crazy to trust you. I heard them, Darren! I heard our fathers talking about their little arrangement and how crucial you were to them being able to carry out their plans. Job well done, Darren. You did it. You made me fall in love with you. You even knocked me up to boot. You even got me to agree to marry you. I hope that means your inheritance is secure. Because this marriage is over!" She started to take off her rings, so she could give them back to Darren.

His hands quickly went to hers and held them. "Don't do that, Alicia. Don't take off the rings. We need to talk. I can explain it all to you. Just let me explain."

She tried to pull her hands free, but his grip tightened. "You don't have to explain. I've heard enough, Darren. Trust me, I understand. It was business. I'm sure being the heir to Whitman Enterprises was worth it all to you—being the savvy businessman that you are. This is where it ends. I'm done." She tried to pull away again, but his grip was too tight. The rings were in such an awkward position when he initially grabbed her hands that the diamond was now pressing into her flesh. "Let me go!"

"I can't let you go, Alicia. Please, I love you. Let me explain." Flustered, Darren's eyes were wide and pleading as he all the while held tightly to her hands.

"Let me go, Darren, please. You're hurting me."

Darren stared at his hand for a moment and loosened his grip a little. "Just, please, don't take off the rings. Listen, I'm going to tell my mother and your mother that we're leaving. Then we can go back to the loft and talk about this. I can explain it, Licia. I know that it seems bad, but it's not what you think." He stepped back.

"Alicia, I love you. Okay. I'm going to let go. Please don't take off the rings. Please just let me tell them we're leaving. I'll explain everything. Okay. Just wait right here, I'll be right back." Letting go of her hands, he backed away slowly all the while not taking his eyes off her.

She stood there motionless, watching him back away. He backed off into the bustling crowd, and soon folks just moved out of his way since he wasn't watching were he was going; his eyes were on her. Standing still, she kept her eyes on him, because as soon as he was no longer watching, she was going to leave; her mind was made up. So she watched, and he watched.

Then, as if confident she would wait for him and not leave, he turned and rushed off to find their mothers. At that moment, Alicia reached for her left hand with her right and listened to the sound of the metal rings hit the marble floor. Darren turned back around and started making his way through the crowd toward her. Satisfied when she saw Reverend Richardson stop him, she ran out of the door.

Once outside, she saw Kendrick and Sonya giving their keys to the valet. She jumped in the back seat of their luxury sedan, and they each turned to her in shock.

"Please get me out of here. Now!"

"Licia, what's wrong?" Kendrick stared past her to the door.

"Now please, Kendrick! I have to get out of here." She glanced at the door first before turning to Kendrick.

Kendrick grabbed the keys that were halfway between his hands and the valet's and got back in the car. Sonya followed.

They heard Darren screaming her name as they pulled off. Kendrick glanced back at Alicia, confusion all over his face.

"Just keep driving please, Kendrick. Just keep driving." Closing her eyes, she willed herself not to start crying.

They made it to the highway, and she was finally able to breathe. If she could hold it together for a little while longer, she wouldn't make a bigger fool of herself in front of Kendrick and Sonya.

"Where do you want to go, kiddo?" Kendrick briefly glanced back with a worried expression.

She didn't know where she should go.

Where can I go? Not the loft. Not my parents' house. Where?

"I don't know." A sob and a hiccup came out of her mouth at the same time.

"Why don't we just go back to our place?" Sonya offered. "The guest suite is yours for as long as you want it."

Alicia sighed. She could stay with them until she got her life sorted out. She felt a small bit of relief, but the nausea returned. She couldn't get sick in Kendrick's new car.

"Kendrick, pull over please. I'm going to be sick."

Screeching off the highway, Kendrick pulled on to the shoulder.

She jumped out and released just about everything that was inside of her. The strawberries and whipped cream did not taste nearly as good as they did earlier, and the memories weren't nearly as sweet.

CHAPTER 24

Once Darren was able to pull away from Reverend Richardson, he barely made it in time to see Alicia drive off with Kendrick and Sonya. If they hadn't been pulling up at that moment, there was no way she would have had time to get away. If he could have cut Reverend Richardson off more abruptly, he could have caught her. If he had been upfront with her about their fathers' plans from the beginning, none of this would have happened. Thinking of the "what ifs," Darren picked up Alicia's rings and headed back into the country club to find his father. Since Alicia was with Kendrick and Sonya, he was sure they would take care of her until he got there.

He pushed the door to the cigar room open with so much force it bounced back and almost hit him when he walked in. He walked straight toward Jonathan, who was sitting in a huge leather chair smoking one of his Cuban cigars. Mr. Taylor sat in an identical leather chair smoking a cigar. The two men appeared to be having their own private celebration—congratulating themselves on a job well done.

Jonathan jumped in his seat a little at Darren's abrupt entry. Seeing it was Darren, he smiled.

"Well, Son, I see you finally made it. We were just talking about you." Jonathan sat his cigar in the marble ashtray sitting on top of the mahogany table between the two chairs.

"Hello, Darren, is my daughter ready for her dance with her dad?" Mr. Taylor put out his cigar and started to rise from his seat eagerly.

"No, she's not. She's not ready because she just left. She left because she overheard the two of you talking about the arranged marriage." No matter how harshly he spoke, it would never come close to how angry he felt. He narrowed his gaze on Jonathan.

"Now you tell me what you said that has her so pissed she would take off her rings and leave her reception?"

"What do you mean she left the reception? Why didn't you stop her? How will this look?" Jonathan sat up in his chair, and his mouth fell open.

"I don't give a damn how it looks. Didn't you hear me?" Darren let out a ragged sigh. "I said my wife has left. She took off her rings and dropped them on the ground, and she left! She left because of what she overheard the two of you talking about. Tell me what she heard so I can think of a way to try and fix this."

He watched as the gravity of his words sank in with the two fathers. Mr. Taylor placed his head in his hands. His shoulders slumped.

Jonathan simply stared into space for a moment before explaining exactly what he thought Alicia might have heard.

Still, Darren didn't trust himself to move. If Alicia heard half of what Jonathan was telling him, he would have a hell of a time getting her to understand. He couldn't even look at Jonathan by the time he finished. Mr. Taylor just sat there slumped over and distraught.

"Son, of course we didn't mean for her to hear us. Eavesdropping is a very bad habit that she should really work on quitting. That's neither here nor there. You will have to fix this," Jonathan implored.

Glaring at Jonathan, Darren snapped, "I know that I have to fix it. I'm not fixing it for you. I'm fixing it because I love her." He let out a frustrated sigh. "You know, Dad, you can keep my inheritance, and I am resigning from Whitman Enterprises, effective immediately."

"Are you insane? Son, don't make a rash decision that you'll regret. You are the sole heir, and you also need to think about your child. Do you feel comfortable giving away his future?"

He figured Jonathan would automatically assume the child would be a boy. Too tired to continue trying to get him to understand, he simply shook his head.

"The inheritance would always be between me and Alicia. If I can get her to forgive me and give us a chance, I don't want anything between us. If you want to leave it to our child, I'm sure that he or *she* would appreciate it. I don't want anything from you."

He walked out of the cigar room and up the stairs without stopping to talk to the people who were trying to wish him well, or the people inquiring about Alicia's whereabouts, or the people who had witnessed the bride take off and wondered just what happened. Let them continue to drink, dance, and party on Jonathan Whitman's dime, he was done. Leaving the country club, he waited for the valet to bring his car around.

Alicia probably didn't go back to the loft, and she would be too pissed to stay in the same house with her dad. So he drove in the direction of Kendrick and Sonya's house, hoping against hope she would be there.

Once close to their home, he realized he didn't know what he would say to her. How would he be able to get her to understand that he loved her? How would he convince her he only wanted to be sure that when she married him she was doing it because she loved him and not because she was fulfilling some family obligation? How could he explain that he'd loved her for so long he needed to be sure she loved him, too?

Darren just sat in his car at the end of the cul-de-sac for what amounted to a couple of hours but felt more like a lifetime. When he finally rung Kendrick and Sonya's doorbell, they were dressed for bed.

Kendrick opened the door in a pair of red silk pajama pants.

"Sorry, I hope I didn't wake you guys. Is Licia here?" He looked his friend in the eye and didn't flinch away from the disappointment he saw there.

"She's here, but she doesn't want to see you, man." Kendrick didn't move aside so that he could enter.

He sighed. "Listen, man, can I please come in? I need to see my wife. I need to explain things to her. It's not what she thinks."

"So your father and my uncle didn't plan for the two of you to get married? An exchange of her for majority rights in Taylor Publishing?" Kendrick's tone was just shy of judgmental, and he gave Darren a pointed glare.

Darren leaned against the doorframe, his mouth tight. "That happened."

Still not budging from his spot at the door, Kendrick continued. "Your father didn't threaten you with disinheritance if you didn't marry the woman he chose for you?"

"That happened."

"Did you or did you not tell them you would be able to make Alicia fall in love with you?" The air of judgment now thick, Kendrick's lip curled in a half snarl.

"Yes, I did. I did it because I didn't want the kind of jacked up marriage my parents have. I wanted my future wife to love me. Is that so bad?"

"Did you get her pregnant as a way to insure she would have to marry you?" Kendrick snapped.

"Hell no! Come on, Kendrick, man. You know me better than that." He slapped the doorframe with his hand. "Would I do something like that? I didn't mean for Licia to get pregnant. But she is, and I'm not sorry. I want both her and my child. So would you please let me see my wife, so I can try and fix this mess your uncle and my father made?"

Both of them eyed each other wearily as they simultaneously calmed.

"I don't know, Darren." Kendrick ran his hand across his chin. "She is really messed up about this. She's going to need some time. Shit, we just heard her stop crying, and it sounds like she's finally sleeping. Why don't you come back in a couple of days? Give her time to get some perspective and think about things."

"Kendrick, don't take this the wrong way, but you really need to move so I can see my wife." His patience with his friend was shot. "If she is upset, I want to have a chance to console her. I need to see her."

"Kendrick, let him see her. They might be able to work this out." Sonya walked up and stood behind her husband in a pink silk robe and slippers.

Darren silently thanked God when Kendrick reluctantly let him past.

"The guest suite is upstairs, the first door to your right. She's in there sleeping. Good luck." Sonya rubbed his arm with encouragement.

Needing all the help he could get, Darren hugged and thanked Sonya, then turned to take the stairs two at a time. Opening the bedroom door softly, he found Alicia in the queen-sized brass bed fast asleep.

He walked over to the bed and gazed down at her. She wasn't resting peacefully at all. With the soft moonlight coming in from the window blinds and the hall light under the door, he could see traces of dried up white lines from the tears she'd cried, and he could also see the pain. It pierced his heart.

He decided not to wake her up. She needed her rest. They could talk in the morning. Maybe by then he could think of a better way to explain.

He didn't want to leave her, so he took off his shoes and tuxedo jacket and carefully slid onto the bed and rested on top of the pink and white floral print comforter. He placed his arm around her waist and said a silent prayer that God would give him the words to make Alicia understand how much he loved her.

When he woke up, it was because he felt a sudden jerk movement from Alicia. She must have seen that she wasn't alone. Darren opened his eyes to find Alicia sitting up in the bed glaring at him.

Pushing his arm away, she snapped, "What are you doing here?"

Darren squinted at the sunshine that was coming through the window blinds. They must have slept through the night. *So why don't I feel well rested? I feel like crap.*

"What are you doing here, and what is that smell?" Alicia sniffed. All of the sudden she went pale. "Oh no, I'm going to be sick." Running into the adjoining bathroom, she dropped to her knees and lifted up the toilet seat.

Realizing his tuxedo jacket reeked of cigar smoke, he ran into the bathroom to help her. He held hair back while she puked. When she was done, he gave her a cup of water to rinse with and assisted her back to the bed.

"Do you want me to go to the kitchen and see if Sonya has any saltines and ginger ale?" He brushed his hand across his head as he waited for Alicia's answer.

She nodded yes, and he went off to the kitchen. They did have saltines, but they didn't have any ginger ale. He hoped that some warm Sprite would calm her stomach a little.

He'd taken his tuxedo jacket with him and left it downstairs to alleviate some of the smell. When he walked back in, he tried to gauge what she was thinking, but her expression was blank.

He handed her the saltines and placed the can of Sprite on the nightstand. "They didn't have any ginger ale." He sat down uneasily at the foot of the bed and watched her.

She nibbled on the saltines and took slow sips of the Sprite, without acknowledging him. He watched her for what seemed like an eternity. As she finally turned to him, her face was still blank and her eyes expressionless.

"Licia, I can explain everything if you give me a chance. I know it looks bad, but you have to know that I love you. Please tell me you know that!"

She continued staring at him.

He sighed. "I don't know where to begin."

"Why don't you begin with the part where you thought it would be a good idea to make me fall in love with you so that you could keep your inheritance?" Although her tone was flippant, he could tell she was disturbed.

"Or why don't you start with the part where you thought it would be cool to get me pregnant as an extra insurance policy?"

"That's not what happened, Alicia. You were there. You know things just got out of hand and we used protection every other time. I did not get you pregnant on purpose."

"Whatever, Darren. Listen, just save it. I don't want to hear it. There's nothing you can say that will make me forgive you. Nothing at all." Alicia turned away.

"I love you." He finally knew what all those R&B singers meant when they crooned that they weren't too proud to beg. If begging would work, he would drop to his knees in a second.

Alicia refused to look at him. "I want this marriage annulled."

"You can't get an annulment. The marriage has been consummated."

"Fine, I want a divorce," she snapped.

"Listen, Alicia, we just need to talk this through. If you would just listen to me, you would see this whole thing is a misunderstanding."

"I want a divorce!"

"I'm not giving you a divorce!" Taking a deep breath, he continued. "Licia, we got married because we love each other. You are pregnant with my child. I told you I won't be on the periphery of my child's life, and I damn sure won't be on the periphery of yours."

"Oh, so that's what this is all about. What, do you not get as much money if you don't raise the heir yourself? Well, I'm sure I can work out a joint custody arrangement that would be to your liking. That way, you get to keep your inheritance." Alicia laughed shakily, and her voice cracked. Her eyes glistened with the beginnings of tears.

"Please, Alicia, we can get past this. You know I love you, and I know you love me." He played the last card he could. "There is the matter of our child."

"Don't you dare! I do not love you anymore, and I don't think you ever loved me. You couldn't have loved me and do what you did." A tear slid down her cheek. She angrily wiped it away. "As for my child…we will work out joint custody arrangements with our lawyers."

Wiping away another tear, she sighed. "Listen, I really need you to leave, Darren. You're no better than our fathers. In fact, you're worse than the both of them put together. I wouldn't wish what you did to me on my worse enemy."

Feeling like he'd been punched in the gut. He couldn't breathe. He stood up. "I'm going to give you some time to think about this. I want you to know that I will fight any move toward divorce, and I will not give away any part of custody for my child."

"You can actually stand there and threaten to take my child away after all you've done? What am I, some kind of bred mare for you and your father? Is that it? I was willing to share because in spite of how badly you have treated me, I really believe you should be a part of your child's life. But for you to stand there and tell me you won't settle for anything less than full custody tells me you don't give a damn about me. So, please, Darren, just leave."

Holding on to the bedpost, Darren took a deep breath. His breathing was starting to normalize, then she went and misconstrued his last-ditch effort to save their marriage as a threat to take their child. That she could even think he would do such a thing let him know how little she thought of him.

He walked over to the nightstand and placed the rings next to the Sprite can.

"I love you, Alicia. And I want you to be happy. I hoped you could be happy with me, but if you can't, I understand. If you file for divorce, I won't fight it. You can have full custody of our child. All I ask is for visitation. I'll provide for both of you including full-time, live-in help so you can finish graduate school." Making an attempt to touch her, he stopped. "Just let me know what you need from me. I'm sorry."

Walking out of the bedroom was the hardest ten steps he ever took. As he closed the door, he could hear her crying, and he felt a throbbing ache in his chest. He never wanted to be the cause of her unhappiness.

He stood at the door with his hand on the knob, listening to her body-wrenching sobs. Although he was tempted to go back in and hold her and beg her to forgive him, he now realized Kendrick was right. She needed time.

Sonya came walking down the hall. He asked her to go in and console Alicia. He left and drove around aimlessly for hours before he finally ended up exhausted at his loft. There were several messages on his phone from his dad, Alicia's dad, his mom, Alicia's mom, Troy, and Jazz, but none from Alicia.

CHAPTER 25

Ann Arbor, Michigan, after some time

The fall semester was over, and Alicia was sitting in the kitchen of her townhouse with her mother, Jazz, and Sonya. Jazz and Sonya had come to town to be there for the birth.

Several days past her due date, even though she was dreading labor and childbirth, she was ready for the kid to come out already.

Karen Taylor had packed up her things, told her husband there was no way she would let her baby go off to graduate school alone and pregnant and moved to Ann Arbor.

Even though Alicia complained about Karen living with her on a daily basis, she was so glad she had someone with her who really loved her.

Karen, Sonya, and Jazz were all sitting around the kitchen table, acting as if they knew better than she did how she should handle her relationship with Darren. She wished they'd just mind their own business.

"Licia, baby, I know you needed some time to try and figure things out. But I think it's time for you to at least talk to Darren." Karen was entering her umpteenth "give Darren a chance" speech. "He has reached out to you on numerous occasions, yet you refuse to talk to him. You're having the baby any day now. You guys are going to share a child. It's time for you to stop being stubborn and talk to the man, see if there's anything left to salvage."

Jazz had grown close to Karen the past few days. She provided the perfect background chorus to Karen Taylor's solos. "Yeah, girl, and I think the fact that you haven't filed for a divorce and you're technically still wearing his ring, albeit on a chain around your neck, means you're not ready to let this go. You know you still love him. I can look at you and tell you do."

"Troy and Kendrick told me Darren left his job at Whitman Enterprises and gave up his inheritance, girl," Sonya chimed in. "He gave it all up because he didn't want you to have any doubts about his love for you. I think that's so romantic. He loves you, Licia."

"Girl, lay off the soaps. That man does not love me. It's all probably a part of some game he's playing. He can't be trusted. I can't trust him." Trying to ignore them, she just wasn't ready to listen.

Because she wasn't ready to deal with the Darren situation, the rest of her life was running somewhat smoothly. She made it through her first semester in the masters program with all A's. She simply focused all her time and energy into taking care of herself and studying. Between her fellowship and what she received from her mom, she was able to live.

She didn't ask Darren for any help even though he set up a checking account for her. She didn't spend any of his money. She unconsciously fingered the rings on her gold chain and nibbled on her bottom lip.

"The boy loves you, baby. Do you think I would have let you marry him if I didn't see the love in his eyes? I would have thrown myself in front of the aisle and refused to let you walk down it." Karen had taken to repeating herself. Alicia had heard it all before during the past seven months.

"I knew all about that stupid arranged marriage deal Kyle made with Jonathan Whitman. I was against it. When he went ahead and formed the deal anyway, I left my job and made it my business to make sure I would raise a child who would know her own mind and who would not let any man, not even her father, run her life. I know I raised that kind of a child. That's why I can't believe you're sitting her like a chicken, scared to work things out with a man you know you love."

"That's right! Momma ain't raise no punks! Girl, get a backbone. Stop tripping and call the man. You could go into labor any minute now, and he should be there." Hyped up by Karen's speech, Jazz almost bounced off her chair with enthusiasm.

"Yes, Alicia, he's so sorry. I saw him the other day, and he seemed so lost. And the night of your reception, I don't know who looked worse, you or him." Sonya got all wistful and somber.

"I really appreciate that you guys love me enough to think you can get all in my business. But I really think I can handle this on my own." Focusing her gaze on a grease spot on the wall behind the stove, still playing with her chain and rings, Alicia tried to ignore the group she affectionately called the "Darrenette Singers" and their same old tune.

"If you could, we would let you. You can't, baby. So we have to try and help." Karen's voice was matter-of-fact.

"Yeah, girlfriend, you're about to mess up and lose a good one," Jazz said. "Yeah, he messed up. He should have been up front with you. But you have to learn to forgive. No one's perfect."

Alicia made a mental note to take Jazz's mom's side against Jazz the next time they were together—*no matter what*. On general principle, Jazz shouldn't have been all gung-ho and co-signing everything Karen had to say. As *her* friend, she should take *her* side or shut-up.

"Whatever, if he could be so deceitful, how can I possibly trust him?" They were clearly not trying to understand or take her side.

"You can trust him, Licia. He did the wrong things for all the right reasons. He loves you. Don't just throw that away without talking to him," Sonya pleaded.

"I'm not talking to him. I'm not ready yet. I don't know when I'll ever be. Now if you guys are done getting all in my business, I'm going to take a nap." Wobbling up from her chair, she started to walk away.

"Fine, be hardheaded," Karen scolded.

"Be stubborn," Sonya judged.

"Be scared," Jazz taunted.

"Be out of my business," she snapped.

Darren hadn't spoken to his father since the night of the reception, and he didn't plan on doing so anytime soon.

Although perfectly happy blaming Jonathan for everything that went wrong with his marriage to Alicia, the more he thought about it, he realized he had to take his share of the blame.

Sure, Jonathan set things in motion that planted the seeds of trouble, but he nurtured those seeds by not coming clean with Alicia about the plans. He was just as much at fault. He was man enough to admit that.

So, he decided to face Jonathan, accept his lunch invitation, and after that, find a way to get his wife to respond to him.

Jonathan Whitman was sitting in the smallest of the three dining rooms in the Whitman mansion waiting for him and appeared to be in deep thought.

When Darren entered the room, Jonathan glanced up. "Hello, Son. I'm glad you came. Have a seat."

He took the seat across the table from his father and didn't say a word.

"How have you been, Son?"

Sighing, Darren opted to speed things up. The more he thought about it, the more he knew he had somewhere else to be. "Can we cut the small talk, and can you just tell me why you summoned me? Jeez, Dad. How do you think I am? My child is going to be born any day now, and my wife won't talk to me."

Jonathan cleared his throat and let out a sigh of his own. "I didn't summon you here. I only requested to have lunch with my son. I haven't seen you in a while, and we don't talk anymore. I guess in a way, I *summoned* you here, as you put it, just to hear some small talk, just to find out what's been going on in your life."

"Dad, there is really nothing to tell. I go to work and I come home. I pray that one day I'll get a call from Alicia saying she wants to work on our marriage, or at least that she wants to talk, because I can't imagine the rest of my life without her."

He spent most of his days building up a small consulting firm he'd started up with half of the money from his small trust fund, all of the money in his portfolio, and the money he got from mortgaging his loft. He'd put the other half of the money from his trust fund in an account for Alicia that she had yet to touch, which meant he was struggling to make it. For the first time in his life, he was hurting financially—hurting but free.

The business was growing in small increments. He was offering advice and consultation to small businesses—mostly minority businesses in Detroit—on how to expand and broaden their markets. Most people came to him because he was Jonathan Whitman's son. That was okay with him because he felt like he was helping people, and that was what mattered. It was different from taking over companies and running people out of business. He was building, and that felt nice.

"Then why don't you go to her, Son? Fight for your family. Don't just let it slip away." Jonathan's voice was full of emotion, and it made Darren stop for a minute before he spoke.

He wondered if he could really get Jonathan to understand his reasons for not pushing Alicia. "Dad, I don't want to make things hard for her, and I don't want to make her unhappy. If she doesn't want to be married, I'm not going to try and force or bully her into staying with me."

I don't want to be like you. That's what Darren felt. Even after all the pain and hurt, he had enough respect left for the man who raised him not to voice it. It was enough that he was resolved to be his own man, not Jonathan Whitman's son.

"I am not saying you should. Don't you think you should at least let her know how you feel?"

Since he'd been thinking he should be trying to talk to Alicia instead of listening to his father anyway, he didn't say anything.

Jonathan sighed. "Son, this is not about me. This is about a man wanting to see his son happy and wanting the best for his future grandchild. I know you would never forgive yourself if you gave up on your family."

"She might not want to talk with me. She'll probably turn me away." He spoke more to himself than to Jonathan, going over all the reasons that had played in his head the past few months that kept him from running after Alicia each time she refused his phone calls, or declined his invitations to meet and talk.

"Then you keep going back until she listens. You keep going back until she takes you back. I didn't raise you to quit because things are difficult. Whitmans do not quit."

"Okay, Dad, I'm going to go to her now. Can I take a rain check on the lunch?"

"By all means, yes. When we meet next time, we will have to have a long discussion about this rejecting your inheritance business and that little consulting company of yours." His father smiled. "I think you should know that there is no way I will allow my only son to walk away from the family empire. And I will not quit until you're back on board. I don't care if I have to buy your business and put you out of business."

It was a playful threat, but Darren knew Jonathan well enough to take it seriously. He shook his head. "We'll talk when I get back, Dad. You should know that I'm very happy with what I'm doing, and I don't intend to stop." Firm, he meant every word.

He got in his car and drove straight to Ann Arbor. When he arrived, he was surprised to find Jazz and Sonya there. He knew that Mrs. Taylor was living with her.

Sonya answered the door and gave him a hug. "Darren, I knew you would come. I knew you wouldn't let Alicia give birth without at least trying to work things out. Come in."

He hugged her back and smiled, heartened by the wonderful greeting.

"Come on back into the kitchen, Alicia's upstairs taking a nap, but we're all back there plotting how to get her to stop being so stubborn and give you another chance."

He smiled and followed her into the kitchen. The women were sitting around the table; it was evident they were having an intense conversation.

"So, Darren, you finally made it here?" Mrs. Taylor asked. "What took you so long? Do you know I have been away from my husband for seven months because you two kids can't seem to get it together?" Mrs. Taylor seemed stern for a minute before breaking into a big grin. She got up and hugged him.

"Sorry, Mrs. Taylor. I would have been here a lot sooner, but I was trying to give Licia time to make her decisions and hopefully get to a point where she could think about forgiving me." He hugged her back.

"Well, you can just head back to Detroit and keep waiting because that's not going to happen. What are you doing here, Darren?" Alicia walked into the kitchen and startled everyone.

"Well, look who's awake? We were just talking about you." Jazz walked over to the refrigerator and pulled out a juice pouch. "Anyone thirsty?"

No one answered her except for Alicia who glared at her friend. "No. And I wasn't sleep. I came down to see who was at the door."

Alicia crossed her arms over her protruding belly and turned her glare to Darren. "And, yes, you guys clearly have a knack for talking up folk. You were just talking about Darren earlier. I'll tell you, speak of the devil."

Beautiful pregnant, Alicia's skin glowed, and her eyes gleamed. Darren knew it wasn't just because he hadn't seen her in a while. She was filled out all around, all her curves even curvier. The stomach that protruded in front of her was perfectly rounded. She put one hand on her hip and rested the other on her belly.

He stopped staring at her long enough to speak. "Hi, Alicia, how are you?"

"Why are you here?" Alicia moved her other hand from her stomach to her hip.

Small talk was not going to work, so he went for the forthright approach. "We need to talk. Can we go somewhere and talk?"

"Y'all don't have to go anywhere," Jazz said. "Please have a seat here. There's plenty of room." Jazz slurped the rest of her juice, pulled out the chair next to her and motioned for Alicia to have a seat.

Mrs. Taylor pulled out the chair next to her and motioned toward Darren. "Yes, at the rate you guys are going, you'll need our help sorting this out if you're going to work things out before my grandchild gets here."

"Guys, they should really be alone." Sonya eyed them all nervously.

"*Please* they are messing everything up on their own." Mrs. Taylor patted the chair with her hand. "They need our help

"Yeah, I agree. They need help." Jazz got up and threw her empty juice pouch in the trash.

He weighed the options of having the discussion in front of witnesses. The women did seem to be on the side of them getting back together. "Alicia, please, can we talk?"

"Okay, but definitely not here. Let's go. I'll be back." Alicia made a point of sending evil glares to her mother and Jazz.

"Okay, baby, see you later." Mrs. Taylor didn't bat an eye before she turned to Jazz. "That worked out lovely."

"Yeah, nice work, Mrs. Taylor." Jazz held up her hand for a high-five. Mrs. Taylor slapped her five.

"Thank you, Jasmine. You weren't so bad yourself." Mrs. Taylor glanced over at her daughter and smiled. "Did you two change your mind? You're staying to talk here?"

Alicia let out an exasperated sigh. "Darren, let's go."

Alicia sat in Darren's car and immediately wished that she had put up a bigger fight. She wasn't ready to talk to him. She didn't know what to say, didn't trust

herself *not* to stay good and mad at him. So far the distance, not seeing him, and not talking to him, helped her to hold on to her anger—to nurture it.

Seeing him would just open up all kinds of feelings and possibly make her vulnerable to him again. She didn't want to do that.

He looked awful. Not in a bad way. He was still *fine.* His eyes were hollow, sad and rather hopeless. Trying to steel herself to his pitiful demeanor, she reminded herself that she was the wronged party. He should have been upfront and honest.

"So, where would you like to go?" Darren tapped the steering wheel.

Good. He should be nervous.

"We don't have to actually go anywhere. I just needed to get out of there. They were working my last nerve." She stared straight ahead, knowing that as long as she didn't look at him, she'd be fine.

"I'm sure they're just trying to be helpful."

"Yeah, I suppose they think they are. That's the only reason I haven't kicked them all out yet. Well, that, and I'd like for somebody to be here when this kid decides to come out." Alicia touched her belly and stared out the side window toward the townhouse.

Although happy her mom and her friends were there, she would have liked to have shared the whole pregnancy with Darren.

She heard Darren give a sharp intake of air. She turned to face him as best she could, given her protruding belly and the limited space in the passenger seat of Darren's sports car. He had turned to look out the window and seemed to be searching for something.

Finally, he turned around, and the minute he did, she was sorry she turned to face him. He seemed so damn sad. Her guilt for keeping him from enjoying the experience of their child growing within her was starting to return. It was easy to ignore the guilt when he wasn't around. She started to turn away, but he reached out and touched her face.

"Licia, I want to be here for you."

She didn't know what to say. He seemed so sincere. He'd also seemed sincere when he said that he loved her, and when he married her. She sighed.

He is sincere.

"I know that, Darren."

"You don't want me here?"

She didn't know how to answer that question without either telling a lie or opening herself to vulnerability. She decided to just ignore it.

"Alicia, I realize I made a big mistake. I should have told you about the stupid arranged marriage thing. You had a right to know. Even though that was not the reason I married you. I married you because I love you. I want to spend the rest of my life with you."

"When did you find out? About the deal between our fathers—when did you find out?" She shifted the conversation, if he said he loved her one more time, she knew she wouldn't be able to hold out because she realized that in spite of everything, she wanted to believe more than anything else that Darren loved her.

Darren hesitated. "My father told me the night I graduated from Andover."

Her mouth fell open, and she felt her eyes grow wide. That had to be heavy for a teenager. "So you knew about it that night at your graduation party?"

"Yeah."

Finally, she asked the one question that had burned her for the past seven months. "So, why didn't you tell me?"

"Honestly, I wanted to be able to know you were marrying me because you loved me—not to save your father's company or some sense of obligation. When I saw marriages like my parents…" Darren paused and shook his head emphatically. "I kept thinking I didn't want that kind of marriage."

"Didn't you think I had the same right to know you were marrying me because you loved me and not to keep your inheritance or to fulfill your father's grand design for your life?"

"When I reflect on it now, yes, I realize that. I honestly thought I was doing the right thing by not telling you." Darren's eyes were pleading.

Not convinced, she shook her head. "How could it have been right? You lied to me, Darren."

"I didn't lie. I kept information from you, yes, and I will regret that for the rest of my life. But I didn't lie to you. Every time that I told you I loved you, I was telling the truth."

Back to love again. It wasn't enough. *Is it?*

"I don't think I can trust you."

"Ever?" The word came out in a strained whisper.

"I don't know."

"Alicia, I have declined my role as heir to Whitman Enterprise and resigned from my position as well." Darren was telling her things she already knew, but she listened anyway.

"I don't want anything to be between us." Darren touched her face. "If you could just tell me what I have to do to make you see that I want to be with you…what can I do to earn a second chance? I don't want to lose you."

Again, she was forced to remain quiet. She couldn't lie, and she was not ready to admit anything.

After moments of awkward silence, she trusted herself enough to speak. "Darren, I'll take everything you said into consideration. I think that I still need a little more time to process everything. It's been rough with school and the pregnancy. I just haven't allowed myself the time I need to think about this—to heal. It hurts too much."

His shoulders slouched, and he placed his head on the steering wheel. She felt the need to voice at least some of what she was feeling. "I'm glad that you came, and I will definitely call you when I'm ready to talk."

Lifting his head, he sighed and forced a smile. "Well, I guess that's better than nothing. What about the baby? I was thinking I could stay in a hotel around here until you go into labor. I really want to be there. I understand if you don't want me to be there. I just… I just would like to be present when our child enters the world."

She thought about it. She wanted Darren to be there, too. He deserved to be there, especially since he missed the pregnancy. "Okay, I'll have Jazz or Sonya call you when I go into labor."

"Thank you."

She got out of the car and walked back to her townhouse. The December air was brisk, and the teardrop trailing down her face felt like ice.

CHAPTER 26

Alicia bypassed the kitchen divas and went right back upstairs to her bedroom. She wasn't in the mood for their questions, comments, or suggestions. She just wanted to be alone with her thoughts and allow herself the space to think about, *really* think about, her feelings for Darren.

Everything was so complicated and wrapped up in so many bad feelings. When she looked at him, when he *touched* her, she just wanted to put it all behind her and go forward.

Touching her belly, she spoke softly to their child. "What do you think, little one? Do you think that your mommy should let bygones be bygones and forgive your Daddy?

"He wants to be there for your birth. He really loves you, and I think it will be good for him to be there. So, Mommy told him yes.

"I can't promise that we will be together right now. I love him. Mommy is just a little scared of being hurt again. I know now that if he had told me about the arranged marriage, I never would have given him a chance. I wish things could have gone differently, but

I honestly don't know what I would have done if I had to make the decisions your Daddy had to make. I think I'm ready to promise to you that I will try and work through the issues I have so that you can have your Daddy and your Mommy together in your life.

"Wooo, ouch, little one. I wonder if I can take that as a sign that you're pleased with my promise."

Suddenly in a pool of water, she knew that her child was ready to come into the world.

"Don't tell me you were waiting for your Daddy to get here? After I've carried you for nine months, you wait for him to show up and you're ready to make an appearance? It figures."

Taking deep breaths, she got up from the bed, and glanced back at the soaked mess.

There goes the mattress.

Once down in the kitchen, she saw that the three busybodies hadn't moved from their spots.

"Well, look who decided to come downstairs. We were just about to come and make you tell us what happened with Darren. Your conversation with him was much too short." Karen's tone half-teasing and half-serious, she shook her head in disappointment.

"Mom, my water just broke, and I think I'm having contractions."

"What does it feel like?" Karen's eyebrows raised in concern.

"Like pain." Alicia glanced down at her belly and rubbed it, just as she felt another sharp cramping pain. "Wooo, ouch. Okay, baby. I get it. You're ready."

"Well, I'll go get the car warmed up and ready." Sonya jumped up, but she didn't move, she just glanced around frantically for someone to give her the okay.

"I'll go grab your suitcase." Dashing from the room, Jazz ran up the stairs.

"I'll help you to calm down. Come on, baby, have a seat and let's see how far apart these contractions are." Karen was the only one who seemed cool and controlled.

Alicia sat down and held Karen's hand. She noticed that Sonya was still standing there panicked. "Oh, Sonya, can you call Darren on his cell phone? He said that he'd like to be there."

"What's his cell phone number?"

"It's… woooo… ouch… wooo… " She struggled to remember the number in the midst of sharp labor pains.

"I'll call Kendrick or Troy from my cell in the car while it's warming up, and they can call him, okay?" Sonya winced. "We need to get moving! I'm going to get the car warmed up!" Sonya ran from the kitchen.

Just Alicia and her mom remained.

"Looks like it's time. Are you ready?"

"No way!"

Darren was halfway back to Detroit from Ann Arbor when he got the call from Kendrick that Alicia was in labor. Taking the next exit, he headed back to Ann Arbor.

Jazz and Sonya were in the waiting room when he arrived at The University of Michigan Hospital.

"Hey, Darren." Jazz glanced up from a magazine and smiled.

"Hi, Jazz, how is she?"

"She's fine. They're waiting until she's fully dilated. You can hear her scream from down the hall when those contractions hit." Laughing, Jazz put the magazine down on the seat next to her.

"Oh, she's not that loud," Sonya offered.

Then they heard a loud "Wooooo shooooot!" in the background, and Jazz smirked at Sonya.

Pretending to rub her ears, Jazz shook her head and smiled. "I told you. I swear she's the loudest one here. That baby better come soon."

"Are you going to go in the delivery room? It's really nice. It's designed to be all warm and home like." Her usual sunshine and happiness self, Sonya rubbed his shoulder in encouragement. "She's doing natural childbirth. I think that's so wonderful. Her Mom is in there now, but I'm sure they'll let both of you stay."

"Yeah, come on…let's tell the nurse you're the husband, so you can get in there. Wouldn't want you to miss any of the fun." Jazz got up from where she was seated and stretched.

She eyed him with mock concern. "Although, judging from the way girlfriend is screaming, you might want to stay out here. She is sure to be cussing you out as soon as those contractions get more intense."

"Woooooo! Oh, shooot!" Alicia's scream greeted them from down the hall.

"Right, enter at your own risk," Sonya warned teasingly.

"Be afraid, be very-very afraid." Jazz gave a haunting pose and broke out laughing.

"Okay ladies, I'm going in." He went to the nurse who promptly took him to wash up. He put on a blue sterilized gown over his clothes and walked in just as Alicia was in the middle of another contraction.

"Hello, Darren. You are just in time. I'm sure my grandbaby is going to just pop right out now—now that Daddy's here." Mrs. Taylor was sitting next to Alicia and holding a wet cloth on her forehead.

"Woooooo! Get out!" Alicia screamed.

Darren backed up.

Between short panting breaths, Alicia snapped, "Not you! Your kid!"

"Oh, don't yell at the baby. I wouldn't come out either with you yelling like that," Mrs. Taylor teased.

Darren took a deep breath and sat down in the chair on the other side of Alicia's bed. With Mrs. Taylor helping her with breathing, he felt utterly useless. Wishing he were her birthing coach, he instead just sat there.

Mrs. Taylor must have taken pity on him, because she let him feed Alicia ice chips when she was in her fifth hour of labor and damn near delirious. Mrs. Taylor must have known that after that much pain, Alicia would take ice chips from anybody, even him. He was just glad to be doing something.

He'd tried to make small talk in the first two hours. She gave him dirty looks and screamed. So, he just sat quietly. Feeding her ice chips was nice. She even managed to smile at him. Well, at least it resembled a smile. By the ninth hour of labor, she even let him hold her hand. Even though she squeezed the shit out of it every time a contraction hit, he didn't mind. It wasn't broken anyway, maybe slightly sprained. Who knew she had such a strong grip?

After eleven hours of labor, at 5:06 a.m., his son was born.

My son.

The doctor allowed him to cut the umbilical cord and let him place the baby in Alicia's arms. Although she had bags the size of quarters under her eyes and her hair was sticking out in every direction, he had never seen her more beautiful, especially when she looked at their child, and her face lit up.

"Well, I think the mother needs some rest now." The doctor seemed to also need some rest, although she wasn't there for the bulk of it like the rest of them.

"I'm fine. Can I hold him for a while?" Alicia kept her eyes on their child.

"Sure, but we'll need to take him and check him out. We'll bring him back to your room for a while, so you and he can get used to feeding." The doctor motioned to the nurse and walked out.

"He's beautiful. Look at my grandson. He looks just like you, Darren." Mrs. Taylor seemed tired, but her eyes where shining, and her smile was bright and cheerful.

Alicia studied the little bundle in her arms. "Yeah, he does. Figures. I carry him for nine months, go through eleven hours of labor, and he comes out looking just like you." Alicia turned to Darren and smiled.

Awestruck, Darren simply stared at his wife and child without saying a word. He couldn't believe they'd created something so precious and beautiful. At a loss for words, he silently thanked God for letting him be there to witness it.

CHAPTER 27

When Alicia woke, she saw Darren sitting in a rocking chair holding their son and talking softly to him. She didn't mean to eavesdrop.

But he is talking about me.

Eyes closed, she listened.

"I want you to know that I love you. I will always be there for you. I'm going to try my best to get your Mommy to forgive me and make her understand how much I love her. I don't want to live without the two of you. I was going to try and let her go. I can't do that. I need her. I need you both. So know that your Daddy loves you, and he's going to do everything he can to make this right."

If Darren were not in such a deep conversation with his son, if he was not talking so softly and didn't seem so oblivious to anything else but the child he was holding, she would have thought he knew she was awake. She would have thought he was trying to use the child to gain her trust again. She knew better.

Even while she was going through the labor and delivery, she found herself thinking she was glad that he was there. When she watched him, she saw the love in his eyes. She only had to decide what she was going to do about it.

Opening her eyes, she watched her husband and her son. "So, are you going to keep him all to yourself?"

Startled, Darren lifted his head with his eyes wide. "So you're awake." He whispered to his son, "I think your Mommy wants to see you. Let's take you over to Mommy."

Darren handed her the baby and continued to stand beside the bed, gazing at both of them.

Letting her finger trace her child's face, she whispered softly. "He really doesn't look anything like me. He's all you. That's amazing."

"Yeah, I can't believe he's ours. Have you been thinking about names?"

"Well, seeing him, I think the name is obvious. We'll have to call him Darren." She gazed down at her son. "How do you like that, DJ? If you don't mind, we can give him Taylor for a middle name. I know he won't technically be a Junior because you guys won't have the same middle name. So, I'll understand if you don't want Taylor to be his middle name. I was thinking I'd hyphenate my name after all, you know. I think it's important that I share the same last name as our kids."

"Taylor would be a great middle name…" Darren gazed sort of glazed over, and she could swear she saw the wheels turning in his head. "Alicia, are you telling me you're going to give me…give us another chance?"

She pretended to mull it over. The joy on his face made her suddenly coy. "If you want to, I'd like to. I understand why you didn't tell me what was going on with our dads, and I forgive you. You better not ever keep that kind of information from me again. I want us to always be upfront with each other, Darren. I'm sorry that I kept you away during the pregnancy, baby. I will regret that for the rest of my life. You should have been allowed to see our son growing inside of me. If I could change any of it, I would."

"Oh, baby, you…you've made me the happiest man on the planet. Thank you. I promise to spend the rest of my life making sure you're never sorry for giving us a second chance. Knowing we have the rest of our lives to spend together as a family, more than makes up for me missing the pregnancy. I'm just happy I got to see my son come into the world."

She stared down at their son. "I'm happy that you got to see it, too. And we're going to hold you to that. Won't we, DJ? Any more secrets and arranged marriages, and we're going to get you. And there will be no arranged marriages for our son."

Darren bent over and brushed his lips across hers. She smiled. His kiss felt like a thunderstorm after a long drought.

"Can some grandparents come in and see their grandchild?" Kyle Taylor came into the room followed by the other grandparents.

"Of course, we can come in. They don't expect us to wait out here forever. We haven't even seen him yet." Jonathan Whitman was his usual overbearing self.

"Oh pipe down! Your loud voice will scare my first grandson." Karen wasted no time putting Jonathan in check.

"Yes, really, Jonathan. This is a hospital." Mrs. Whitman was getting a backbone. She rushed over and eyed the baby.

Alicia smiled and handed the baby to her.

"Oh my, look at him. Oh, my God. Oh, he looks just like you did as a baby, Darren. It's like holding you all over again." Mrs. Whitman cooed at her grandson.

Karen walked over and gazed lovingly at her grandchild. "I know, if I wasn't right here in the delivery and hadn't seen Alicia give birth with my own eyes, I would swear Darren had that baby by himself. He's like a little clone."

"Well look at this, my grandson. The heir to Whitman Enterprises." Mr. Whitman's chest puffed with pride.

"Or the heir to Taylor Publishing." Kyle stared at his grandson, also beaming with pride. He walked over and touched Alicia's head. "How are you, Princess? Your Mom tells me you had a rough time."

She took a deep breath. She hadn't spoken to Kyle since the night of the reception. When he called the townhouse to speak to Karen and she answered the phone, she just handed over the phone with no conversation. When she looked at him, she saw how desperately he wanted her forgiveness, and she couldn't help herself. In spite of how much he tried to control her life, she loved her father. After all, he'd picked the right man for her.

"It wasn't so bad. Actually, I think I was a trooper. After a while, I was laughing at the pain." She lifted her chin in a boastful manner.

"Yeah, if you call that hysterical cackling sound you were making toward the end laughter," Darren teased.

"Yeah, I thought we were going to have to perform an exorcism because surely you were possessed." Karen laughed.

Giving her mother and Darren a pointed stare, she said, "Oh, stop it. I was good. I'd like to see you handle eleven hours of labor."

"Please girl, I was in labor for fifteen hours with you. Why do you think I don't have any more kids?."

Just like a mother. There must be a switch in the DNA that triggers as soon as you give birth that makes you think that no matter how rough your child has had it, you have always suffered worse.

"I was in labor for almost seventeen hours with Darren." Mrs. Whitman, not one to be outdone, added her own labor horror story.

Alicia sighed. "Well, do you see how big DJ's head is? My head was not that big, Mom. Mrs. Whitman, I remember Darren when he was a kid, so I think you're the only person in this room who can empathize with me on this one."

"Ouch." Darren feigned hurt feelings.

"Oh, you know you had a big head. You grew into it rather nicely though," she offered.

"What did you call him?" Piqued, Mr. Whitman's raised his eyebrows.

"Who? Bighead?" Alicia asked.

"No, the boy." Mr. Whitman motioned hastily to little DJ and Alicia mused that he could easily be moved to irritation. *Maybe I'll be able to have some fun with this man after all.*

"Oh, DJ, we're going to call him Darren, so I thought DJ would be a nice nickname, even though he won't technically be a Junior. His middle name will be different. His middle name will be my maiden name, Taylor."

Mr. Whitman mulled it over. "Darren Taylor Whitman. I like the sound of that."

"So do I." Kyle paused. "What do you mean your maiden name? I thought you were keeping Taylor?"

"I am. I've decided to hyphenate, so I can share the same last name as our kids." She smiled and waited for her words to sink in.

Mrs. Whitman cuddled her grandson to her chest. "Your kids? So are the two of you...Oh, this is wonderful. I was so dreading having to explain a divorce to the Links and my sorority sisters. That reception was awkward enough, not to mention the separation."

"That's wonderful, Princess. I'm glad." Kyle rubbed her arm.

"Me too, now I can move back home with my husband," Karen teased.

Kyle's face lit up. "Amen! I'm off punishment and out of the dog house."

"Well, I haven't said all that. You have served some time. We might let you off for good behavior with time served." Karen put a stern expression on her face and wagged her finger.

"Well, I for one am just happy this matter is settled. Now, about your position at Whitman Enterprises—"

"Not now, Dad. Not now." Darren cut his father off before his gaze fell on Alicia. "I'm really happy with my life just the way it is right now."

"Me too, baby. Me too." She let the words and Darren's loving gaze penetrate her, and the warmth spread throughout her heart. The lump in her chest was finally gone, and she knew without a doubt it was gone for good this time. Everything would be all right from then on.

EPILOGUE

Martha's Vineyard, sometime in the near future

Alicia ran out to the backyard of their house on the Vineyard to the sound of a bloodcurdling scream. DJ and Samantha, whose family lived next door, were playing nicely one minute. The next minute, little Samantha was screaming as if someone was killing her.

After reaching the children, she saw Samantha sobbing uncontrollably and DJ standing there kicking the sand and glaring at Samantha.

"What happened, Sam? Are you okay? Did you fall down? Did you hurt yourself?" She knelt in front of the little four-year-old girl who was dressed in a pink and white short set and wore big pink and white ribbons in her pigtails.

Samantha took big gulps of air and shook her head wildly in the negative.

"Well, what's wrong? What happened, honey?" She patted the child's head.

The four-year-old let out a sigh. "DJ pulled my hair and pushed me. He called me ugly." She started sobbing again.

"Darren Taylor Whitman, did you do that? Did you push her and pull her hair? You are five and a boy. That means you are older and bigger." She gave her son a stern stare.

"You should not push her, and you should *never* put your hand on a girl. Boys aren't supposed to hit girls. Do you understand me?"

"Yes, but—" DJ glanced anxiously from Samantha to his mother.

"Don't 'but' me." She sighed. "Don't ever put your hands on another person in anger. Now apologize."

"But, Mommy, she started it. She—"

Giving her son another pointed stare, she said through clenched teeth, "Darren Taylor Whitman, you apologize."

"I'm sorry," DJ mumbled reluctantly.

She glanced toward the house, needing to take Samantha to her mom.

How am I going to explain this tear-struck child to her mother?

"Darren! Darren!"

"What?" Darren came to the screen door.

"Come out here for a minute, please."

Darren came outside. "Yes, dear?"

"I'm going to walk Sam next door." Examining their son, she saw that his head was bent, and he was still kicking the sand. "Please talk to our son about how it's not right for boys to hit girls or pull their hair or call them names." She picked up Samantha, and the little girl put her head on her shoulder. Patting the child's head again, she tried to soothe her before taking her home.

"That's okay, sweetie, I'm going to take you to your Mommy. If DJ doesn't know how to play nice, he can play by himself for the rest of the summer."

Darren knelt down next to his son. When he saw an expression of rage and horror come across his son's face, he glanced up to see what made him so angry. He got a glimpse of *dear sweet* Samantha sticking out her tongue and rolling her eyes at DJ.

Shaking his head, he smiled. "So, you want to tell me about it, Son?"

DJ sighed. "She started it. She's a pest. I don't care if I don't have anyone else to play with the whole summer. I will not play with her. Stupid. Ugly. Girl." The little boy kicked the sand, all the while looking at Alicia and Samantha.

Clearing his throat, Darren patted his son on the head. "Why don't you come inside and have a little ice cream and tell me all about it? I might just have a little story to tell you about another little pigtailed girl who was an even bigger pest than Samantha."

"*Really?* A bigger pest than Samantha? I don't think *anyone* can be a bigger pest than Sam." DJ stared up in amazement, his anger slowly dissolving.

"Oh boy, let me tell you…" He took his son's hand, and they walked back toward the house.

2009 Reprint Mass Market Titles

January

I'm Gonna Make You Love Me
Gwyneth Bolton
ISBN-13: 978-1-58571-291-5
$6.99

Shades of Desire
Monica White
ISBN-13: 978-1-58571-292-2
$6.99

February

A Love of Her Own
Cheris Hodges
ISBN-13: 978-1-58571-293-9
$6.99

Color of Trouble
Dyanne Davis
ISBN-13: 978-1-58571-294-6
$6.99

March

Twist of Fate
Beverly Clark
ISBN-13: 978-1-58571-295-3
$6.99

Chances
Pamela Leigh Starr
ISBN-13: 978-1-58571-296-0
$6.99

April

Sinful Intentions
Crystal Rhodes
ISBN-13: 978-1-585712-297-7
$6.99

Rock Star
Roslyn Hardy Holcomb
ISBN-13: 978-1-58571-298-4
$6.99

May

Paths of Fire
T.T. Henderson
ISBN-13: 978-1-58571-343-1
$6.99

Caught Up in the Rapture
Lisa Riley
ISBN-13: 978-1-58571-344-8
$6.99

June

Reckless Surrender
Rochelle Alers
ISBN-13: 978-1-58571-345-5
$6.99

No Ordinary Love
Angela Weaver
ISBN-13: 978-1-58571-346-2
$6.99

2009 Reprint Mass Market Titles (continued)

July

Intentional Mistakes
Michele Sudler
ISBN-13: 978-1-58571-347-9
$6.99

It's In His Kiss
Reon Carter
ISBN-13: 978-1-58571-348-6
$6.99

August

Unfinished Love Affair
Barbara Keaton
ISBN-13: 978-1-58571-349-3
$6.99

A Perfect Place to Pray
I.L Goodwin
ISBN-13: 978-1-58571-299-1
$6.99

September

Love in High Gear
Charlotte Roy
ISBN-13: 978-1-58571-355-4
$6.99

Ebony Eyes
Kei Swanson
ISBN-13: 978-1-58571-356-1
$6.99

October

Midnight Clear, Part I
Leslie Esdale/Carmen Green
ISBN-13: 978-1-58571-357-8
$6.99

Midnight Clear, Part II
Gwynne Forster/Monica
    Jackson
ISBN-13: 978-1-58571-358-5
$6.99

November

Midnight Peril
Vicki Andrews
ISBN-13: 978-1-58571-359-2
$6.99

One Day At A Time
Bella McFarland
ISBN-13: 978-1-58571-360-8
$6.99

December

Just An Affair
Eugenia O'Neal
ISBN-13: 978-1-58571-361-5
$6.99

Shades of Brown
Denise Becker
ISBN-13: 978-1-58571-362-2
$6.99

2009 New Mass Market Titles

January

Singing A Song…
Crystal Rhodes
ISBN-13: 978-1-58571-283-0
$6.99

Look Both Ways
Joan Early
ISBN-13: 978-1-58571-284-7
$6.99

February

Six O'Clock
Katrina Spencer
ISBN-13: 978-1-58571-285-4
$6.99

Red Sky
Renee Alexis
ISBN-13: 978-1-58571-286-1
$6.99

March

Anything But Love
Celya Bowers
ISBN-13: 978-1-58571-287-8
$6.99

Tempting Faith
Crystal Hubbard
ISBN-13: 978-1-58571-288-5
$6.99

April

If I Were Your Woman
La Connie Taylor-Jones
ISBN-13: 978-1-58571-289-2
$6.99

Best Of Luck Elsewhere
Trisha Haddad
ISBN-13: 978-1-58571-290-8
$6.99

May

All I'll Ever Need
Mildred Riley
ISBN-13: 978-1-58571-335-6
$6.99

A Place Like Home
Alicia Wiggins
ISBN-13: 978-1-58571-336-3
$6.99

June

Best Foot Forward
Michele Sudler
ISBN-13: 978-1-58571-337-0
$6.99

It's In the Rhythm
Sammie Ward
ISBN-13: 978-1-58571-338-7
$6.99

2009 New Mass Market Titles (continued)

July

Checks and Balances
Elaine Sims
ISBN-13: 978-1-58571-339-4
$6.99

Save Me
Africa Fine
ISBN-13: 978-1-58571-340-0
$6.99

August

When Lightening Strikes
Michele Cameron
ISBN-13: 978-1-58571-369-1
$6.99

Blindsided
Tammy Williams
ISBN-13: 978-1-58571-342-4
$6.99

September

2 Good
Celya Bowers
ISBN-13: 978-1-58571-350-9
$6.99

Waiting for Mr. Darcy
Chamein Canton
ISBN-13: 978-1-58571-351-6
$6.99

October

Fireflies
Joan Early
ISBN-13: 978-1-58571-352-3
$6.99

Frost On My Window
Angela Weaver
ISBN-13: 978-1-58571-353-0
$6.99

November

Waiting in the Shadows
Michele Sudler
ISBN-13: 978-1-58571-364-6
$6.99

Fixin' Tyrone
Keith Walker
ISBN-13: 978-1-58571-365-3
$6.99

December

Dream Keeper
Gail McFarland
ISBN-13: 978-1-58571-366-0
$6.99

Another Memory
Pamela Ridley
ISBN-13: 978-1-58571-367-7
$6.99

Other Genesis Press, Inc. Titles

A Dangerous Deception	J.M. Jeffries	$8.95
A Dangerous Love	J.M. Jeffries	$8.95
A Dangerous Obsession	J.M. Jeffries	$8.95
A Drummer's Beat to Mend	Kei Swanson	$9.95
A Happy Life	Charlotte Harris	$9.95
A Heart's Awakening	Veronica Parker	$9.95
A Lark on the Wing	Phyliss Hamilton	$9.95
A Love of Her Own	Cheris F. Hodges	$9.95
A Love to Cherish	Beverly Clark	$8.95
A Risk of Rain	Dar Tomlinson	$8.95
A Taste of Temptation	Reneé Alexis	$9.95
A Twist of Fate	Beverly Clark	$8.95
A Voice Behind Thunder	Carrie Elizabeth Greene	$6.99
A Will to Love	Angie Daniels	$9.95
Acquisitions	Kimberley White	$8.95
Across	Carol Payne	$12.95
After the Vows	Leslie Esdaile	$10.95
(Summer Anthology)	T.T. Henderson	
	Jacqueline Thomas	
Again My Love	Kayla Perrin	$10.95
Against the Wind	Gwynne Forster	$8.95
All I Ask	Barbara Keaton	$8.95
Always You	Crystal Hubbard	$6.99
Ambrosia	T.T. Henderson	$8.95
An Unfinished Love Affair	Barbara Keaton	$8.95
And Then Came You	Dorothy Elizabeth Love	$8.95
Angel's Paradise	Janice Angelique	$9.95
At Last	Lisa G. Riley	$8.95
Best of Friends	Natalie Dunbar	$8.95
Beyond the Rapture	Beverly Clark	$9.95
Blame It On Paradise	Crystal Hubbard	$6.99
Blaze	Barbara Keaton	$9.95
Bliss, Inc.	Chamein Canton	$6.99
Blood Lust	J. M. Jeffries	$9.95
Blood Seduction	J.M. Jeffries	$9.95

Other Genesis Press, Inc. Titles (continued)

Bodyguard	Andrea Jackson	$9.95
Boss of Me	Diana Nyad	$8.95
Bound by Love	Beverly Clark	$8.95
Breeze	Robin Hampton Allen	$10.95
Broken	Dar Tomlinson	$24.95
By Design	Barbara Keaton	$8.95
Cajun Heat	Charlene Berry	$8.95
Careless Whispers	Rochelle Alers	$8.95
Cats & Other Tales	Marilyn Wagner	$8.95
Caught in a Trap	Andre Michelle	$8.95
Caught Up In the Rapture	Lisa G. Riley	$9.95
Cautious Heart	Cheris F Hodges	$8.95
Chances	Pamela Leigh Starr	$8.95
Cherish the Flame	Beverly Clark	$8.95
Choices	Tammy Williams	$6.99
Class Reunion	Irma Jenkins/	$12.95
	John Brown	
Code Name: Diva	J.M. Jeffries	$9.95
Conquering Dr. Wexler's Heart	Kimberley White	$9.95
Corporate Seduction	A.C. Arthur	$9.95
Crossing Paths, Tempting Memories	Dorothy Elizabeth Love	$9.95
Crush	Crystal Hubbard	$9.95
Cypress Whisperings	Phyllis Hamilton	$8.95
Dark Embrace	Crystal Wilson Harris	$8.95
Dark Storm Rising	Chinelu Moore	$10.95
Daughter of the Wind	Joan Xian	$8.95
Dawn's Harbor	Kymberly Hunt	$6.99
Deadly Sacrifice	Jack Kean	$22.95
Designer Passion	Dar Tomlinson	$8.95
	Diana Richeaux	
Do Over	Celya Bowers	$9.95
Dream Runner	Gail McFarland	$6.99
Dreamtective	Liz Swados	$5.95

Other Genesis Press, Inc. Titles (continued)

Other Genesis Press, Inc. Titles (continued)

Other Genesis Press, Inc. Titles (continued)

Meant to Be	Jeanne Sumerix	$8.95
Midnight Clear (Anthology)	Leslie Esdaile Gwynne Forster Carmen Green Monica Jackson	$10.95
Midnight Magic	Gwynne Forster	$8.95
Midnight Peril	Vicki Andrews	$10.95
Misconceptions	Pamela Leigh Starr	$9.95
Moments of Clarity	Michele Cameron	$6.99
Montgomery's Children	Richard Perry	$14.95
Mr Fix-It	Crystal Hubbard	$6.99
My Buffalo Soldier	Barbara B. K. Reeves	$8.95
Naked Soul	Gwynne Forster	$8.95
Never Say Never	Michele Cameron	$6.99
Next to Last Chance	Louisa Dixon	$24.95
No Apologies	Seressia Glass	$8.95
No Commitment Required	Seressia Glass	$8.95
No Regrets	Mildred E. Riley	$8.95
Not His Type	Chamein Canton	$6.99
Nowhere to Run	Gay G. Gunn	$10.95
O Bed! O Breakfast!	Rob Kuehnle	$14.95
Object of His Desire	A. C. Arthur	$8.95
Office Policy	A. C. Arthur	$9.95
Once in a Blue Moon	Dorianne Cole	$9.95
One Day at a Time	Bella McFarland	$8.95
One of These Days	Michele Sudler	$9.95
Outside Chance	Louisa Dixon	$24.95
Passion	T.T. Henderson	$10.95
Passion's Blood	Cherif Fortin	$22.95
Passion's Furies	AlTonya Washington	$6.99
Passion's Journey	Wanda Y. Thomas	$8.95
Past Promises	Jahmel West	$8.95
Path of Fire	T.T. Henderson	$8.95
Path of Thorns	Annetta P. Lee	$9.95
Peace Be Still	Colette Haywood	$12.95

Other Genesis Press, Inc. Titles (continued)

Picture Perfect	Reon Carter	$8.95
Playing for Keeps	Stephanie Salinas	$8.95
Pride & Joi	Gay G. Gunn	$8.95
Promises Made	Bernice Layton	$6.99
Promises to Keep	Alicia Wiggins	$8.95
Quiet Storm	Donna Hill	$10.95
Reckless Surrender	Rochelle Alers	$6.95
Red Polka Dot in a World of Plaid	Varian Johnson	$12.95
Reluctant Captive	Joyce Jackson	$8.95
Rendezvous with Fate	Jeanne Sumerix	$8.95
Revelations	Cheris F. Hodges	$8.95
Rivers of the Soul	Leslie Esdaile	$8.95
Rocky Mountain Romance	Kathleen Suzanne	$8.95
Rooms of the Heart	Donna Hill	$8.95
Rough on Rats and Tough on Cats	Chris Parker	$12.95
Secret Library Vol. 1	Nina Sheridan	$18.95
Secret Library Vol. 2	Cassandra Colt	$8.95
Secret Thunder	Annetta P. Lee	$9.95
Shades of Brown	Denise Becker	$8.95
Shades of Desire	Monica White	$8.95
Shadows in the Moonlight	Jeanne Sumerix	$8.95
Sin	Crystal Rhodes	$8.95
Small Whispers	Annetta P. Lee	$6.99
So Amazing	Sinclair LeBeau	$8.95
Somebody's Someone	Sinclair LeBeau	$8.95
Someone to Love	Alicia Wiggins	$8.95
Song in the Park	Martin Brant	$15.95
Soul Eyes	Wayne L. Wilson	$12.95
Soul to Soul	Donna Hill	$8.95
Southern Comfort	J.M. Jeffries	$8.95
Southern Fried Standards	S.R. Maddox	$6.99
Still the Storm	Sharon Robinson	$8.95
Still Waters Run Deep	Leslie Esdaile	$8.95

Other Genesis Press, Inc. Titles (continued)

Stolen Memories	Michele Sudler	$6.99
Stories to Excite You	Anna Forrest/Divine	$14.95
Storm	Pamela Leigh Starr	$6.99
Subtle Secrets	Wanda Y. Thomas	$8.95
Suddenly You	Crystal Hubbard	$9.95
Sweet Repercussions	Kimberley White	$9.95
Sweet Sensations	Gwyneth Bolton	$9.95
Sweet Tomorrows	Kimberly White	$8.95
Taken by You	Dorothy Elizabeth Love	$9.95
Tattooed Tears	T. T. Henderson	$8.95
The Color Line	Lizzette Grayson Carter	$9.95
The Color of Trouble	Dyanne Davis	$8.95
The Disappearance of Allison Jones	Kayla Perrin	$5.95
The Fires Within	Beverly Clark	$9.95
The Foursome	Celya Bowers	$6.99
The Honey Dipper's Legacy	Pannell-Allen	$14.95
The Joker's Love Tune	Sidney Rickman	$15.95
The Little Pretender	Barbara Cartland	$10.95
The Love We Had	Natalie Dunbar	$8.95
The Man Who Could Fly	Bob & Milana Beamon	$18.95
The Missing Link	Charlyne Dickerson	$8.95
The Mission	Pamela Leigh Starr	$6.99
The More Things Change	Chamein Canton	$6.99
The Perfect Frame	Beverly Clark	$9.95
The Price of Love	Sinclair LeBeau	$8.95
The Smoking Life	Ilene Barth	$29.95
The Words of the Pitcher	Kei Swanson	$8.95
Things Forbidden	Maryam Diaab	$6.99
This Life Isn't Perfect Holla	Sandra Foy	$6.99
Three Doors Down	Michele Sudler	$6.99
Three Wishes	Seressia Glass	$8.95
Ties That Bind	Kathleen Suzanne	$8.95
Tiger Woods	Libby Hughes	$5.95
Time is of the Essence	Angie Daniels	$9.95

Other Genesis Press, Inc. Titles (continued)

Timeless Devotion	Bella McFarland	$9.95
Tomorrow's Promise	Leslie Esdaile	$8.95
Truly Inseparable	Wanda Y. Thomas	$8.95
Two Sides to Every Story	Dyanne Davis	$9.95
Unbreak My Heart	Dar Tomlinson	$8.95
Uncommon Prayer	Kenneth Swanson	$9.95
Unconditional Love	Alicia Wiggins	$8.95
Unconditional	A.C. Arthur	$9.95
Undying Love	Renee Alexis	$6.99
Until Death Do Us Part	Susan Paul	$8.95
Vows of Passion	Bella McFarland	$9.95
Wedding Gown	Dyanne Davis	$8.95
What's Under Benjamin's Bed	Sandra Schaffer	$8.95
When A Man Loves A Woman	La Connie Taylor-Jones	$6.99
When Dreams Float	Dorothy Elizabeth Love	$8.95
When I'm With You	LaConnie Taylor-Jones	$6.99
Where I Want To Be	Maryam Diaab	$6.99
Whispers in the Night	Dorothy Elizabeth Love	$8.95
Whispers in the Sand	LaFlorya Gauthier	$10.95
Who's That Lady?	Andrea Jackson	$9.95
Wild Ravens	Altonya Washington	$9.95
Yesterday Is Gone	Beverly Clark	$10.95
Yesterday's Dreams, Tomorrow's Promises	Reon Laudat	$8.95
Your Precious Love	Sinclair LeBeau	$8.95

Order Form

Mail to: Genesis Press, Inc.
P.O. Box 101
Columbus, MS 39703

Name _____

Address _____

City/State _____ Zip _____

Telephone _____

Ship to (if different from above)

Name _____

Address _____

City/State _____ Zip _____

Telephone _____

Credit Card Information

Credit Card # _____ ☐ Visa   ☐ Mastercard

Expiration Date (mm/yy) _____ ☐ AmEx   ☐ Discover

Qty.	Author	Title	Price	Total

Use this order form, or call 1-888-INDIGO-1

Total for books	_____
Shipping and handling: $5 first two books, $1 each additional book	_____
Total S & H	_____
Total amount enclosed	_____

Mississippi residents add 7% sales tax